THE SPRINGS OF ANAHITA

MARK HOWARD HENDERSON

MARK HOWARD HENDERSON

The SPRINGS of ANAHITA

PART ONE

THE YAZDAN TRILOGY

For Kaz and Rhun

"From what I can tell, there are no gates in Hell."
— The White Demon

SAMJARI SETTLEMENTS
KUH-E-SANG
GREAT PLAINS OF NAMAK
KUH-E-AB
RAYDUR
RUD-E BARIK
SANG~E PIR
KUHHA-YE SABZ
RUD-E HAYAT
JARAK
MILES
5   10   20   30   40   50   60

N
W
E
S
DASHT-E-MARG
KUHHA-YE SIYAH
ZAD
RUD-E MAH
JABIRI RUINS
RAH-E FARAZ
DANZARDAN
KUH-E ZUZE
JARAKI GARRISON
GHELI-KHAST
KUH-E SHOELE
Z-E RHUN
SIN
VISGARI SETTLEMENTS

CONTENTS

PREFACE

Though the tale told within these pages is fictional, the setting is rooted in the late Sasanian period of pre-Islamic Persia. In every respect, I have sought to reflect the culture and traditions of a people and civilization I deeply admire.

The kingdoms were inspired by the ancient adobe citadels of Arg-e Bam and Arg-e Rāyen, located in today's Kerman province. Tragically, the former was nearly leveled by an earthquake in 2003.

It is the people of Bam to whom this story is dedicated.

PROLOGUE

"**I** used to look at dead bodies—for a living.

You brigands are right to question how I've come to my conclusion, this notion that chaos will soon break loose in Zad. But you must understand I've had a unique insight into that which afflicts my desert kingdom. I've examined all types of death, from air deprivation and ballistic trauma to organ failure and infection. Causes include old age, drowning, warfare, parasites, and one's physical composition or deficiencies. But what I've seen in Zad is death by, shall we say, sinister means.

Despite my wife's objections, I have no quarrel with your confiscation of our treasures. With my wrists bound behind my back, I'm in no position to demand that you return them. Besides, given the itinerant destiny awaiting us, such keepsakes would prove cumbersome. All I ask in exchange, which I submit humbly before you, is that you *not* release me and my family. We don't require much, and we eat even less. As for my medical knowledge, I promise you will find it most beneficial.

You asked earlier what I expect will happen. Who knows? The drought gripping the land might be all of our undoing. Until such a time, however, the fate of the world hangs in the balance. Please do not ask me which side is good or which side is right. We both know that since the dawn of civilization, all who seek power claim moral justification. In the end, it comes down to will. Those whose wills are strongest lay claim to the tomes of antiquity. They also lay claim to those yet to be written.

I used to be the coroner of Zad. Loras is my name."

THE ONE HOPE (SORT OF)

Adarbad scurried around his laboratory like a starving rat, nosing behind books and beakers and looking in bowls and drawers. "What did I do with them?" he said to himself, the bags under his eyes more pronounced than usual.

It was midday in the kingdom of Zad, and the alchemist stood before three magical elixirs, their putrid byproducts wafting into the air. "Corks, where are you?"

He stared at the floor for an extended period and retraced his every action. With anything work-related, this was a skill he could perform with stunning precision.

At length, he patted the pockets of his faded green robe and felt something knobby. "Ah, hiding from me, were you?"

Adarbad pressed the corks into the vials and placed them into a small wooden crate. Cradling it in his arm, he shuffled through the citadel's primary residential corridor and made his way toward the king's quarters. As he entered the bedroom, walking through light and shadows, he saw that the ailing Khavar had been propped against some pillows.

Queen Shanaz sat beside her frail husband, spoon-feeding him a bowl of *ash-e anar*, or pomegranate soup. "What are you doing here?" she said. "The meeting isn't until later."

The alchemist had arrived earlier than expected. He set the crate on a beautifully hand-crafted console table at the foot of the bed. "Please forgive the intrusion, my lady. But I must speak with the king about a matter of grave importance."

The queen, still shocked by the sudden passing of her and Khavar's only son, was in no mood for surprises. "Can't it wait until Lilya gets here? We're eating."

"There is no time."

The king raised his hand and beckoned the diminutive alchemist closer.

Adarbad approached, a sense of foreboding in his expression. "My lord, you'll recall that I recently finished making an elixir of precognition."

"We'll take your word for it," the king muttered.

"Well, whatever doubts I had of its efficacy were immediately dispelled after drinking it."

"What do you mean?"

"The time horizon—I was able to see over it, and bad omens portend."

"Omens? What sort of omens?"

"Blood and fire—the land will shake and turn to dust." Adarbad fidgeted and looked at the king hesitantly before adding, "I raise this not to worry you. Heaven knows your heart is already burdened enough."

"Does it? Then why do my prayers fall on deaf ears?"

Shanaz set the bowl down and placed her hand on her husband's shoulder, hoping to comfort him. "Ada, please sit. Tell us what you've seen."

Adarbad moved to the edge of the bed. "You've been made aware of the unusual weather that has hit the kingdom—the fierce northerly winds, the lack of rain. But there is more. This pattern is not an aberration. It'll continue much longer. The people will grow agitated, and war will come to the lands."

Indeed, usually at this time of year, storms moved in from the southwest over the *Kuhha-ye Sabz*, or Green Mountains, but the rains had all ceased. Only the occasional cloud had been spotted, and the alchemist, knowledgeable in meteorology, began to hear rumblings of concern through the farming communities, their crops struggling to break the surface of the arid soil. He spoke with the *magi* who had translated and collated scores of ancient holy texts and were completing the first full-scale standardization of the *Avesta*. What they told him was unnerving.

"How are you so sure of this?" the king asked. "You've always professed skepticism regarding visions of foresight."

"Early this morning, I spoke with the priests. Their findings confirm not only what I've seen, but also what I've deduced from the planetary positions. One of the ancient texts they've translated, only recently discovered in the Jabiri ruins, is the long-lost *Yasht* of *Tishtrya*. It foretells his battle with *Apaosha*."

"The demon of drought," Shanaz confirmed.

"Precisely. We will be called upon to wage war against the forces of darkness that *Ahriman* is unleashing. The drought underway is the evil one's first volley, the groundwork for all the wickedness yet to come."

The king pondered what he had heard. "You said you raised this not to worry me but to tell me something important?"

"Yes, my lord."

"Well, you have failed miserably. Good grief, Adarbad, I don't need to deal with this. I've suffered a stroke, our beloved Mahyar is dead, and the last thoughts of my life will be filled with tidings of the apocalypse."

The king began to sweat profusely.

Shanaz blotted her husband's forehead with a towel. "Please, Ada, go on."

"The magi speculate that Tishtrya has grown weak from centuries of neglect, the result of failing to show the rain god due reverence or paying him proper tribute. That also goes for *Warahram, Mithra,* and the rest of the ancient pantheon. I was under the impression we had moved past these myths. Were they not reinterpreted as mere manifestations of *Ohrmazd*?"

"What you speak of euphemistically," the king said, "was a movement of iconoclasts that swept over the lands three centuries ago. Reinterpreted? That's one way to put it. From *Kuh-e Zuze* to *Kuh-e Ab* and all the places in between, the ancient places of pilgrimage were razed to the ground and abandoned. Our ancestors may have been through with the old gods, but it would seem the *Yazdan* are not through with us."

"Such is the peril of dismissing our inheritance," Shanaz said.

The king nodded in agreement. "Call it the conceit of the living. What else did the magi tell you?"

"That to achieve victory, we must be agents of good to see it through. But there are no guarantees that it will all end well."

"Enough with the riddles. Get to the point."

"There is one hope for the future."

"What is it?"

"Not 'what' but 'who,'" the alchemist said.

The king and queen looked at each other, puzzling over the possibilities. No one came to mind.

Adarbad scooted in closer. "It's your grandson, my lord."

"Afshad?"

"No, Prince Yaya."

"Yaya? Our scrawny Yaya? You must be kidding. He doesn't even eat meat."

"My lord, you'll recall the brightness in the sky on the night Yaya was allegedly born. Our royal celestial tables, recently compiled by our astrologers, place that date as the most recent conjunction of the two largest planets in the solar system. Such a merger is exceedingly rare. By all accounts, the boy's birth was a sign of providence."

Khavar looked into the alchemist's eyes with steely resolve. "Then, by all means, find a way to protect that boy."

Lilya soon entered the king's quarters and stood near the foot of the bed, her arms folded. She curiously observed the vials Adarbad had since removed from the crate and placed on the table.

Unlike Shanaz, whose lineage descended from the Zadian administrative class, Lilya hailed from royalty, specifically from the eastern kingdom of Danzardan. Her father, the late King Vanitar, had arranged his daughter's marriage to Khavar to help quell territorial disputes between the rival kingdoms and to solidify political ties. However, the agreement nearly unraveled when he learned that Khavar's new bride, eighteen-year-old Shanaz, was already pregnant. To keep the arrangement on track, Khavar's father offered Vanitar two concessions: Shanaz would not be permitted to bear any more children, and future Zadian kings would descend solely through Lilya's progeny.

"I have news to share with both of you," the king said, looking alternately at his wives. "And because my days are few, there is little time to spare."

"Need he be in here?" Lilya questioned, motioning toward the alchemist. "I thought this was a meeting of the spouses."

"Never mind him. Now listen, all fathers desire to leave their children something of value when they die, so I had instructed Adarbad to make *wish* elixirs to be drunk upon my death."

"Very well, but why do I see three vials when *your* Mahyar is no longer with us?"

"The vial—" The king began to cough, his face red with irritation.

Shanaz adjusted the pillows, providing Khavar a moment to ponder his second wife's peculiar use of a possessive adjective.

"Yes, *my* Mahyar is now in God's loving embrace. But since you ask, I want my dear son to understand, wherever his spirit may be, that I had every intention of honoring him. You might find that senseless, but there you have it. The other two vials are for Zahan and Kamran."

"Won't the elixirs lose their potency if not drunk immediately?" Lilya asked.

"The elixirs are fermented," Adarbad said. "They won't spoil."

Lilya turned back toward the king. "You do have grandchildren, you know? Why not let Afshad have the extra elixir?"

Shanaz snickered, shaking her head. "He never gets top billing, does he?"

"I beg your pardon."

"Your other grandchild. Not once have I seen you prioritize Yaya over Afshad. One would think that after nearly fifteen years, you would have done so—if not intentionally, then at least by mistake."

"But I don't make mistakes, Shanaz. You know that."

"Lilya, please," the king said, trying to diffuse the tension. "I need rest. You can sort it all out after I'm gone."

BEATING HEARTS AND SKIPPING STONES

The name she gave was Yazdegerd. His father called him Yaz. To everyone else, he was just Yaya. No one knew precisely when he began to stutter, but it started around the age of three.

Queen Lilya blamed it on a choking incident, often telling the story of smacking him on the back and shooting the lodged obstruction into a visiting king's iced-rose water.

"He began to stutter right after that," she often proclaimed.

The boy's uncle, Prince Kamran, was certain it had to do with his son knocking his cousin in the head with a *chogan* mallet, damaging his left ear drum and making him slightly deaf.

Whatever the reason, Yazdegerd couldn't get his name out. When asked, "What's your name, little one?" he would reply, "YaYaYa, Yaya…" So he became Yaya. Mostly, he grew out of his stutter, but the name stuck.

Years later, Yaya wondered about his grandmother's real motive for whacking him: expelling the pistachio shell or having a chance to smack the *daevas* out of him. In short, she wasn't very fond of the boy, and this was through no fault of his own. As it happened, Yaya's father, Prince Zahan, had fallen in love with a *vastryoshan*, or commoner, and defied Lilya's explicit orders to end the relationship.

When the queen first laid eyes on him, she said, "Look at that face and those legs. They didn't come from this side of the family."

Yaya's mother was never seen again after his birth. What might have happened to her was a parlor game of speculation.

"She was left in the desert," some would say.

"She was dropped off with the roaming brigands," others would say.

Since she belonged to the lower caste living in the villages beyond the city walls, little fuss was made about her.

Why Yaya didn't disappear remained more of a mystery among the ruling elite. After all, he was a bastard child lacking the requisite genetic disposition for royalty. His prominent nose and long legs even prompted his grandmother to call him *shotor*, which meant camel. To her mind and among many others, having him done away with while an infant would have been the sensible thing to do.

In discussing the matter with the king, Lilya commented, "One doesn't shed tears for runts. Why should we care about a mongrel?"

Yaya was nearly fifteen years old and reluctantly handsome—all the right pieces were there; they just didn't fit properly. Ever since Lilya bequeathed to him the cruel moniker, the name "Shotor" had spread among his peers. But during that time, something odd happened, as if the boy gained attributes from the dromedary to which he was compared. He rarely became thirsty, and while not the fastest of youths, his endurance was unrivaled.

Such was the way of Yaya. But that wasn't all.

During the festivals of sacrifice that honored Ohrmazd, he would demand that his friends eat the abundant grains and fruits that the kingdom provided instead of the goats and lamb. Sometimes, he would go so far as to lecture them about their complicity in the slaughter. Had it not been for his royal lineage and the deferential treatment it induced, the boy known as "Shotor" might have realized sooner that his moralizing tended to be bothersome.

Rather than follow the path prescribed for someone of his station, like learning to play chogan or wrestle, Yaya could usually be found relaxing in the gardens or joining the vastryoshan in pilfering pomegranates from the bazaar vendors.

Lilya knew that her grandson was drawn to the commoners because they linked him with the mother he never knew. Once, when he was old enough, he asked about her, and the queen told him never to do so again.

Yaya's disposition hinted at an indolent nature, but like other boys his age, he was only trying to act cool. It was no secret that he was smitten with Gulzar, the grand magus's granddaughter. Unfortunately for him, so was his cousin, who had pulled the girl into his circle of friends and discreetly courted her. To cope with what he saw as rejection, Yaya sometimes took refuge outside the city walls.

⸺⬦⸺

Early that evening, the grandson, best known in his grandfather's mind as "the vegetarian," lay on the banks of the

Rud-e Barik. The river serving as the lifeline to the walled city and adjoining villages looked unusually low. Except for the dry winter months, he couldn't remember ever seeing the water so shallow. As he drifted off and began dreaming, he felt a tickling sensation on his cheeks.

Yaya opened his eyes to find a girl hovering over him, her long, black hair sweeping against his cheeks like spun silk.

"What are you doing?" Gulzar asked, glancing around to make sure none of the chaperones was observing her immodest behavior.

"Resting," Yaya said through his yawn. "Why?"

Gulzar sat back on her heels. "We're heading to the orchards. Come with us."

"I can't."

"Why not?"

"I have to study. I have class first thing tomorrow morning with the *Grand Magus*. Talk about a bore. I'd rather lie in a pit of vipers than listen to his tedious lectures. You wouldn't happen to know him, would you?"

"Very funny," she said. "Actually, you won't be having class tomorrow. My *pedar bozorg* has other matters to tend to. He told me to tell you should I see you."

Upon hearing what Adarbad had told him, King Khavar requested a meeting with the council of magi, of which Gulzar's grandfather was the leader. As the most learned man in matters of the Avesta and prophecy, the king thought it wise to get confirmation from Rustem of what he had already been told.

The prince sat up. "Well, in that case, I suppose I could go to the orchards." His grin vanished when he noticed Afshad and several other boys and girls standing by the river and skipping stones.

At least to his mind, Yaya felt that his cousin cared more about denying him Gulzar than truly wanting her. After all, it was only when he showed interest in the girl that Afshad had done the same. Battles of this nature marked their shared history. Outside the royal formalities, the boys had difficulty masking their mutual enmity.

Afshad walked up the bank and called out to Rustem's granddaughter. "Gulzar, let's go. If Shotor doesn't want to come, let him be. No need to twist his arm. Besides, you might break it."

Gulzar took Yaya's hand and met his eyes with compassion. "I'm so sorry," she said, her voice full of emotion.

"For what?"

"For your *Amoo*. Everybody loved Prince Mahyar. You will ask if you ever need anything, won't you?"

Yaya nodded, his eyes falling onto the girl's lips.

Gulzar stood up. "Well, come on. You want to come, don't you? Or am I as boring as my pedar bozorg?"

"You know what? I'm feeling a bit tired. You go ahead."

"I don't know, Yaya. I think you need to be among friends."

Yaya looked at his cousin, who was watching intently, then motioned to Gulzar that he wasn't interested.

"Very well," she said, running off to join the group. "Suit yourself."

Afshad looked back at his cousin and gave him a cocksure smile. He wrapped his arm over Gulzar's shoulder and whispered in her ear, prompting her to take good-natured offense and push him away.

Yaya felt jealous at the apparent flirtation, but he wasn't in the mood for his cousin's games.

As the teens departed for the orchards, the prince crossed his legs and began to reflect on his uncle's burial. One bothersome thought kept returning to his mind. During the ceremony, everyone shed tears except his Uncle Kamran and Queen Lilya. His grandmother's black silken gown hung on her like loose skin, and he imagined it propped up by a fleshless skeleton made from the femurs and ribs found on the burial grounds. The more he tried to wrestle the image away, the more it seared into his thoughts, as visions of the grotesque often do.

Looking for a distraction, Yaya wandered through a cluster of tamarisk trees near the river. As he scoured the dirt for a proper rock to skip, he heard a voice from behind.

"I bet I can beat you."

Standing at the end of a path that cut through the trees was Queen Shanaz. She excused her attendants and joined Yaya at the water's edge.

"I know," Yaya said, his tone confessional, "I shouldn't be alone here without a chaperone."

Shanaz repressed a smile. "I didn't say anything. I only happened to see you down here and figured you might want some competition."

"Huh?"

"Before you accept my challenge, you must know that in my youth, I was the most feared stone skipper this side of the Green Mountains."

Yaya looked bemused.

"I'm not kidding."

The prince picked up a round stone and handed it to Shanaz, his hand trembling with feigned fright. "Promise you'll go easy on me?"

"Never." The queen looked the stone over before discarding it into the river. "I'll choose my own, thank you."

"Well, that's one skip. My turn."

"That doesn't count."

After sharing a laugh, Shanaz and Yaya enjoyed a heated game of stone skipping. When it finished, and as much as he was loath to admit, Yaya learned that the queen's bravado had not been misplaced—most skips: Shanaz 10; Yaya 7.

Given the levity of the moment, Shanaz risked asking the prince about Gulzar.

Yaya reacted with a dismayed expression. "Really? It's that obvious?"

"I do have eyes."

Yaya glanced at the queen's three attendants loitering on the other side of the tamarisk trees. "Apparently, many."

"Don't be silly. They're not charged with spying on the family. I see how you gaze at the girl and how you seem to be everywhere she and her friends are."

"Yeah, well, same with Afshad." Yaya became sullen as he scratched the sandbank with a stick. "It's nothing you can help me with unless you can get rid of my cousin." He tossed the stick hard into the slow, moving waters. "Wait a moment. You're a queen."

"Very observant."

"Can't you get Pedar bozorg to banish him? Maybe drop him off in the *Dasht-e Marg*?"

"Well, I can't help you by decree, nor do I believe you'd want the king to abandon his other grandson to the scorpions and dunes."

"What do I have to do to convince you?"

Shanaz's expression turned grave. "The king's condition has worsened, you know?"

With the bigger picture presented before him, Yaya felt embarrassed by his petty jokes about having his cousin left for dead in the desert. He looked down and nodded.

Shanaz hiked up her dress and embroidered cloak and sat on the riverbank. She invited Yaya to join her.

The beautiful consort and the prince sat shoulder to shoulder and talked for the rest of the afternoon. Mostly, Shanaz listened. Her only advice concerning Gulzar was that "things will work themselves out." To Yaya, the words were uninspiring, as was her trite analogy of life and the winding river. Nevertheless, he felt better, if only for the talking.

"Come," the queen said. "Let's go see your pedar bozorg."

THE UNFOLDING

S hanaz and Yaya were moseying through the chogan field when they saw a company of cavalry, or *savaran*, emerge into view past the orchards. The men were returning after a tour of duty at the southern garrison near the *Kuhha-ye Siyah*, or Black Mountains. Yaya knew his father and Uncle Kamran were among the riders and had been anticipating their arrival. The queen knew as well, giving the boy leave before he even had a chance to request it.

Eager to be the first to welcome his father home, Yaya took off running.

After a quarter mile, the prince came upon the savaran's right flank, where the riders and their horses were moving in a slow, three-row cavalcade. As he made his way to the front, he was struck by the grim and downcast faces. Every rider slumped in his saddle. Nobody spoke. It was hardly the homecoming the boy had imagined. At the vanguard, he recognized his uncle and General Baraz, both men's eyes fixed on the road ahead.

When the prince failed to recognize the rider on the far side, he began to panic. "Where's my father?"

The question caught Kamran off guard, and he flinched as if waking from a trance. He glanced at his nephew before turning to Baraz and mumbling some orders.

In response, the general raised his hand and spurred the savaran to an easy trot.

As the company neared the southern wall, the many villagers leaving the bazaar scrambled to the roadside with their baskets and pushcarts.

Meanwhile, Yaya made his way around the rear of the cavalry and ran toward the front. After passing many riders and their horses, he came to one bearing a limp body. It was the corpse of his father, belly down and arms dangling to the side. Despite efforts at concealment, the rider tasked with securing the body had let the cloak slip just enough to reveal the face.

With the company in full view of the vastryoshan, it took only a moment for someone to realize his identity.

"It's Prince Zahan!"

And with those words, the news of Yaya's father's death spread like a contagion. Other voices cried out.

Fearing the savaran might get bogged down among the villagers wishing to touch the fallen royal, General Baraz called the riders to move apace.

The prince chased after the cantering horses until he became too overcome with grief, his tears streaming as he stumbled down the road into a trail of dust.

Upon entering the city, the vanguard split from the rest of the savaran and took a less traveled route to the citadel complex, the royals' residence perched high on a rock formation.

Once inside, General Baraz, Kamran, and a group of horsemen bore the slain prince down a corridor and past the council chamber. After climbing a few flights of stairs, they pressed on, passing many courtiers, several of whom held their hands to their mouths in disbelief.

Seeing their faces made Baraz fret, unsure how the sick king could weather the loss of another son.

Lilya was the first to react as they moved through Khavar's quarters and into his bedroom, springing from the king's bedside and rushing toward the deceased.

"My son," she said, gently pulling him to the floor.

As she cradled Zahan in her arms, tears in her eyes, the queen caressed his cold face, still regal in its countenance.

The king, unable to lift his body due to partial paralysis, had attendants assist him to a seated position against the headboard. He put his hand to his face and began to whimper.

"Does Ohrmazd not have pity on a dying man?" he said, slurring his speech. "What on God's earth happened?"

Before the general could speak, Kamran interjected. "We had camped at the usual watering hole, Father. In the morning, we were loading our horses when they came..." Kamran's voice faded, his eyes lurching from side to side as he pieced together his memory.

"When what came?" the king asked.

"Arrows—arrows from all directions. Roaming brigands ambushed us. We had no time. We tried to return fire, but the bastards got away. Fearful of a more elaborate trap, we thought it prudent to flee."

General Baraz gave Kamran a studied look.

Lilya restrained her crying and turned her anguish upon her enfeebled husband. "All of this is your fault. Had you taken my counsel, my son would still be alive. Shame on you. Shame."

"Enough," the king said. "My body is broken, and now my heart. Please, do not break my spirit."

"I told you to change the routes to the garrisons. The brigands couldn't have been handed easier targets." Lilya looked at the general, standing by the foot of the bed. "As the leader of this expedition, you most of all should have known better."

"But my lady, with all due respect to Prince Kamran, I'm not convinced brigands were—"

"Know your place, General. The prince has spoken of what happened."

"Please, dear wife," the king said, pleading for restraint. "No more of this bickering."

"Save your 'dears' for the other one."

After laying her son's head on the woolen rug, Lilya pushed her slender frame from the floor and drew herself up to her full height. She took a deep breath and wiped the tears from her face. "Ask the priests to begin the ritual of preparing Zahan's body. Ask them to summon me when he is ready."

With her back to her husband, Lilya reached for Kamran, taking him by the arm. "I need to lie down. See me to my chamber."

As his wife and sole surviving son left his room, Khavar motioned to the general to bring Zahan's body to the bed. Once there, the king drooped over him, touching his face while he muttered in paternal tones.

Meanwhile, in the doorway stood a breathless Yaya, the boy stunned, and his face covered with a paste of dust and tears. He could not bring his feet to move, fearful that seeing his dead father's face would sear itself into his memory and haunt his dreams forever.

◆

As canorous whistles from wind tunnels filled her quarters, Lilya walked outside to the balcony. Her countenance was calm yet pensive. In the distance, a large billowing cloud of dust, unusual for that time of year, slid over the sand like the feet of a skulking thief. It moved fast and grew in depth and breadth, sweeping over everything in its path.

Kamran joined her at the balustrade. "Everything is going according to plan, Mother. All that stands in our way is a dying king. When should I take care of him?"

"Don't worry about your father. We must let some time pass so as not to raise any suspicion. My contacts in Danzardan showed their incompetence by sending less-than-discreet assassins. Why does General Baraz harbor doubts about who killed Zahan? You heard me cut him off."

"The fletching and the nocks."

"The what?"

"The feathers and notches on the arrows point to Danzardani craftsmanship."

"That explains why my cousin was put in the unenviable position of running their garrison at *Gheli-Khast*. I pay him a small fortune, and he has the foresight to arm his brigand mercenaries with his *own* arrows? What an incompetent fool."

Kamran turned to face his mother. "Then what are we to do? We can't let General Baraz sour any willingness to end the conflict. Assassinating a prince will be viewed by him and the savaran as an act of war. Were we not to retaliate against Danzardan, we would appear weak and ineffectual. And you'll be accused of dual loyalties."

Lilya tapped her chin, her mind churning. "While I've never been too impressed with the general's valor, I have been with some of his other qualities. He's intelligent and well-versed in war. But more than that, he's shrewd."

"What is it you're implying?"

"That Baraz is going to wait and see how this unfolds before saying anything."

"And if he doesn't?"

"One thing you must understand about generals is that they can always be bought off. More than anything, they crave influence or tools for their trade. Find ways to feed them, and they'll be as obedient as the next dog."

"Well, if the general knows what's good for him, he'll be obedient. To be anything but will get you killed around here."

"Your unruly and impertinent brother was too much like your father. To have let him take over the kingdom would have been an abdication of responsibility."

"And Mahyar? What was his sin? He could only ever function as regent."

"Edicts are broken all the time. When one tastes power, rarely is it ever forsaken." Lilya straightened out the flap of chain mail that protected her son's neck. "Anyway, my problem with your half-brother is of a different matter, his different nature. To be thirty-six and unmarried tells you all you need to know."

"Zahan never married."

"Only to spite me."

After a moment of self-reflective guilt, the queen stared at the *haboob* that roiled the otherwise placid landscape. "Ohrmazd knows we are doing this to preserve the kingdom."

KAMRAN'S TURN

The summer winds swept spring aside. In their wake, and still clinging to life, was King Khavar. Since his stroke three months prior, he had survived a severe bout of pneumonia and suffered extreme weight loss. While some would characterize his tenure as king of Zad as somewhat lacking—given his penchant for leisure over the rigor of rule—the harbinger that is death's shadow compels even the most derelict to put his house in order.

Most concerning in his view was how tumultuous transitions of power could be. It happened in Danzardan after the death of Lilya's father only five years ago. King Vanitar's youngest sibling seized the throne and had Lilya's brothers executed. So Khavar well understood how circles of trust were smaller than perceived. Bed-ridden, with only his thoughts to occupy his time, he began to wonder who might be disloyal.

Khavar loved both of his wives dearly, a love that he knew was reciprocated. Even though politically savvy Lilya was prone to jealousy, the two queens had learned to coexist and manage any tension between them. Whenever flare-ups happened to occur, the king trusted his abilities to mollify his temperamental second wife. Despite what others may have whispered behind closed doors, he never doubted her loyalty to the kingdom or him.

After dismissing the magi, who were more preoccupied with their internal hierarchy, Khavar's thoughts turned to his and Lilya's younger son. Unlike Zahan, he feared that Kamran was not prepared to run a kingdom. Lying in his bedroom chamber, with Shanaz napping by his side, the king concluded he had to get better until he deemed Kamran ready. He called for his alchemist, hoping his friend could save him from the grasp of death's clenched hand.

Little did the king know that, across the citadel, his fate was about to be sealed.

⸻ ◆◉◆ ⸻

In Kamran's quarters, Lilya reclined on a cushion-covered bench and watched with much interest as her daughter-in-law and grandson played a game of twenty squares on the floor.

"It's your turn," Afshad said. "You had better get me. My scorpion is one roll from winning."

"Don't get too confident." Vira picked up the stick dice and tossed them on the carpet. "Seven." She began to move her piece while enumerating her words. "One-two-and-your-scorpion-is-dead." Vira knocked the piece over and raised her arms in victory.

In a fit of anger, the prince shoved the board. "Stupid game."

Lilya shook her head and sighed. "Oh, how the date doesn't fall far from the tree."

Kamran entered the room as if he had heard her disparaging comment. His face was tense. "Seeing that board game reminds me. Vira, why don't you take Afshad to the bazaar and buy a new pair of stick dice? And let him pick out a new piece while you're at it."

The request took Vira by surprise. Yet from her husband's piercing eyes and set jaw, she knew when he desired to speak privately with her mother-in-law. She took a gold coin from a drawer and hurried after Afshad, the boy already halfway down the corridor.

Lilya laughed at her grandson's exuberance and then turned to her son, his visage full of anxiety. "Well, that was creative. But you'll only spoil him."

"I can think of worse things."

"Of that, I have no doubts. Anyway, you've gotten rid of them. What's on your mind?"

"We can't wait anymore."

"Wait for what?"

"For the old man to die. He's incapable of rule. The government is paralyzed much like his body."

"I have no quarrel with your assessment."

"Mother, the kingdom is in decline. Father inherited a solvent treasury, but because of the war and his lavish spending, Zad has run out of money. Our trade agreements have stalled, and the people are taxed too heavily. The system is grinding to a halt, and I'll be damned if I let him pass onto me a throne destined for failure."

Kamran sat in a wooden chair embossed with gold and rested his head in his hands, running his fingers through his thinning hair. Impatient, he stood back up. "And to think that he seems to be hanging on. What kind of witchcraft is Adarbad helping him with?"

Lilya took a sip of rose water. "You know what must be done. Were he to live much longer, Zad might be on an intractable path to ruin. It certainly isn't fair that he inherited a prosperous kingdom while you'll be forced to deal with one that's nearly bankrupt." Trying to guide her son, the queen pushed even harder. "It's also better for a king to be more feared than loved, even by his children."

"What are you suggesting?" Kamran asked as he toyed with his dagger.

Setting down her cup, Lilya walked over and directed the blade toward the floor. "The time has come to be king. Be discreet. No blood."

"What if Shanaz or Adarbad are there?"

"It's my evening to be with him."

"Then you'll be suspected of his murder."

"Spindly Lilya? Not a chance. As far as I'm concerned, your sickly father will pass away in the night. Leave no trace of the killing. And when Afshad returns, be sure to take him with you."

The queen headed for the doorway, pausing to gather the scorpion game piece from the floor. She studied it briefly, weighing the odds such a tiny creature faces when confronted by a mighty predator. Like the desert arthropod, she knew there would be no second chances.

Lilya tossed the scorpion to Kamran. "You mustn't fail," she said, before leaving the room.

Outside, a full moon marked the summer solstice. An interlude to the oppressive heat scorching the kingdom brought much-needed relief to the people. From the brisk southwesterly winds, one could detect the faint smell of caraway fruits abundant in the mountain ranges.

Along with his son, Kamran passed sentries outside the king's quarters and strode to his father's chamber. A few torches ensconced on the walls lit the way.

Resolute in his task, Kamran entered the bedroom and shut the door behind him. The change in air pressure caused a few candle flames to flicker from the draft. The king, having eaten, was on his side, facing away from the entrance. Kamran could see his torso slowly rise and fall under the sheets. The time between breaths seemed oddly long, as if the king was running out of air.

Sensing a presence, Khavar rolled over. "Who is it? Lilya? Who's there?"

"Sorry, Father. We didn't mean to startle you."

"Kamran?"

"Were you sleeping?"

"No, no... just resting. At least, I think I was. I can't tell anymore whether I'm awake or dreaming."

Kamran walked over and sat on the edge of the bed. He glanced at the elixirs on the table. "I can assure you that you're awake."

"I'm so happy to see you both," the king said, laying his hand upon his son's.

"Are you?" Kamran pulled away to scratch his chin.

With his grandson nearby, the king felt embarrassed by the accusation. Indeed, it hurt him. "Of course, I am. Why do you doubt me?"

Kamran stood up. After gathering his thoughts, he launched into a bitter critique of his father's rule. At times, he was rude.

The king moved from being stunned at his son's bizarre behavior to growing increasingly angry. "Kamran, the kingdom will be yours soon enough, and you can do with it what you will. Until then, I'm still in charge."

Khavar began to cough but was overwhelmed by regurgitated mucus.

Kamran responded to his father's apparent discomfort with indifference. "I know you planned for Zahan to become king. Did you have any plans for me?"

The king took a moment to wipe his mouth. "You were groomed as he was. But you were not next in line. That's all. You would have been the new king's advisor or..."

"Or what?" Kamran said, his hands tightening into fists. He walked toward his father and leaned over him. "My time has come to be king. Nothing will stand in my way, and your continued refusal to die won't either."

Khavar's eyes filled with fear. Despite his best efforts, the king could no longer ignore the circumstantial evidence surrounding the untimely deaths of his other sons. In light of his alchemist's premonitions, everything at that moment coalesced to confirm his suspicions.

With resignation setting in and bitterness in his voice, the king pressed for answers. "Why, Kamran? Why did you do it? Did I not love you enough?"

"I don't want your love. I want to save this kingdom. What I have to do is for Zad and our people. Don't you understand that?"

"How could you have orchestrated Zahan's murder, your own mother's son?" The king, saddened and hurt, shed a tear.

"Don't waste my time with this false concern for Mother. She has always felt like a second-class citizen to your precious Shanaz."

"Your mother is most beloved. From the moment she arrived in Zad, our people embraced her as queen."

"Certainly more than you."

"How dare you question my feelings for her?"

Kamran again sat on the bedside, this time caressing the old man's face with a morbid affection. "Whether I question them is not important. What is important, Father, is that she does. You are a weak king, a dying king." Kamran looked over his shoulder. "You see, Afshad, every son should fear his father; even more when he is king. I never feared mine."

The king reached for Kamran's sleeve and pulled him close. "You speak in the past." Shaking from the strain, he added, in a low voice, "Not in front of the boy."

"Goodbye, King of Zad." Kamran yanked a pillow from under his father's head and pressed it over his face with all the force he could muster.

A stunned Afshad, his gaze fixed upon the gruesome scene, could only mutter a horrified "No" amid the king's desperate, muffled grunts.

The dying man contorted a little, but in his weakened state, life slipped away from him quickly, and he was soon dead, his one free hand gripped around the wrist of his son, his eyes open and devoid of all the vitality they had held in life.

Kamran raised the pillow from the king's face. He stood slowly, straightening his clothes, and turned the dead body to its side, covering it with the sheet. The tenderness in the way he cared for the corpse was more than he had ever shown to his father alive.

Kamran walked over to the magical elixirs, taking one and handing another to Afshad. "This is the other reason why I brought you here."

"What will it do?" the boy asked.

"Provide an answer to that which you have always longed for."

"But I don't even know what that is."

"You do in the deeper recesses of your mind. Hurry. Drink. We don't need to linger here."

After drinking the concoctions, Kamran and Afshad stood in defensive postures.

The effects struck fast. Kamran's body began to shake, and his skin burned as if it were on fire. Violent, gut-wrenching spasms consumed his muscles, dropping him to one knee. His organs felt dislodged. Another sharp pain brought him fully to the floor, causing him to writhe in anguish. Gritting his teeth, it took all of his willpower not to cry out.

The torment moved to Kamran's extremities, pulling at his arms and legs like a thief on the rack. As he was about to yell in agony, no longer able to endure the pain, his lungs took a deep, involuntary gasp, and the ordeal ended. Soaked with sweat, he brought himself to his feet and clenched his hands. He felt energized, his muscles still twitching rapidly.

During the frenzy of his transformation, Kamran had lost track of Afshad but found him on his hands and knees. "Son?" he said, kneeling to the floor. "Are you all right?"

What Kamran saw was shocking, for Afshad's complexion had changed. The acne that marked his face had all but disappeared. Even the few pockmarks that blemished his skin had seemingly healed. What was more, his hair, both wiry and coarse, had become soft and fine. No longer would the prince be a prisoner to his physical anxieties.

Afshad rubbed his face which felt strangely tender. "I feel ill."

Kamran pulled Afshad to his feet with an effortlessness he had never known, realizing what his elixir had brought him—extra-human strength. And he knew why. His lack of brawn relative to his older brother had always troubled him, and he resented how Zahan leveraged his superior strength to his advantage. He observed Afshad to see if he realized how easily he had been lifted, but the boy was too distracted by his grandfather's corpse.

The thrashing chaos that accompanied the drinking of the elixirs had knocked the king's bed from its normal position, rolling the body onto its back, mouth open and eyes bulging.

Heeding his mother's advice, Kamran slid the bed to its original position. He then divvied the last elixir equally into the three vials and topped them off with water from a pitcher. While his son corked the bottles, he returned the king to the tucked-in position he had found him.

Kamran hastily ushered Afshad to the doorway. "Word of Father's death will come in the morning. As hard as that was for you to watch, you must understand that the interests of a kingdom always transcend those of a king. I did what I did for Zad. Never speak of what you saw."

As they left the king's quarters and entered the torch-lit corridor, one of which had burned out, Kamran bade the guards a good night. The dimness of the hall and Afshad's discreet bearing provided enough cover to hide his face.

"What has happened to me?" the prince asked.

"One look in the mirror, and you shall see your gift. Come, I feel famished."

PIECING THE PUZZLE

Like his sons before him, King Khavar was taken to *Sarza-min-e Mordegan*, a burial site northwest of Zad. The cemetery was where the kingdom brought all its deceased, laid their corpses within a circular structure known as a *dakhmeh*, and let the scavengers of flight feast on the flesh. The bones that remained would be swept into a central pit or ossuary.

The repeated funeral processions for members of the royal family turned a somber mood among the people into one of fear. The logical question had become, "Who's next?"

Beyond that was a general malaise and feeling that the kingdom was adrift. The war with Danzardan had taken a severe toll on the military. Soldiers complained about the long tours of duty, especially since both garrisons on the front had been completed and needed to be manned at all times.

What was more, the city's infrastructure and civil works projects had been neglected. One involving underground canals, or *qanats*, to channel mountain water to Zad and the surrounding cropland had all but ceased. Cracks in the ramparts and walls caused by frequent tremors had not been repaired. Death not only filled the air; it was a heavy, pungent scent that everyone could smell. What the people desperately wanted and yearned for was hope.

Queen Lilya was attuned to the people's need for action, and a litany of orders soon followed: she and General Baraz would travel to her former kingdom to negotiate an end to the conflict; taxes and tariffs would be slashed; investments would be made in new weapons and armor; and the crowning of the new king would be done with such extravagant fanfare that it would imbue Kamran with a savior-like quality.

"Never waste an opportunity to use the power of the throne," Lilya had often reminded her son.

But the charade she had hatched with Kamran was beginning to fall apart.

———— ◄○► ————

The following evening, as twilight gave way, Shanaz hurried, face draped and garbed in a plain cloak, through the city gates and along the road until she reached the orchards. After shuffling past several rows of date palms, she stopped and scanned the barely visible tree lines. With her nerves on edge, the restive queen fought to calm her belabored breathing when she heard the voice she had sought.

"I'm over here." A figure approached Shanaz, unfurling his hood to reveal his face.

The queen took Adarbad by the hand. "Let's move farther in. I don't want to take any chances."

The pair moved deeper into the orchards until the queen felt insulated from spies and eavesdroppers.

"My lady, can you please tell me what this is about? I must leave for Raydur immediately."

"You were right, Ada," she said, her voice stricken with panic.

"Right about what?"

"Your premonitions—everything you said. You, me, the entire kingdom is in peril."

"Tell me what happened. Something must have happened to upset you."

Shanaz fought to hold back tears. "I found something in the king's mouth."

"What do you mean?"

"After receiving news of his passing, guards escorted me to his chamber. I excused them so I could be alone with him one last time. But you should have seen his face. His eyes bulged. His mouth hung open. It was an expression unbecoming of a king. So, to preserve his dignity, I closed his lips only to pull a piece of red silk from his teeth. Naturally, I gave it no consideration until I turned his pillow and discovered it had been torn."

"What am I missing?"

"Ada, his pillowcase is red silk." Shanaz reached over and clutched the alchemist by the shirt. "My husband didn't die a peaceful death the other night. He was murdered, suffocated to death. There are even stains around the tear, most likely saliva."

Adarbad's heart sank, but he remained skeptical. "I don't see how Lilya would have the strength to... are you certain? You spoke to the coroner?"

"Nobody has seen Loras or his family since yesterday morning. Seems convenient, doesn't it? Ada, it all makes sense. Think about it. The savaran was ambushed by alleged brigands. Why, then, was only Zahan killed?"

"It would seem unlikely."

"I'm telling you, he was assassinated. And my dear Mahyar? Loras said he succumbed to a ruptured gall bladder. Yet, he showed no previous symptoms. He died out of the blue." Shanaz put her hands to her head in exasperation. "It has to be Lilya. Besides, she and Kamran have been thicker than thieves lately. Who knows what other surprises they have in store?"

Adarbad rubbed his beard as he pondered the claims.

"Are you still not convinced?" Shanaz asked. "You think Mahyar and Zahan's deaths so soon after the king fell ill are merely coincidental?"

"That would seem unlikely, but there's one piece to this puzzle that makes no sense. Why would Lilya go to such lengths to kill her own son?"

"Because she no longer loved Zahan. As one of the king's wives, I was privy to the intimate details of the families. I heard things that the king was not able to see. Lilya could never control Zahan, and she despised him for it, especially after the twins drowned.

"And daring to love a commoner? For Lilya, that was the last straw. I could see the love loss in her eyes. As for Mahyar, he was just in the way. Make no mistake. Kamran will be king, but Lilya will rule the kingdom. The longer I remain here, the more my life is in danger. I fear my days are few."

"Listen—calm down. We are going to be fine. I have seen that, too." Adarbad hadn't seen Shanaz in his visions, but at the moment, he needed to say something to fortify her spirits.

"You trust me, don't you? Ever since we were children, haven't I always proven you wrong whenever you doubted me?"

"Except once, when you told me you would never marry the king." The alchemist smiled, but underneath lay a deep sadness.

He took Shanaz's hands and looked her in the eyes. "I believe you."

The queen warmly touched his face. "Now listen. Lilya and General Baraz leave soon for Danzardan, so until they return, we are probably safe. But in the meantime, you said you needed to travel to Raydur?"

"You'll recall the king had tasked me with making an elixir of protection for Yaya. Unfortunately, I can't seem to get the proper concentration of ingredients. After failing so many times, I've run out of essential minerals. I know that my counterpart in Raydur will have them."

"What will the elixir do?"

"I dare not say for fear of jinxing the outcome."

"Well, until you return, I'll lay low and look after our dear boy. He's still in shock with all that's happened." Shanaz looked through the trees toward the citadel. "My heart breaks for him."

Taking all necessary precautions, the two departed the orchards separately.

With his horse loaded with gear and waiting for him at the city gates, Adarbad made haste toward the kingdom of Raydur. By the time of his arrival, Kamran would be king.

Lagging behind, Shanaz walked through the gates to empty streets and headed for the citadel, her mind turning toward her growing fear for Yaya.

Since his father's death, the prince had been staying with the queen, rarely leaving the room where he slept. The unexpected loss had taken a toll. His appetite had waned. He slept during the day and took to wandering the city at night. The features that had given him his nickname were made all the more prominent from a face rawboned with grief.

Entering the doorway to her quarters, Shanaz called out to him. She checked his room, pulling back the canopy around his bed and lifting the sheets. She searched the veranda and then the washing basin. Yaya was nowhere to be found.

A Shortcut to Alchemy

As night settled in before the day of the crowning, Lilya summoned Kamran and Afshad to the council chamber. When the two entered the room, they saw Sarvin standing beside the queen, his hand on her shoulder and grinning ear to ear. Lilya found whatever her alchemist had been telling her amusing and her peal of laughter filled the space.

A fellow Danzardani, Sarvin had been Lilya's pick-me-up for years, and his tongue was as sharp as his mind. Whenever she felt down or overlooked by the king, she could always depend on his wit or drugs to brighten her mood. Compared to Shanaz, Lilya suffered bouts of insecurity. Fortunately, Sarvin's penchant for lobbing disparaging and bawdy remarks at the more buxom wife gave her the reassurance she needed.

Also in the council chamber was the thick-fingered blacksmith, Bezan, who was hunched over and arranging a complete set of gold-colored scale mail against the wall. Already propped up and gleaming with astonishing brilliance was a massive two-handed sword, metallic in composition and as smooth as a wind-swept dune.

Lilya brought her son and grandson to the finely crafted pieces. "Sarvin and Bezan, at my behest, have been working on these items for weeks."

Their curiosity piqued, Kamran and Afshad began to inspect their new war toys.

The queen added, "They are imbued with the rarest metal alloys, making them both extremely light and strong."

"How strong?" Afshad asked, running his hand over the glistening armor.

Holding a spear, the blacksmith asked everyone to stand clear. He cocked the weapon and threw it with force, striking the scale mail dead center.

Bezan walked over and pointed to the area where the spear had struck. "You see there, not even a scratch. This armor is impenetrable."

The blacksmith approached Afshad and handed him the helm. "Unless you run into the horn of the mythical *karkadann*, there is nothing for you to fear. No arrow, sword blade, or lance will ever draw your blood."

Lilya stepped to her grandson and placed the helm and adjoining face mask on his head. "How does it fit?" she asked, backing away to get a more complete view.

"It's perfect, *Madar bozorg*."

"And forever will you remain my perfect grandson." Lilya kissed his forehead.

The queen turned to Bezan, who held the new sword and a rusty *shamshir* in his hands. She motioned for him to proceed.

The blacksmith handed the weapons to Kamran. "What takes a normal man two hands to swing will take you only one. Do you notice the difference in weight?"

Kamran held out each sword to judge for himself. Intrigued, he passed the weathered shamshir to Sarvin and traced his finger along the new blade's metallic edge, realizing that any more pressure would open his skin.

"Just how strong have you become, my lord?" Sarvin asked.

Sensing an opportunity to display his strength, Kamran exchanged swords with the alchemist and bent the old blade in one fell swoop, snapping it at the tang and hilt.

Sarvin was astounded.

"You asked," Kamran said, handing back the remnants.

Nodding with satisfaction, Lilya addressed her son. "With the strength of ten warriors, you will be an unstoppable force in battle. Take Afshad and your new toys with you to your rooms. Play with them. Pretend. More importantly, enjoy them in their clean state, for I suspect they won't always remain so."

The queen beckoned Kamran and Afshad to come closer and took each by the hand. "Tomorrow is the coronation, a day that symbolizes hope. It would be wise to have these gifts accompany you so that our people, who have suffered immeasurably, will see that a new power has come to Zad."

❖

After the others departed, Sarvin ushered Lilya to three gilded bowls embossed with images of kings of yore in battle. Inside them were powders of various hues. Frankincense and rue filled the air.

"My lady, I have labored hard and learned much from the myriad tomes on alchemy my team found buried in the Jabiri ruins. Despite unseemly praise for Ahriman, which we translated in his diary, Uzava's skills as an alchemist exceeded all but the great Danush. And here we are, nearly one millennium after their deaths, and still much to learn."

Sarvin lifted a silver vase and poured enough water into the first bowl to dissolve the powder. "Please, drink," he said, handing it to her.

Lilya tilted the bowl to her mouth and consumed the concoction. No sooner had she set the empty vessel down than she winced and clutched her abdomen. She bent over and placed her hands on her knees, groaning as if suffering from extreme indigestion.

Soon, the discomfort passed. Lilya stood straight and took a few deep, tentative breaths. She extended her fingers and clenched them into fists.

"How strong have I become?" she asked, feeling her sinewy biceps and forearms. "And how did you pull this off?"

"Fortunately, I was able to add chemicals that blocked the receptors in your brain, isolating the elixir's effects to your physiology rather than your psyche. In that way, it differs from what Prince Kamran consumed."

"My wishes and insecurities can wait."

"As to your first question, and if my calculations are correct, you probably have the strength of two to three men. My supply of the necessary ingredients was somewhat lacking."

Lilya folded her arms. She wasn't happy.

"But, but," Sarvin said, sensing her disappointment, "these next two will be most pleasing to you."

The alchemist added water to the other bowls, and Lilya duly drank the mixtures.

But unlike the strength elixir, she experienced no immediate physical effects. "Have you failed me, Sarvin? I feel nothing."

The alchemist wore a look of mischief, rubbing his hands with childish glee.

It prompted the queen to excoriate him. "I don't have time for this. Can we move on from the high jinks?"

"Yes, of course, my lady," he said, his tone professional. "The power within the elixirs you consumed comes from what you say. They were created for summoning and represent the first of Uzava's secrets I have mastered. Listen to me and repeat these words: 'In praise of Ahriman, I call upon you to rise.'"

Sarvin repeated the phrase for Lilya's benefit, noting her expression, which suggested discomfort in extolling the evil spirit.

The queen moved to the middle of the council chamber. "What should I be bracing for?"

"Something wonderful. Say the words."

Lilya did as she was told, but nothing happened.

A panicked Sarvin slapped his forehead before retrieving a pinch of coarse, black hair from his pocket. "I forgot to give you this," he said, placing the hair in Lilya's palm. "I borrowed some from Adarbad's stash of animal ingredients."

"Borrowed?"

"In a manner of speaking. Go ahead. Toss it onto the floor when you say the chant."

Lilya recited the words, this time throwing the hair.

When it landed, a cloudburst of amorphous matter, gelatinous in nature, congealed into solid forms. There before the queen were two jackals with black fur. They stood over three feet at the shoulder and were larger than any wolf or leopard that roamed the mountains.

They shuffled toward their creator like toddlers to their mother, nuzzling the queen with their narrow snouts and showering her with their excited yips.

Lilya praised Sarvin for his efforts. "You have outdone yourself, my dear friend. But tell me. How is it that you have mastered the art of summoning before Adarbad? Even from the books I've recently been studying, what you've done is nothing short of extraordinary."

"Because I view summoning as an art. Adarbad prays to the altar of science and has faith in its laws. Well, you can see how that's worked out for him. I have merely sped up the process by taking what I gleaned from Uzava's ancient texts. Call it... a shortcut to alchemy?"

Lilya knelt in front of one of her jackals. As she rubbed under its chin, she regarded her friend thoughtfully, musing about his comments. She wondered how to reconcile her devotion to Ohrmazd with powers that derived their effect from the dark spirit. Her thoughts, however, were fleeting, for the tingly rush that she had felt from summoning the jackals surpassed even the best of Sarvin's stash of sedatives and mild hallucinogens.

The queen stood. "Well, if it's a shortcut you need, then so be it. The creator works his will in ways that can appear contradictory. Am I right?"

Sarvin nodded.

Lilya smiled as if her friend's affirmation gave her pardon. "I do hope there are more surprises in store?"

"There are indeed, but they will take time. Adarbad's secrets are many, and his collection of rare minerals and cellular specimens is invaluable. But I can't rummage through his laboratory willy-nilly. When he returns, I fear he'll learn that someone has been in his chamber. Of course, he'll suspect me."

"Returns? Returns from where?"

"Raydur. He went in search of some specific minerals."

"He knows better than to skip the coronation." Lilya fumed with anger, her eyes glaring and hard. Her mind moved to Adarbad's possible rationale. "As you know, I leave for Danzardan following the crowning. While I'm away, I want you to keep one eye on Yaya and two on his sneaky alchemist friend."

"And Shanaz?"

"I'll deal with her soon enough."

Sensing the queen's anxiety, the slightly smaller of the two jackals began to lick Lilya's hand. This seemed to calm her, and she returned the gesture by rubbing behind the animal's ears, images of grandeur flashing in her head.

After dismissing Sarvin, she sent for tailors to get her measurements so that Bezan could fashion proper garments. No longer would she conform to the silken dresses and overgarments of a king's wife when she could instead don battle gear like the great queen warriors of years past.

While she waited, Lilya tossed a cardamom cookie from a nearby platter onto the floor and summoned the guards.

Two spear-wielding men entered the council chamber but froze at the sight of the jackals fighting over the treat.

"Do you like my new children?" the queen asked.

The men were too transfixed by the jackals' piercing red eyes to answer.

"Bring twenty *mina* of meat and two bowls of water."

Their continued hesitation drew a sharp rebuke.

"Should I feed them lamb or feed them you? Go."

WRESTLING, I

With summer underway, the Rud-e Barik feeding the grounds around Zad had shrunk to a shallow creek. Irrigation barely trickled, and villagers were coming to blows along the riverbanks as they jostled for access. The restlessness that had spawned the unusual spats of violence began to weigh on Lilya. Before departing for Danzardan, she gave explicit orders to finish the construction of the qanats sloping down from the Kuhha-ye Sabz.

While the newly crowned king led an expedition to the Green Mouhtains to oversee the progress on the underground channels, workers at home busied themselves with final preparations for his inauguration. Having assumed power four days earlier, the king's inaugural was a more celebratory affair, giving dignitaries from other kingdoms, including Kings Delawar and Mazad, time to make the journey.

It was also fitting that *Jashn-e Tirgan*, the water festival, would fall on the same day. Canopies draped in silk were erected around the chogan field. Goats and lambs were slaughtered by the dozens. Cooks and bakers worked around the clock preparing loaves of bread, soups, and delectable desserts. Ice blocks from the *yakhchal* were carved to chill desserts like *faloodeh* and drinks like *sekanjabin* made from honey and vinegar.

Perhaps more than his father, Afshad's transformation had an overtly powerful effect on his behavior. He had become, in the words of one observer, "almost born anew," and always found himself surrounded by admirers and sycophants. Being a prince has its share of perks, but a handsome one culls even more. Many of his insecurities had vanished, replaced instead with a confidence that was to reveal itself as both arrogant and cruel.

⸺◆⸺

Two days before the celebration, Yaya and Gulzar strolled together through the orchards. As they talked, Yaya tried to piece together the puzzle that was this girl. But for all his self-professed wisdom, he remained baffled by her intentions.

Gulzar stopped walking. "Hold on. I have something to give you." She reached into her pocket and pulled out a woven rainbow-colored wristband. "I know it's early, but with Jashn-e Tirgan around the corner, I wanted you to have mine."

Yaya smiled as she placed it on his wrist.

"Oh, and one other thing," Gulzar said, kissing him on the cheek. "That's for your birthday."

The two hugged before wandering toward the chogan field.

Afshad was given illusory authority over the inaugural preparations. He happened to be leaving one of the ice houses when he saw the exchange of affection. Stung with jealousy, he corralled his gang and approached the apparent couple.

"Well, well, well... is this a budding romance I see? I didn't think anything could grow in this godforsaken land."

"That's enough, Afshad," Gulzar said, attempting to bypass him. "This isn't the place."

Afshad grabbed her arm. "Just a moment—hang on. This is nothing to be ashamed of. The thing about Shotor is that once you get bored with him, you can ride him. Isn't that right, Yayayaya,yayayaYaya?"

The other boys and girls laughed uncomfortably at Afshad's fake stuttering.

Yaya only listened, expressionless, a tactic he always relied on around his cousin because he knew it upset him. "Yeah, well, camels are good for something. At least I can be ridden."

"Ooh, clever."

"I admire you, Afshad. I do. Whether it's with girls or chogan, you always come to play. But they're tough games to master when you don't have a mallet or any balls."

Yaya began to walk away, an amused grin across his face. He didn't get far. His cousin tackled him and wrapped his arm around his neck like a vice.

Pinned face-down in the dirt, Yaya struggled to squirm free. As his breathing grew labored, he heard Gulzar and a few other voices imploring his cousin to release him.

But Afshad ignored their pleas and instead whispered into his ear. "I know this is your good ear, so you had better listen well. I've had it with your wisecracks over the years. The next time you humiliate me, mark my words, you'll get the same fate as your father. Do you understand?"

"Yes, prince of smugness."

Afshad tightened his hold and only released his cousin after workers noticed the mayhem.

With his head down to hide a bloodied nose, Yaya pushed himself to his feet and walked away.

Two boys who had ahold of Gulzar released her.

"*Nakas*," she said with a scowl before storming off. She stopped by Afshad and gave him a scornful look. "What has happened to you? You used to be nice."

Afshad reached for her tentatively.

But Gulzar swatted his hand and sped away.

"Fine—be with him. But I'll be king one day, not Shotor."

Gulzar ran around one of the conical-shaped yakhchals. She found Yaya sitting against the earthen wall and staring at the cloudless sky. His sleeve was bloody from where he had wiped his face, and his eyes welled with tears. But they did so less from any pain than the sheer embarrassment of his drubbing.

When Yaya saw Gulzar, he fled down a few stairs leading to the icehouse's interior.

Gulzar chased after him, calling his name.

Light entered the yakhchal through an air portal and illuminated the cavity. Large iron tongs and other tools used to move and cut the ice blocks lay on the ground. The space whirred as vents and slats on the walls funneled in strong drafts that aided the refrigeration process.

Gulzar held her hair back and headed below ground to the chill room.

There, on a block of ice, its surface covered in grass and thatched insulation, sat the prince, the boy armed with an icepick and digging into the *sarooj* of the wall.

"What are you doing?" Gulzar asked.

"Checking the quality of construction. Pedar bozorg always worried that not enough goat hair was used in its formation. 'Less on the ash; more on the goat hair,' he would say." Yaya tossed the pick to the side and glared at Gulzar. "Why don't you go to your boyfriend?"

"He's not my boyfriend. We're only friends."

"Then why were you kissing him the other day?"

Gulzar looked away. "It's not what you think."

Yaya shook his head, unconvinced. "I don't understand. I really tried. I know I'm not as handsome as he is, but did I ever have a chance? Did you ever think of me in that way?"

Gulzar walked over to Yaya and sat beside him. "Don't make this hard on me. I'm confused, too."

"Your lips don't seem to be. I'm telling you, Afshad's no good. He's always putting you down."

"That's not true. Most of the time we're together, he's very sweet."

"Sweet? If he's 'sweet,' I must be saffron pudding."

Gulzar sighed. "Don't you realize that you intimidate him? That's why he acts up."

"So it's my fault he turns into the prince of darkness? How do I intimidate him? He knows me like a brother."

"And you know him like one, which means you know all his insecurities. I understand Afshad can be an arrogant jerk, but you know it's only a mask. When he and I are alone, he can be quite charming."

Yaya's eyes filled with sadness. "I guess I'm not charming enough."

"Of course you are. But you're also aloof."

"What does that mean?"

Gulzar looked at Yaya hesitantly. "I understand you've been grieving, but ever since your father's death, you've closed your-self off—from me, our friends. Sometimes, I get the sense you don't want me around."

"I do want you around. It's just... I don't know how to explain it. I have a lot on my mind."

"You have too much on your mind, Yaya. Half the time, you seem to be in a different world. Part of me loves that mysterious side of you, but—"

"But what?"

Gulzar looked down.

"You don't have to say anything. I know you don't like me that way."

"Yaya, stop it."

"I guess the better man won. As they say, 'To the victor go the spoils.'"

"Why are you making this so difficult? You're as confused as I am."

"I've never been more certain of anything."

Gulzar began to cry. "I'm not some prize for you and Afshad to fight over."

Yaya reached for her hand.

But Gulzar rebuffed him. She rose from the ice block and ran up the stairs, the cool breeze rippling around her silken dress.

Yaya felt his lungs collapse, and though air was all around, he couldn't breathe.

BEGGAR IN THE NIGHT

It was the night before the rain festival. Kamran stood in all his regalia while his wife adjusted and primped his clothing.

Having just returned from the kingdom of Danzardan, where she had negotiated an end to the conflict, Lilya looked on and critiqued her son's attire.

"I see too many wrinkles."

Vira ignored the comment and turned her focus to the silken headdress beneath her husband's crown .

"Mother, you have succeeded in ending the war, but were you able to set the terms in our favor? Were you able to secure the garrisons?"

"They viewed dismantling the garrisons as a prerequisite for returning their gains near the northern bend of the Rud-e Barik."

"But Mother—"

"Relax. Before you jump to conclusions, what did I teach you about survival?"

Kamran drew a blank.

"Think. You are king. You must remember what I've told you."

"To live to fight another day?"

"I agreed to dismantle the garrisons... but not for two years. I convinced King Syamak that trust must first be established, given the enmity between our peoples. Having the garrisons manned well into the foreseeable future will not only give us eyes at the border, but it will also give us deterrence. And with the ensuing peace, however tenuous, we'll have the time necessary to get our house in order. Once we do, we'll vanquish that no good uncle of mine and reclaim what rightfully belongs to me. My brothers will not have died in vain."

"Two years may be a luxury we don't have."

"How so?" Lilya asked.

"The drought is severe. The qanat system may not replenish what the Rud-e Barik has failed to supply. Cries of hunger are beginning to fill the night."

"I know that," Lilya said, taking over the assembling of the silken headdress. "I have ears, you know. I hear the unease within the villages."

Vira sighed and walked off to remind the servants to properly press her husband's clothing.

"But I think there is more to our lack of potable water than meets the eye."

Kamran searched for an answer to her riddle before conceding. "I'm listening."

"King Delawar is amiable enough and has always been one of our most stalwart allies, but don't think for a moment, based on the severity of the drought, that Raydur is not hoarding water. After all, the Rud-e Barik passes through his kingdom first."

"What are you implying?"

"Pressure," she said. "We'll charm the king during his visit, and I'll arrange a meeting in Raydur upon his return. I'll have a surprise for Delawar that should leave quite an impression."

"What kind of surprise?"

"You'll see soon enough. I suggest you and Vira get some sleep." Lilya searched the room for the new queen. "Where is she anyway? We have a busy day tomorrow."

Kamran walked over to the mirror to inspect his appearance. He tightened the red sash around his gold embroidered tunic and inspected the white shoulder girdle. "You are not the only one with a surprise."

"No?" she said, her eyebrows arching. "Pray tell."

"I ordered the blacksmith to corral several old spears and shamshirs for me to bend—give the people a show. Besides, shouldn't they see how powerful their king has become? It'll give them hope."

Kamran finished adjusting his gem-studded *kulah*, or crown, and presented himself to his mother. "So, how do I look?"

Lilya walked toward the foyer. "One sword bending in the council chamber wasn't enough?"

Kamran looked at his mother nervously, fearing disapproval of the carnival idea.

"You're like an elephant in musth," she said with a smirk, bidding him good night.

⊷◆⊶

Apart from crews working late to assemble the inaugural tents, most Zadians had turned in early in anticipation of the big event. A few beggars wandered the bazaar looking for food scraps, while guards here and there strolled in tandem and engaged in mundane conversation. Among these night crawlers was Yaya, whose personal grief and sense of rejection had led to thoughts of running away.

At first, the idea excited him, but his feelings were soon tempered by the logistics: where he would go, when he would leave, and whom he would tell. He knew he would miss Shanaz terribly. In many ways, she was the mother he never had. Leaving Zad also meant giving up his apprenticeship in Adarbad's laboratory just as he was about to begin learning metal transmutation.

Immersed in his thoughts, the prince walked past a group of vendors packing their belongings for the night.

Out of the shadows, a hooded and hunched beggar in dingy garb approached him with an outstretched hand. His hood was pulled down low, affording no glimpse of his face.

"Young man, can you spare some change?"

Not in the mood to be hassled, Yaya refused. "Sorry."

The prince headed north. At the end of the bazaar was a four-pillared hemispherical dome that functioned as a juncture. From there, he walked to the fire temple where the coronation had happened several days earlier. The immediate space around the edifice was insulated from the encroaching houses by bushes and small trees, making it the most serene part of the city.

As Yaya sat on the steps separating the temple from a shallow pool of water, he noticed the beggar skulking his way. Taken aback by the tramp's persistence, he searched his pockets for money. In one, he found a few pistachio shells and some dirt left behind from his scrape with his cousin. In the other were two silver *drahm*.

The old man stretched out his hand once again.

"Here," Yaya said, placing the coins in the beggar's palm. "Now let me be."

The beggar leaned closer to the prince and pulled back his hood, revealing his face for the first time.

Yaya was dumbfounded. "Ada?"

"Shh, be quiet. Follow me to the bushes."

The alchemist led the prince into a cluster of shrubs.

"Why are you dressed like this?" Yaya asked. "You look ridiculous."

"Never mind that. You must listen to me carefully. We don't have much time."

"Fine, but can you give me my coins?"

"This is no time for jokes. I'm dressed this way because I fear my whereabouts are being monitored, and not for benevolent reasons."

The fear and intensity in Adarbad's eyes had a sobering effect on the boy. "I'm listening," he said, somewhat frightened.

"Your grandfather didn't die a natural death. He was suffocated, murdered by Kamran himself."

"What?" Yaya's face crumpled with horror. "What are you talking about?"

"Shanaz and I also believe that Mahyar was poisoned. At first, I was skeptical of the charge until I took inventory of my supplies and cross-checked them with my daily record of activities."

"I don't understand."

"Back in March, I purchased several pieces of arsenopyrite from a trading caravan. As you know, the king was keen on me learning more about metal transmutation, and the arsenic they contain adds critical strength to copper alloys. However, my records indicate that I've used three pieces of the rock-sized sulfide."

"What does that mean?"

"I purchased four. Somebody pilfered the last piece from my laboratory. It had to be Sarvin."

"To do what?"

"It's poison, something very few people know. He must have extracted some and then mixed it with food or tea. It's the only explanation."

Yaya put his hands to his face and shook his head in disbelief. "I don't want to hear any more of this."

"Understandably. Youth shouldn't be burdened with such things. But the fact remains that there is evil in the world."

Yaya thought of his father's funeral and the lack of remorse shown by his grandmother. "And my father?"

Adarbad placed his hands on the boy's shoulders, looking him in the eyes. "This will be difficult for you to understand, but your grandmother was willing to do whatever it took to put Kamran on the throne, even if it meant assassinating a prince."

Yaya's expression grew distant.

"What is it?" the alchemist asked.

"Just something Afshad said. We fought yesterday, and he threatened me with the same fate."

"It's all true. Shanaz and I are in danger as well. We have to leave the city."

Yaya began to panic. "What about me?"

"You, most of all, must leave. Ancient religious texts have validated my visions. Ill omens portend. There will be war and untold suffering. And time is running out. When did you last see a cloud?"

"I can't even remember."

"Nor can I," the alchemist said. "The skies have been barren for weeks. But we understand why. Ahriman has unleashed his minions of darkness, including the demon of drought. As we speak, it is engaged in an epic battle with Tishtrya."

"Tishtrya?"

"You would know him as Tishtar, the namesake of our water festival."

"But why now?"

"Because the ancient yazdan have grown weak. We have failed to venerate them as our forebears once did. That's where you come in."

"Me? What can I possibly do?"

"You are the champion of Ohrmazd himself. On the day you were born, the planets aligned, heralding a special birth. It's the reason your father was so protective of you. Contrary to what most think, the peculiarities you have are God-given. They have a purpose."

"A purpose for what?"

"To save us. When I told your grandfather of this burden, he instructed me to create a new elixir to aid you. Let me tell you—it wasn't easy. I had to travel to Raydur to finish the job." Adarbad reached into his robe and pulled out a blue ceramic bottle encased in twisted copper threads. "Here, drink the contents."

Yaya took the bottle. "What will it do?"

"You'll know soon enough."

Yaya popped the cork and drank a dense and bitter concoction. His nose turned up at the unpleasant flavor. "That's disgusting."

"You must travel to Raydur at once. Southwest of the city is *Kuh-e Ab*, the highest peak in the Kuhha-ye Sabz. Somewhere at the base of the mountain, you'll find the temple ruins of

Anahita and her sacred springs. They are the life source of our rivers."

Yaya remembered the stories about the springs his father had told him. "All right, what do I do then?"

"Fill the bottle you are holding with the sacred water. All four elements must be gathered and presented to Tishtrya. Together, they represent the rain cycle, making them the ultimate offering. Only then will the rain god have the strength to defeat Apaosha."

"What about the other three?"

"A few months prior, my colleague in Raydur made a pilgrimage to *Sang-e Pir*. He retrieved sheddings from the sacred *haoma* plants that grow there. They represent the earth element. He will give you some to add to the bottle."

"And the other two elements?"

"The priority is getting to the springs of Anahita."

Yaya felt overwhelmed. "As if it were that easy."

"I have faith in you."

"I've heard you say, 'Faith is for fools.'"

"That's only when I'm having a bad day. Don't take every nonsensical thing I say to heart."

"But why aren't you coming with me? I can't do this alone, Ada."

"You won't be alone. Shanaz and I will meet you on the bridge over the Rud-e Barik. If we are delayed, go to Raydur without us, and we'll meet you at the fire temple. You remember where it is, yes?"

Yaya nodded.

"Fill your haversack with only necessities and prepare to leave at the end of the water festival. It'll be dark, and everyone will be drunk from celebrating. Go through the orchards. They'll provide you with cover. I must leave you now and get answers to some pressing questions."

"Answers to what kinds of questions?" Yaya asked.

"Earlier, I heard yipping sounds from your grandmother's quarters."

"Those are her jackals. Did you see them?"

"I peeked around the hallway corner and saw her embrace them. I swear, I've never seen her look happier. Funny how it took a pair of bloodthirsty carnivores to bring out her affections. But you know what that means, don't you?"

Yaya's eyes darted to and fro—then it hit him. "They were summoned."

"Precisely."

After a reflective moment, Adarbad looked at Yaya, who seemed strangely serene in light of all he had learned. But the alchemist knew better. The boy was in shock. "Think you'll be all right?"

Yaya feigned a smile.

The alchemist embraced his "little" apprentice before slipping away into the darkness. He let the tears fall only after he was a fair distance from the fire temple, for in his visions, he didn't see himself with the prince—only images of savage animals, marching armies, and a lone youth in the mountains.

Still, Adarbad was determined to make it to Raydur. He knew he couldn't see everything beyond the horizon, the elixir of precognition he had concocted being too weak to elicit more than sudden flashes of second sight. He had to hope.

Yaya remained there a while longer, thinking about the quest. He felt lonelier than ever and more afraid. He knew his chances of surviving the many predators in the ranges were slim. But if the kingdom truly depended on him, as he'd been told, then he would avenge his father's death by saving it.

Yaya headed back to the citadel to begin packing his supplies. He would leave tomorrow night after Jashn-e Tirgan.

DINNER FOR TWO

The day's festivities were winding down. As a final act, Lilya listened to a poetry recital under a lavender and yellow canopy alongside Kings Delawar and Mazad. Earlier, Kamran had enthralled the crowds with his weapon-bending spectacle. Afshad, for his part, strutted around with his regular entourage of sidekicks, including Gulzar, with whom he had seemingly reconciled. The two often found themselves paired together during the festival's many dances.

The grandiosity of the event, coupled with Kamran's newfound strength, was meant to intimidate the kings of Raydur and Jarak. To Lilya, diplomacy was only effective when backed by force. During her talks with King Delawar, she insinuated as much, warning that any excessive siphoning of the Rud-e Barik would damage relations between the two kingdoms. She was convinced his reasonable nature would prevail during her scheduled visit to Raydur, three days hence.

With dinner set to begin, Lilya excused herself to speak with Kamran.

The two kings, alone at last, took the opportunity to assess the power transfer in Zad.

"It would appear your relationship with Zad has its downside," Mazad said. "Perhaps now you understand my kingdom's propensity for self-reliance. Your past overtures to my late father, Delawar, were refused not out of distrust, but caution. The more strings there are between peoples, the harder they are to sever."

"King Khavar was a reasonable man," Delawar said, "as was his and Lilya's elder son. But the fact that the younger, less predictable one has ascended to the throne has forced us to reassess where things stand. This all smells of treachery if you ask me."

"Indeed, it does." The king of Jarak looked past Delawar's shoulder to a young woman with plaited blonde hair, dressed in a linen kaftan. "Would this be your daughter, Delawar?"

"Oh, yes, forgive my manners. I believe you last saw Mahzarin a year ago during your state visit."

"It's a pleasure to see you again, Princess. I must say, your name is most befitting—a golden moon, and none could deny it."

Mahzarin blushed and adjusted her shawl with long, slim fingers. "It's nice to see you as well, Your Highness. And the queen? Is she not here?"

"She has more important business to tend to at home."

Mahzarin was puzzled. "I'm sorry?"

Delawar couldn't help himself and divulged the good news on Mazad's behalf. "Her Majesty is expecting."

The Jaraki king beamed with pride. "I'm to be a father for the third time. Hopefully, she'll provide me with an heir to the throne."

"I'm sure she won't let you down," Mahzarin said, "but don't discount a woman's ability to lead. The history of our lands is replete with queens who not only ruled but ruled effectively."

"A point well taken, my lady, which explains why your father bears none of the trademarks of a man his age. The confidence you instill in him is a testament to your capability and your mother's before you; peace be upon her." Mazad smiled his most winning smile, wishing to charm the princess.

"You're too kind. Now, if you'll excuse me." Mahzarin rose from her seat and headed to a table serving various *sharbats*, her silken shawl fluttering in the breeze.

The young king of Jarak, running his fingers through his beard, was seemingly lost in thought as he watched her walk away.

This prompted Delawar to clear his throat. "Ahem, we were speaking about Zad's intentions?"

"Yes, of course," Mazad said, resuming a dignified tone. "As you were saying?"

"The drought is deep, but I will not sacrifice my people for Zad."

"You have the leverage. You have the water."

"You don't understand," Delawar said. "The mountain brooks and streams that feed into the Rud-e Barik have greatly diminished. Even if I wanted to bargain with Queen Lilya—and, make no mistake, it would be Lilya, for this King Kamran is more interested in showmanship than governance—I have nothing to bargain with. The question is, will she take that for an answer?"

Mazad saw Lilya walking their way. "I have no doubt she'll let you know."

"Forgive me, gentlemen. The king of Zad will soon speak. But first, let us enjoy the feast that Ohrmazd has graciously bestowed upon us."

"Indeed," Mazad said, "and let us not only pray for rain, but also pray." His eyes met Delawar's.

Sitting nearby were Queen Shanaz and the alchemists.

Over the last few days, it had become clear to Shanaz that her daily movements were being monitored. Around corners or behind bushes, wherever she ventured, spying eyes were sure to follow. Likewise, what should have been an innocuous greeting from a royal guard carried a lingering gaze that was unmistakable in its intent—"we are watching you."

Hence, she advised discretion in both her and Adarbad's departure to preclude suspicion. Yaya would leave first, after the festival ended, and she would follow last.

"Besides," Shanaz had told the alchemist, "There is someone I must first visit."

Yaya and his cousin sat at end of the table. More than once, he imagined ways of hurting him. But he knew better. Vengeance for his father would have to wait. So, while Afshad enjoyed his *halva*, a fudge-like sweet, the prince tried to focus on the journey ahead. He glanced at the date palm orchards where he had left his horse and hid his haversack and woolen cloak. It was only a matter of time before he would 'disappear.'

Kamran rose and addressed the rapturous throngs. The people of Zad had been seduced, and a confidence and feeling of rebirth cut through the festering despair.

For Lilya, everything was proceeding as planned. She even felt exultant this evening. Yet the queen was shrewd enough to know she could only control events for so long before they conspired against her. That meant eliminating any perceived internal threats, including her grandson. Coups were not uncommon, and neither was the rise of boy kings.

The feast ended, and everyone left the grounds, save for a handful of workers taking apart canopies. Some festival-goers headed to the Rud-e Barik to toss in their wrist ribbons as was tradition, while others staggered home in a drunken stupor to sleep off the drink that had been lavishly supplied.

Yaya reached his horse without incident. He packed his crescent-patterned felt hat into his haversack and swapped his formal attire for his favorite blue, scale-patterned tunic—one he wore so often that people who didn't know him might suspect his royal position. Over his tunic, he donned his cloak and waited for twilight.

A short while later, the prince took one last scan of the chogan field when, beyond the trees, he spotted several spear-wielding guards heading his way. Their steps were purposeful. Yaya cursed under his breath. He had suspected all along that his slipping away so easily had been too good to be true.

Needing a diversion, he whispered a command to his horse and smacked it on the hip.

The horse whinnied and trotted off through the orchards, prompting the guards to give chase.

Yaya quietly back-pedaled until, by chance, he came to an orchard station—a small shed housing ladders, baskets, and various implements. He took advantage of the hiding place and went inside, biding his time while sitting on a bench. Next to his feet was a pile of five-inch date thorns plucked in late winter. They made him contemplate that every living thing has its special defense. What his defense was, he didn't know.

"So, it has come to this," he thought, regarding his grandmother's actions.

Startled by a gruff voice, Yaya took a step toward the narrow doorway only to see it blocked by a member of the *pushtigban*, or royal guard.

"I thought as much." Standing there was a middle-aged man whose baritone voice wielded authority well. "Come now, you have nothing to fear from me."

Yaya didn't move. Realizing his hesitation looked incriminating, he straightened his posture and puffed out his chest as much as his skinny frame would allow. "Let me pass, Piruz. That's an order."

"I'm sorry, but the king's carry orders more weight than yours. You are to report to your grandmother forthwith."

"For what?"

"I don't ask for explanations."

Yaya stayed still, ignoring the words of the veteran sentry he had known since he could remember.

"Don't make this difficult on me, *shahpur*."

Yaya remained defiant and backed up to the bench.

"Very well," Piruz said. "You leave me no other choice."

The guard lunged forward but tripped over a chopping block. He stumbled past Yaya, who managed to sidestep his advance, and barreled into an array of harvesting tools hanging on the rear wall.

The prince rushed to the doorway when he heard an anguished groan. He turned to find the guard lying on the pile of date thorns, one of his hands to his throat. Deep in his neck was the curved blade of a hand-held sickle. Blood spilled out like a tipped-over decanter of wine.

Piruz reached for the boy, for help this time, but his outstretched arm held for only a moment before steadily descending to the floor. He gasped once, then his arm fell.

After fleeing the gruesome scene, Yaya ran through the orchards until he reached the main road. With no sign of his horse, he headed farther east. A quarter mile on, and at a juncture, he was startled by a heavy, familiar snort. There was Ruh, hidden behind a tamarisk shrub. Yaya hoped to find him but didn't think the gelding would appear where he had been told to go. Even the telling, in retrospect, seemed preposterous.

The prince mounted and began making his way through the outer villages. Despite giving the guards the slip, he donned his hood and kept his head down. Nothing was to be left to chance.

Not long after, a wave of thirst and nausea hit him. He recalled what Adarbad had told him about the elixir: to expect strange sensations until the chemicals fused with his body.

The villages looked dilapidated even in the dim light. The modest mud-brick homes often sheltered extended families and grew even more crowded as the drought forced people to husband their resources.

For some time the prince wound his way through the streets and alleyways of the vastryoshan settlements. When he reached the byway that led to the east-west road, he nudged his horse into a slow trot. They would soon be on their way to Raydur.

⸺◆⸺

In the citadel, Shanaz moved through her son's quarters. Seeing where she had found his body made her shudder—his head on the floor, a pool of saliva and mucus near his mouth. His room remained as it had the day he died, and she walked around touching his items as if to touch him. The smell of his garments made her sob, for his scent still lingered. Just as she gathered herself and wiped away her tears, she heard a racket outside the room.

Shanaz hurried to the foyer and peeked down the corridor. What she saw sent a shiver through her limbs: four royal guards strode in lockstep toward Adarbad's quarters. With her departure now foiled, the queen had to focus on her and Yaya's survival. Adarbad's fate, she assured herself, was in the hands of Ohrmazd.

When the pushtigban turned the corner, she fled in the opposite direction, down a lesser-used stairwell. Any escape hinged on getting to her horse, the mare saddled and waiting in the royal stall.

The guards and their commander, a man named Dadgar, met General Baraz at the door of Adarbad's laboratory. Together they barged in and found him holding a half-packed bag of supplies. The commander motioned to his men to make an arrest.

Outmanned, the alchemist surrendered and listened to the charges levied against him.

"By order of King Kamran," Dadgar said, "You are hereby under arrest for treason and inciting mutiny."

Struck by a sense of fatalism, Adarbad uttered softly, "I have let you down, my boy."

As the guards ushered the alchemist to the dungeon, General Baraz entered Kamran's quarters, where the new king had convened his wife, Lilya, and Sarvin. The jackals lay on the rug, panting to cool themselves. Their ribs protruded with each breath, stretching the skin around them.

"My lord," Baraz said, "The *pushtigban-salar* has taken custody of Adarbad, but Yaya somehow escaped in the orchards. Dadgar has told me that one of his men was found dead, the blade of a billhook sticking in his gullet."

Lilya was stunned by the news. "What about Shanaz? Where is she?"

Baraz shook his head. "We don't know."

"She was seen returning to the citadel, was she not?"

"We've checked her private quarters and King Khavar's. We've also looked in the bathhouse and the watchtower. She's nowhere to be found."

"'Nowhere' doesn't exist, General. Alert the gatehouses. Search the villages. I want that woman brought to me. Do you understand? Don't worry about Shotor."

Baraz made a hasty exit.

"How can we not worry about Shotor?" Kamran asked, his expression earnest. "You yourself have seen omens of the boy. And by all accounts, he's a murderer. Mother, he needs to be dealt with."

Sarvin sought to bolster Kamran's argument. "He'll go to Raydur, my lady. Delawar was an ally of the late king. It only makes sense that the boy would take refuge there."

With her plan already hatched, Lilya summoned her jackals to their feet. Rubbing the nape of their necks, she knelt and whispered words of ancient Jabiri into their ears. The animals' eyes filled with blood lust. Drool dripped from their jowls. Like arrows tight on a bow, the jackals whined to be set loose.

Lilya relished the taunt before sending them off. "Leave nothing but his bones."

The animals dashed through the doorway.

Vira looked visibly distressed. "Queen Mother, he is your grandson."

Lilya responded with an icy stare. "That's exactly why you need not worry about him. Your role is to see to the needs of my son." She glanced at the young queen as she walked to a small balcony. "Take care of the king, Vira. I'll take care of the kingdom."

When Lilya reached the balustrade, she saw the two jackals hurling along the torch-lit inner wall leading to the citadel gatehouse. Her eyes narrowed for what she hoped would be Yaya's gruesome fate.

LAND OF THE DEAD

T he kingdom of Raydur was a two-day ride. If unburdened by sandstorms or monsoons, a rider of stamina could halve the time by foregoing the usual overnight stop in the ancient temple ruins.

Yaya needed no incentive to mount such a vigorous push. Cloaked in darkness, his late departure also afforded him the benefit of a deserted passageway. Indeed, night travelers were an anomaly on the dusty road, which meant that brigand raids from the Samjari settlements were equally rare.

Once on the main road out of Zad, he commanded his horse into a steady canter.

The prince pressed on until he arrived at the bridge spanning the Rud-e Barik. There he waited, listening to the small eddies struggling around the contours of the riverbed. The near silence unsettled him, as the lifeblood of his people had been all but choked off. Rumor had it that if the qanats failed to deliver, the river's meager supply would last only weeks.

Yaya dismounted and shared a few pistachios with Ruh, a gift from his father when he turned eight and was deemed old enough to ride a full-grown horse. He scratched the gelding's chin, much to Ruh's delight.

"Don't get too relaxed. When my friends to arrive, we're out of here."

The animal snorted and rubbed its muzzle into the boy's palm, more interested in the nuts than the conversation.

Yaya obliged, sharing what was left. He wiped his hands on his cloak and looked toward Zad, its citadel watchtower basking in torchlight.

After a long yawn, the prince heard the rhythmic thudding of two figures moving in stride and fast approaching. He remounted, eagerly awaiting the sight of familiar faces. Only when the silhouettes of the riderless animals became apparent did he have a clue as to what they were. His heart raced, beating its way into his throat.

Wasting no time, he spurred his horse over the bridge and onto the dusty road. Knowing the animals would catch him in the open flats, he banked toward the cemetery, the ground covered in briars, mugwort, and grasses.

As Ruh barreled through the foliage, risking cuts to his skin, Yaya could hear the pounding thrum of his pursuers draw closer.

Soon, they happened upon Zad's burial grounds and the ruins of the ancient dakhmeh.

Yaya led Ruh behind a partially collapsed wall in hopes of hiding, but it proved a brief respite against predators equipped with night vision and an acute sense of smell.

Slinking through the rubble came the creatures that Yaya had rightly guessed were his grandmother's jackals. He had seen them in the citadel but steered clear of their unnatural gaze.

With his horse trapped against the edge of the pit, he could no longer avoid them.

A fierce determination lit the beasts' eyes as they stealthily moved in for the kill.

Yaya went for his sword, but Ruh's nervous shifting forced him to use both hands on the reins lest they both fall into the ossuary. He couldn't believe that his quest was about to end before it ever really began. In a moment of macabre lucidity, whether crushed or eaten alive, he thought it fitting that his bones would lie where they were meant to be.

As the jackals prepared to strike, a rustling disturbance caught their attention.

Yaya took advantage of their being distracted and slid off his horse and over the edge of the pit. When his feet hit the gound, he heard the most awful sounds above—those of carnage. Yaya knew his horse was being torn to shreds. He crouched and covered his ears so as not to hear the slaughter.

Looking up with bated breath, Yaya saw the jackals peer at him over the edge of the ossuary. They were panting heavily. A glob of bloody saliva fell and landed on his chin.

Fearful they would pounce, the boy fled to the center of the pit, stumbling over bones. The jackals reacted by pacing back and forth. Their apparent frustration gave Yaya hope that the twelve-foot drop was enough to end the chase.

"What do you think?" one jackal said to the other. "Should we leap in after him?"

"Then what—pull out our wings and fly out?"

"All right, all right, I get your point."

"Look, he's as good as done, and so are we. Let's eat."

The jackals turned around and sniffed their kill. Like most killers, they went straight for the belly.

Yaya's mind reeled, dumbfounded that he had understood the animals' yips and high-pitched barks as if they were words in his own language.

While the animals feasted on the carcass, the prince took solace that they had stopped pursuing him. But he also knew they were right. He was trapped. Nor was there any reason to believe that Adarbad and Shanaz would find him. After all, why would they look in Sarzamin-e Mordegan?

Before long, the jackals had eaten their fill and scurried off into the deepening dark. In their wake was the chitter-chitter of cicadas.

Yaya looked up at the star-filled sky when an urge to laugh or cry came over him. Whether from relief or the simple absurdity of where he found himself, he wasn't sure. While he worked out his emotions, he began to pile bones at the base of the wall, all the while wondering which ones might belong to his family members.

When the pile seemed high enough, Yaya used it to try to reach the edge of the ossuary. Again and again he jumped up, but with each failed attempt the bones shifted and lost critical height. By the time he rebuilt the pile, his legs were too weak for another go. All he could do was rest until he was ready again.

This pattern repeated throughout the night. Twice, he managed to grip the edge but couldn't hang on.

Finally, after many hours, Yaya gave up and sat against the wall, his knees drawn in. He watched as darkness slowly gave way to light. The sun cracked the horizon and shone on the top of the dakhmeh wall. His urge to keep jumping was fleeting as exhaustion set in.

At first, the prince thought it unwise to sleep. After all, he was a much sought-after commodity. But after further reflection, it didn't matter. Asleep or awake, he couldn't get away. With that line of thinking, he lay down against the stone. His last thoughts as he drifted off were for his poor horse. Fortunately, sleep came soon enough.

When Yaya awoke, the air was still and hot. He ditched his cloak and began piling up the bones. Afternoon slipped into dusk. Hope slipped into despair. Time was running out, a fact confirmed by two buzzards loitering on the edge of the pit. Patiently, they watched as the boy floundered to escape the ossuary. The birds didn't speak, but the prince could sense their thoughts. It was always the eyes of the prey they wanted.

Enraged by their callous desire, Yaya rushed the birds and threw a few bones at them. The buzzards bounded away before taking flight and settling into a circular pattern, biding their time. Yaya stared at them, almost enviously. Here he was, a much more intelligent animal, trapped by his physical constraints. Then, he noticed an engraving on the wall before him.

Resentful and upset with ravenous onlookers, the prince hurled a bone at what appeared to be the likeness of a face.

"*Akh*!" a voice said.

"Huh? What?" Startled and unsure of what he had heard, Yaya took a wary step forward.

"I said, 'akh.' That hurt."

"Don't mind her," another voice added. "She's always complaining."

"Look who's talking," another said.

Yaya walked up to the wall and discovered three faces in the stone, their bearings etched in a white phosphorus glow that grew brighter in the darkening shadow. They were set in a deeper layer of masonry than the surrounding stone, part of which lay crumbled on the ground. Yaya knew the outer wall must have recently collapsed as he had no memory of it during the funerals.

"Who are you?" he asked.

"Let me introduce us. We are he, we are she, we like to give, we like to receive. To my left are Meesha and Gulbahar. I'm Nasrine."

"We are three lonely sisters," Gulbahar said, "who must spend eternity trapped in this earthen wall."

"Well, I'm sorry to hear that."

"He's handsome, isn't he?" Meesha said. "Do we have to offer him the riddle? Let's keep him instead. Please?"

"We must offer him the riddle," Nasrine said.

"A riddle for what?" Yaya asked.

"For you to escape."

"How?"

"You'll have to trust us, you naughty *div*," Meesha said, her eyes resplendent with a come-hither expression.

Seeing that he had nothing to lose, Yaya accepted the challenge. "Very well, what's the riddle?"

"We are he, we are she, we like to give, we like to receive. To my left are Meesha and Gulbahar. I'm Nasrine. What are we?"

Yaya rubbed his chin as he pondered the possibilities.

"Come on," Gulbahar said. "I'm getting impatient."

"Don't worry about her, my *jan-e del*," Meesha said. "You take your time. Take as much time as you need."

"How will I get out of here if I'm right?" Yaya asked.

"You won't be," Gulbahar said.

"Are you sure about that... hermaphrodites?"

With Yaya's answer, the ground began to shake and rumble. Mortar dust spewed forth from the wall as individual stones protruded, one atop the other. Once it had settled, steps led from the base of the ossuary to the top.

Yaya couldn't believe his eyes. "How did this get here?"

"Torture," Nasrine said. "This used to be the dakhmeh of an ancient Jabiri garrison. To satiate their morbid pleasures, successive *argbedan* would toss criminals in the pit and force them to battle wild animals. When no animals were available, they'd sometimes leave an odious criminal to starve but taunted him with hopes of escape if he could answer our riddle. You are only the second criminal to have answered Uzava's riddle correctly."

"I'll take that as a compliment."

"So, how'd you figure out the answer?" Nasrine asked.

"Beginner's luck? Well, each of your names is a flower. That helped. Anyway, I'm a bit of a gardener if you want to know. And I suppose in some people's eyes, even a criminal."

Ready to leave, Yaya retrieved his sword but stopped short of the steps. "I don't suspect I'll be seeing your faces any time soon," he said, sheathing his shamshir. "I certainly hope not."

The phosphorus glow of the faces dissipated as the prince escaped the confines of the ossuary. He considered walking over to where the jackals had attacked Ruh but couldn't bear the thought of looking upon his ravaged horse. A glance that direction led him to believe that most of the carcass had been dragged off anyway, a testament to an unnatural savagery. Besides, with darkness beginning to set in, he didn't see much utility in lingering.

As Yaya left the cemetery, he pondered the lengths his grandmother was willing to go to have him killed. And while he hoped she thought him dead, at least for now, he knew it wouldn't be long before she took another swipe at him. That line of thinking led him to ditch the open road in favor of following the river. Due to its meandering nature, the Rud-e Barik would prove an unsuspecting pathway. It also led to his destination.

The sounds of slaughter played on a loop in Yaya's head. The pounding of his feet as he ran only served to punctuate them. Then he recalled the moment he heard the jackals' words.

"That must be my gift," he thought.

Questions arose in his mind. "That I can understand animals means what? What kind of gift is this when Kamran can bend swords?"

The prince was confused but trusted that his grandfather, in his wisdom, must have had his reasons.

He reached the river, but fatigue was taking a toll. With a few hours until dawn, it only made sense to rest while he still had the cover of darkness. A small berm cut by erosion seemed the perfect spot. So he tossed his haversack on the ground and lay beside it. A breeze brought little relief from the heat, but the boy was so exhausted that his eyes closed anyway. A shooting star streaked across the sky, and thoughts of Gulzar lured him to sleep.

When he awoke, his heart racing, the curve of the sun had eclipsed the horizon, lighting the open plain toward Zad. He stretched his arms, dusted off his bag, and began trudging along. His legs felt so heavy and weary that if the jackals found him, he figured he ought to lie down and give himself up for dead. A few dates helped to energize him and loosen his muscles. Soon, he was off and running.

To the north, Yaya observed a ridge of igneous rock all aglow in sunlight. He was so enthralled with the splendor that he nearly missed a form standing in the foreground. It was an animal of some sort. The prince briefly panicked, but the heft of the animal ruled out any jackal or similarly sized canine. Then he realized—it was Ruh. He recognized his white coat and the black spot between his eyes.

Yaya ran toward the animal, waving his arms and calling him by name. As he approached, the prince held his hands out in disbelief before touching the gelding on the muzzle. "You're alive," he said, his eyes welling up.

"I'm sure that comes as a shock to you."

Yaya stood back. He *was* shocked. "I understood that. And you understand me?"

"Funny, huh? I never did before until you told me in the orchards to meet you 'down the road.' Somehow I knew what you were saying. How'd that happen?"

"It came from a magical elixir. I don't know the reason why, but I suppose I'll find out soon enough."

"It seems you already have."

Yaya gave a puzzled expression.

"I went to the road, didn't I?"

Yaya smiled. "You're right. You did." His thoughts went to the bloodletting by the pit. "But I heard the jackals attacking you. I heard you whinny."

"You *thought* you heard the jackals attacking me."

"I don't understand."

"Well, after you abandoned me to my certain death, a wolf came out of nowhere, apparently drawn by all the uproar."

"Sorry about that."

"Eh, forget about it." Ruh's thoughts returned to the scene, which prompted him to chuckle. "I don't think that wolf was expecting to see what he did."

"What happened?"

"The jackals lunged for him instead of me. Maybe they felt threatened. I don't know. Anyway, I wasn't about to ask them so I fled. I was convinced they had gotten to you, too. But here you are."

"Then you forgive me?"

"Give me some pistachios, and I will."

Yaya smiled and reached into his haversack. He pulled out a handful of nuts and offered them over. "I should've stayed with you."

Ruh gobbled up the treat. "Eh, it's water under the bridge. Go ahead and get on. I want to get away from here as fast as possible. Where are we going anyway?"

"To the kingdom of Raydur," Yaya said as he mounted. "If we hurry, we can make it by evening."

"In that case, hold on tight." Ruh bolted away.

One by one, the miles ticked off, drawing into view the domed roof and archways of the ancient temple ruins. For a boy tasked with paying homage to the gods and goddesses of yore, he figured he'd start by praying to the god of war for whom the temple had been built. Unfortunately, Yaya knew none of the sixty-five verses dedicated to Warahram, so he settled on the first yasht of the Avesta instead. In his guilt, he resolved to do better.

MANTICORES, MILK, AND HONEY

Lilya walked down a cool, dimly lit corridor, followed by General Baraz and two other guards. A whiff of raw sewage wafted in the air.

When they entered the dungeon, Adarbad rose from a small stool, a hint of anxiety in his expression. Against one wall were a few shackles. Though the room was clear of clutter, there was the lingering odor of urine and feces coming from a few empty buckets.

With a studied look, Lilya approached the captive. "You're a good man, Adarbad."

"Thank you, my lady." The alchemist could see she had formulated a strategy in how to cross-examine him.

"Please, sit."

Adarbad obliged and began to twist his beard nervously.

"I know we haven't always seen eye to eye," Lilya continued, "but that hasn't diminished my admiration for you. Without fail, the late king valued your counsel and service. It's also no secret that he valued your friendship and found comic relief in your absent-mindedness—much to my annoyance. Despite that, you are an exemplary citizen and one of Zad's finest servants."

Lilya ambled to the wall and casually inspected a rusty manacle.

Adarbad knew she hadn't come to praise him, and having never expressed an interest in metalworks, he knew she didn't give a damn about the shackles either.

Finally, she spoke. "So, how did it come to pass that you've decided to turn against my son?"

"But I haven't," Adarbad said, the dungeon beginning to brighten from the morning light. "There must be a misunderstanding. This charge you speak of has no basis."

Lilya slammed the chain against the floor. "Don't take me for a fool. Are you telling me you know nothing about Shanaz and Yaya's whereabouts?"

Adarbad shrugged. "I don't."

Lilya walked over to the alchemist. She looked into his eyes, taking stock of the man she had known for over thirty years. Though their relationship had been cordial, she had always resented his influence on the court. For that reason, she put much of the blame for the woeful state of the kingdom on his shoulders.

"We are facing a drought," she said, "the severity of which we've never seen, not in my lifetime anyway. You understand what will happen if this continues, don't you? When word gets out that the qanats are flowing, others will be tempted to wage war against us for our water."

"I was unaware of that, my lady."

"What is it you are aware of?" Lilya moved behind the alchemist. "I envy you, Adarbad."

Adarbad was perplexed by her intimation. "I beg your pardon? For what?"

"For how you use your forgetful and untidy demeanor to mask a more cunning side. While your hapless act may have worked on the king, I've always been on to you. So I'm going to try this again." Lilya stepped closer and leaned down to the alchemist's ear. "What do you know?" she asked, her breath hot and morning stale.

"The boy was deeply saddened and troubled by the loss of his father." Sweat began dripping down Adarbad's scalp. "I wouldn't put it past him to have run away. I've known Yaya his whole life, and he has it in him to do something like that. He is impetuous."

"But not reckless," Lilya said, coming around full circle. "Don't forget that I've known him as long as you have. He wouldn't run away willy-nilly."

"Yes, my lady," the alchemist conceded.

"Anyway, I'm asking about Shanaz. We caught Yaya heading to Raydur yesterday."

"I've never understood why you despise him so."

"Despise him? He is wanted for murder."

"Impossible."

"Tell that to our beloved Piruz, who was found in the orchards with a billhook through his neck."

Adarbad's heart sank, then he suddenly remembered that his limited visions saw Yaya walking in a mountain forest. It couldn't be. He calculated that Lilya was being purposely deceptive.

The queen instructed her guards to flank the prisoner.

Adarbad tensed as they moved behind him.

"And your absence at the king's coronation is worthy of reprimand," Lilya added. "Raydur couldn't wait?"

"I had run out of essential minerals."

"For what? More elixirs? Regardless, a person of your position should have been there."

"Not elixirs. Just restocking. Always working, my lady. You know me. Everything I do is in service to the crown."

"Yes, I do know you, and you are a liar. You've been lying to me since I walked into this damn sewer. Get up."

Adarbad brought himself to his feet.

"My patience is hanging by a thread." Lilya's eyes seared into the alchemist. "I'm going to ask you one more time. Where is Shanaz? If you don't talk, we'll make sure Yaya does."

Adarbad thought of his young apprentice, affectionate memories flooding his brain. He trusted his vision and steeled himself for whatever unpleasantness was about to come. "I've told you all I know."

Lilya nodded to the guards, one of whom delivered a solid blow to the alchemist's lower side, bringing him to his knees. The other guard struck his jaw, scattering blood and sending him crashing upon the hewn stone floor.

Still conscious, Adarbad lay motionless in a fetal position. Blood from his broken lip and split tongue drained down his throat.

The queen crouched beside him. "I have some business to tend to in Raydur. When I return, you'll tell me what I want to hear. Don't doubt what I'm capable of, Adarbad."

Lilya stood and regarded the alchemist with contempt. "Chain him to the wall," she said, addressing the guards. "No water. No rations."

As she and Baraz left the dungeon, the general was puzzled by what he had heard. "My lady, I didn't know the qanats were working. Shouldn't I have been informed of such a development?"

"They're not working. They're as empty as our coffers. I was trying to appeal to Adarbad's sense of duty. Obviously, that didn't work."

"I don't understand. The surveyors had all but guaranteed a sufficient swell of groundwater."

"I guess the lesson is 'don't promise what you can't see,' which is why I want to visit Raydur and see to what extent King Delawar is controlling the Rud-e Barik. We'll know by mid-afternoon when we arrive."

"Mid-afternoon? But that's impossible. It's a long day's trip at best."

"Not anymore."

The queen and general exited the citadel and headed toward the royal stable.

As they passed by individual stalls, Lilya paused at Yaya's, which was empty, and her thoughts turned to her grandson. One byproduct of her summoning powers was limited telepathy. Upon her jackals' return, she gleaned that they had found the boy. Indeed, as their blood-stained muzzles made clear, the encounter had gone most unfavorably for the prince.

Yet Lilya felt a nagging unease—the last image she glimpsed from her jackals' eyes was the dakhmeh, not the boy's dead body. She would not be satisfied until she saw the proof for herself.

At the end of the stable was an isolated stall usually reserved for expectant mares. Lilya removed a sizable piece of timber that secured the gates. Baraz took notice, for removing the slab was no easy task, not even for a man of considerable brawn like himself. She opened one gate and escorted the general past feeding troughs. Anticipation filled her eyes, the kind a child would recognize in gift-bearing parents.

When they reached a grooming space, Lilya directed Baraz's attention to a straw-filled enclosure.

His jaw dropped. "Manticores."

Wary of the intrusion, the four animals came to their feet. One manticore yawned and stretched, its enormous bat wings—armed with spikes at the joints—unfurling like a black banner.

Lilya led the way into the pen.

The creatures reacted nervously, uncertain of the male newcomer, and began snorting and flapping their wings. Dust swirled beneath the romping of their massive lion bodies. Some beasts growled, others flashed fangs or lashed barbed tails. None seemed pleased at having their post-feeding naps disturbed.

"Do you like our creations?" Lilya asked. The queen's proximity to the manticores soothed them. They ceased their aggressive posturing and settled into heavy panting. "Come, General. It's safe. Just be careful of the tails."

Baraz edged closer. "But these are myths."

"Myths that have come alive."

"But how? It's beyond the bounds of alchemy."

Lilya led Baraz to the largest of the manticores, its lip quivering from a subtle growl. "Sarvin's knowledge has grown a great deal—as has mine. Our increased capabilities will provide you with an army unmatched in battle."

Lilya joined hands with Baraz and placed her other one on the beast's head. With eyes closed, she muttered some words in ancient Jabiri. In response, the animal pulled in its wings and crouched down.

Not about to pass up the invitation, the general glanced at Lilya with wondering gratitude before cautiously mounting. As he settled onto the manticore, taking notice of its defined musculature, he felt a sudden surge of power and excitement. He imagined leading a company of savaran and their flying beasts into battle. Triumphant pride flowed through him.

"Are they difficult to control?" he asked.

"Easier than a horse." Lilya ran her fingers through the manticore's mane, maternal joy beaming from her face. "They have such a keen intelligence—mind you, this is only the beginning. Once Sarvin and I create dozens more, we will have changed the face of war in the span of weeks."

"I'm at a loss for words, my lady."

"I have instructed Bezan to create new armor and a sword befitting the leader of Zad's army. For too long, you have relied on outdated equipment. All that I ask in return is your unwavering loyalty."

Baraz bowed. "And you shall have it."

The queen wore a mischievous grin as she looked at the manticore. "Imagine old Delawar's face—he might die from fright when he sees these animals. Not that I'd mind."

"Then I should have them readied to leave."

"Their saddles and headgear are hanging on the wall. I'll summon Kamran and Afshad, for they'll be joining us. But on the way, we must first stop at Sarzamin-e Mordegan."

"May I inquire as to the purpose?"

"There is something I must verify."

After Lilya left, the general set off to fetch the makeshift bridles. His beast followed him like a stray cat that had just been fed, sometimes nipping at his fingers.

Moved by the sudden display of affection and all alone, Baraz decided to take a moment to get to know his new pet. He scratched vigorously behind its ears until the beast plopped onto the ground and rolled over. Taking the hint, the general rubbed its belly. Soon after, the manticore he had named Juju settled into a low, gravelly purr as its new master spoke of visions of conquest and greater glory.

⬧◆⬧

Adarbad sat chained to the dungeon wall. The air had become so hot and dry that the breezes entering through the wind slats made him feel like a piece of *naan* in a tannur oven. His throat was parched. He had also lost the ability to control his bowels, convinced a broken rib was the reason.

Sitting there in his soiled clothing, the alchemist began to hum his favorite song, *Bagh-e Shahryar*, knowing full well that a far worse fate awaited him.

The door to the dungeon soon swung open, and the pushtig-ban-salar and six of his royal guards entered. They carried several earthen jugs and an odd assortment of items.

After arranging them near the center of the floor, they unlocked Adarbad from his manacles and carried him over, setting him down in front of the stool and a few woolen linens.

Having figured out what was coming, the alchemist cried out to the commander, a man whose severe temperament was only exceeded by Queen Lilya's.

"Don't do this, Dadgar. I beg you."

While four guards pinned the alchemist onto his back, another knelt behind him and placed a wooden vice around his head. Once secured, he forced a hollow tube of imported bamboo into Adarbad's mouth and held it firm. The last guard, the one of rank, picked up a jug and poured a mixture of milk and honey into the alchemist's throat.

Adarbad gagged, coughed, and sputtered out the first mouthful.

Perhaps owing to the prisoner's reputation, the guards relented until the coughing fit was over.

This only served draw Dadgar's ire. "Enough with the coddling. Do you want me to die of heat stroke? Hurry it up."

Little by little, jug after jug, Adarbad was force-fed the concoction. When it finally ended, he knew he'd never see Yaya or Shanaz again. His visions of the boy making the long journey without him had been right all along.

HIDE AND SEEK

S hanaz took a few expectant slurps of her pomegranate soup. She sat cross-legged on a faded blue carpet, while a large extended family, anxious for her verdict, clutched their wooden spoons and waited.

Amid the silence, the young woman who had prepared the soup rocked her fussing newborn.

"The ash-e anar is most wonderful," Shanaz said. "How'd you learn to cook so well at such a young age? It took my *madar* years before she mastered its delicate balance of flavors."

The new mother, still in her teens, smiled modestly at her royal guest yet was visibly distracted by her inability to pacify the infant child.

"May I?" Shanaz said, reaching for the baby.

Having her newborn held by someone of the queen's stature felt like a blessing, and the young peasant woman gladly handed the girl over.

Humming her favorite song, *Bagh-e Shirin*, Shanaz danced while cooing at the baby. After escaping the citadel two nights earlier, she had abandoned her plan to meet Yaya at the Rud-e

Barik for fear of leading the enemy to him. She trusted the boy would only wait so long for her and Adarbad before heading to Raydur alone, just as they had rehearsed.

So instead, Shanaz sought sanctuary in the villages, hoping to buy enough time to devise a plan to rescue Adarbad. She prayed that a family of good grace would take her in despite the precarious hour of her calling. Fortunately for this refugee on the run, she knew of one, but only after the family patriarch, having met Shanaz many years ago, vouched for her identity. After all, very few commoners ever saw the royals up close in person.

With scores of pushtigban making random house searches, Shanaz had spent much time hidden behind the family's tannur oven.

Twice, guards stopped to inquire about a "person of interest," but they avoided searching the house—a quick scan from the doorway was enough to survey the small abode. In keeping with Zad's rhythms, the patrols decreased midday so the guards could eat or shelter in the shade.

Shanaz peeked out a window toward the citadel watchtower. In the dry air, the structure stood stark against the blue sky. While mulling over her options, she observed four objects rise above the city and move west. They were winged yet much too big for birds. "What on earth?" she thought. Whatever the creatures were, she suspected Sarvin had a hand in their making. After all, Lilya's oversized jackals sprung from nowhere.

The queen's pulse quickened. With four winged beasts likely bound for Raydur, it stood to reason that Lilya, Kamran, and perhaps General Baraz were aboard. If she ever had a chance to find Adarbad, it was now. Her eyes shifted side to side as myriad thoughts raced through her mind.

Unable to fully pacify the baby, Shanaz handed the girl to her mother and addressed the family. "The time has come for me to leave. I want to thank all of you for accepting a stranger into your home. You've been most gracious."

The family members began to stand and come forward, including the old man of the house, a produce vendor whose frail frame barely filled out his tunic.

"You're hardly a stranger," he said. "And you'll always be welcome. I'm just sorry for the messy state of our home. We weren't expecting a guest."

"You've been most hospitable, just as you were all those years ago. But I'm afraid the fate of Zad has taken a grave turn. You must be vigilant—all of you—especially for the sake of the children." Consumed with emotion, Shanaz gently touched the infant she had been holding. "If only my husband were still alive."

Shanaz kissed the baby and bade the family farewell, turning toward the doorway. Her best effort at concealment was the hood of her cloak.

"May I offer some advice?" the old man said. "If you venture to the citadel, walking as you are, you'll never again see the light of day. Neither will the alchemist."

"I appreciate your concern, but I've already overstayed my welcome."

The old man walked over to Shanaz. "If war is coming, so be it. But I, for one, refuse to stand by and do nothing." He looked at his family, which only steeled his resolve. "I think I have a way to sneak you inside. But it's not without risk."

So here was Shanaz, pinned in the storage section of the old man's produce cart.

The ride in the heat was by itself bad enough—made barely tolerable by a few gaps in the side planks—but the ruts and bumps in the road were worse. Shanaz endured painful jolts, a crick in the neck, and fits of sneezing from the stale, dusty air. As best she could, she distracted her mind by trying to recall the twelve names of the family with whom she had stayed.

When the queen reached the name of the family patriarch, the produce cart stopped.

"Sorry, Xani," a guard said. "All traffic in and out of the city must be inspected. King's orders."

"For what?"

"That's none of your concern." The guard looked over Xani's paltry amount of produce and snuck a peach from a basket. "Planning for a short shift, I see."

"Times are tough," Xani said, glancing up at the sky. "In all my years, I've never seen a drought so relentless, so... what's the word I'm looking for? You know, in some ways, it seems almost deliberate." He turned his attention to the guard, whose face wore a bothered expression. "Are you a praying man?"

"Everyone prays."

"Of course they do. But that's not what I asked. I asked if you were a *praying* man."

The guard shifted uncomfortably as if he had been repri-manded. He knew what Xani meant.

"Would you be a good lad and help an old man down?"

The guard obliged, extending his hand. "Is there a problem?"

"No problem at all," Xani answered, raising his voice so Shanaz could hear his words. "When you get to be my age, one does need to stretch. Anyway, my main business today is with the alchemists. They've been so kind to let me to bring my eldest daughter in for treatment, which, as you know, they do from time to time."

Right on cue, Shanaz began to moan.

The guard glanced suspiciously at the old man before moving to the rear of the cart. He tapped the storage section with his shamshir, prompting more distressing sounds from Shanaz.

"This may be a dumb question," he said, bemused, "but is she so sick she needs to be stuffed in the cart? Fresh air is often the elixir for what ails us."

The guard moved in for a closer inspection, placing his hand on the tailgate.

Xani intervened. "Don't do that, good man. For your own sake, do not open that gate."

"You know... all right, what exactly is going on here?"

Xani nervously looked around. "Come closer," he said, beckoning the guard. "This is something that should be whispered."

The guard indulged the old man one last time. When he heard what Xani had to confess, he recoiled in horror and nearly fell, then beat a hasty retreat away from the cart. Without delay, he waved the old man through.

Xani smiled at his interrogator, "You're a good lad." After climbing on the cart, he muttered, "Much better if you were a praying one."

The cart jolted forward.

After a short distance, Shanaz could hear the bustle and banter of the bazaar. Soon, the noise faded and she could sense the cart was moving uphill and nearing the citadel. Eventually, it stopped. Through its warped, citrus-stained boards, she heard Xani greet the guards at the citadel gatehouse on the inner wall.

From his seat, the old man once again explained the purpose of his visit, this time with matter-of-fact assurance.

Shanaz perfectly played her part, punctuating Xani's words with dramatic moaning. Then she saw a shadow round the cart. She braced for the tailgate to open, but the guard smacked it instead and permitted Xani to proceed.

The cart lumbered on, turning west and moving parallel to the rocky foundation of the royal residence. The queen found herself trembling and realized she hadn't taken a breath. At last, the cart halted and the tailgate lifted.

"Come, my lady," Xani said as he helped Shanaz slide out.

Too stiff to stand, the queen leaned over and rested her hands on her knees.

Xani bent down to her, his eyes wide with elation. "We made it."

"Good thinking, my friend."

"Nothing weakens the knees like the threat of leprosy. It worked like a charm—twice."

"I suppose it did."

Shanaz stood straight and arranged a ragged *rusari* around her head, a hand-me-down from Xani's family. She looked at the old man with apprehension.

"What's the matter, my lady?"

"Your cart could barely hold me. How will two of us fit?"

"It'll be tight, but we'll manage." Xani handed the queen a straw broom he had stored on the cart. "Now, hurry on. I'll be here waiting for you."

Shanaz gave a half-hearted smile before shuffling off, her face kept low. She passed through an open-air corridor into the barracks—a rectangular building with peripheral housing and a large courtyard.

A score of soldiers were busy with training exercises. Otherwise engaged, they hardly noticed the hunched figure dressed in borrowed peasant clothing as she scurried under the portico, sweeping the thresholds of each doorway she passed.

Without incident, the queen drifted like a shadow until reaching the rear of the citadel. Here and there, a few courtiers passed her, but none spared her a glance. Why would they? Servants are to serve, not to be seen. A final flight of stairs and hallway led to Adarbad's quarters. Opposite this was his laboratory. The door was open.

Shanaz entered a room that had been ransacked. Chairs, papers, and laboratory equipment were strewn across the floor, and various powders and liquids had mixed into a putrid burning stench. She tiptoed around the debris—then froze at the sound of voices coming down the corridor. With broom in hand and head down, she played her role and began to sweep.

Amid a toppled bookcase, Shanaz spotted one of Adarbad's favorite reads: *Alchemy and the Science of Genetic Hybridization* by Nouri Mirza. Next to the book and under a chair, she found what she had been hoping for—a small green chest of dyed cypress wood. With the footsteps in the corridor fading, the queen risked picking it up and removing the lid. She cursed when she saw it was empty.

A familiar voice startled her from the doorway. "Your work doesn't involve inspecting the rubbish."

"Yes, *agha*."

"When you finish here, I want you to sweep the other lab."

"Yes, yes," Shanaz said, her back to Sarvin.

"I didn't catch that?"

"Yes, agha."

"Remember to whom you're speaking," the alchemist said before striding down the corridor.

After catching her breath, Shanaz abandoned her search in the laboratory and made her way down a narrow set of service stairs. A small annex led to the food prep room located above the dungeon. Inside were buckets, ropes, cutting utensils, and a rudimentary table covered with vegetable scraps and remnants of lamb. On the floor was a barred window through which food was lowered.

Shanaz hurried to the opening but tripped over a bucket. The sound reverberated in the space.

Getting on her hands and knees, she peered down, thinking that if the alchemist had been free, he would have come to inspect whatever vile rations he had been allotted. But below, all was still.

Shanaz held onto the bars and called out to her friend in a hushed voice. "Ada, are you down there?"

With no response forthcoming, Shanaz came to two conclusions: either the alchemist was dead in part of the dungeon she couldn't see or not there at all. Inclined to hope, she assumed the latter, but then came the question of where he could be.

As the queen stood, someone greeted her. "Hello, *Khaleh*."

Shanaz's heart sank. She turned. "Vira. How'd you know I was here?"

"I know how servants sweep." Vira's posture was stiff, her eyes cast down. "I was with Sarvin when he spoke to you, and I could see what he couldn't—that you were no servant. Don't forget, I've had a lot of experience hiring them. So I followed you."

Lilya wasn't in the room, but Vira's discomfort made her presence palpable.

Shanaz approached the new queen. "Where is he? Where's Adarbad?"

Vira briefly covered her face with her hands. She choked up. "I'm so scared."

"I know you are, but if you don't help me, he will die."

A swift tear ran down Vira's cheek. "They've taken him away. I can tell you no more than that. Please, don't ask me any more questions."

"You followed me here for a reason. What would Ohrmazd want you to do?"

Vira wrung her hands in anguish. Though quite fond of Shanaz, she had kept a formal distance in spite of herself for fear of provoking Lilya's ire.

Shanaz knew as much and respected the unspoken bound-aries, even if she wished she had been closer to Vira, especially since she had no daughter of her own.

"It's all right," Shanaz said. "You can tell me."

"He's north of the river in the *boats*."

Shanaz gasped.

"He won't last long," Vira said. "You must hurry."

"I have someone waiting for me at the stable, but I need water and supplies. Adarbad is probably in desperate need of medicine, assuming he's even alive. Can you get those things for me?"

Vira turned away in fear.

"Please, Vira, I need your help."

The new queen looked at Shanaz reluctantly since she knew the risk involved. Already, her actions constituted treason, and in her brief hesitation at the request, perhaps that realization propelled her to act. In effect, she had crossed the line, and what she said next unnerved Shanaz beyond the pale.

"There's something else you should know." Vira began to cry. "It's Yaya, he—"

Shanaz grasped the queen by the shoulders. "What is it? Tell me."

"Lilya sent her jackals after him the other night. I tried to stop her, but she shut me up while everyone just watched." Vira's eyes grew distant as the memory came back to her.

"Have the jackals returned?"

"Yes, but I don't know what happened. I haven't heard anything, and Lilya and Kamran have left for Raydur."

"Anybody else with them?"

"General Baraz and Afshad. War is coming. I can feel it."

"Then we have no time to lose. Hurry, Vira. I need supplies."

Vira hastened out of the room, leaving the elder queen alone. Her thoughts turned to Yaya and his struggles against such a formidable adversary. And she wasn't thinking of the jackals. It was Lilya, and Lilya alone, who was orchestrating events. Everyone else was a mere puppet on her strings. To end the madness and the march toward war, she had to be stopped. The prince's fate, at least for now, lay beyond Shanaz's control.

But first things first. If Adarbad were still alive, Shanaz would rescue him and flee to Raydur. With tears replaced by resolve, she settled into prayer and reflected on her childhood with the alchemist. The memories were vivid. She could still picture a youthful Adarbad, so skinny that his shoulder blades stuck out like wings, sunbathing along the banks of the Rud-e Barik. She drifted in reverie until the sound of footsteps came down the stairs.

Vira entered the room, carrying a basket of linens. "Here," she said, thrusting the bundle into Shanaz's arms. "I found what

I could. I'll walk you to the stable, but keep your head down. Everyone will assume you're a laundry servant."

Mid-afternoon set in, and the citadel was relatively calm. The courtiers were napping or soaking in the bathhouse while most soldiers sheltered in the barracks to escape the sun.

The timing was perfect, and Vira led Shanaz to the stable with little notice—save for two workers who paused briefly, pitchforks in hand, to regard the scene.

After receiving an icy glare from the young queen, they returned to corralling their hay.

Xani anxiously watched the women approach, bowing to Vira after Shanaz introduced her.

"But where is the alchemist?" he asked, rubbing his hands together.

"He's tied down in the desert. I don't have time to explain. I need to get to my horse."

Shanaz had Xani put her basket on the seat.

Vira folded her arms. "Everything you need is under the linens, including what you were looking for in Adarbad's laboratory."

Shanaz was moved by the revelation. "You found it?"

Vira forced a smile. "Where will you go?"

Shanaz looked at the citadel where so many of her memories lived. "I don't know. But I suspect you won't see me again."

Vira nodded, for she already knew.

Shanaz embraced her and whispered, "You have a pure heart, my dear. Remember that always."

With tears beginning to stream down her cheeks, the elder queen pulled herself into the cart.

Vira latched the tailgate shut and watched the cart move along the wall until it finally turned toward the citadel gatehouse. For some time, she remained standing on the stable grounds, alone, unable to move, as if frozen under the sun.

THE BOATS

Xani wound his way through the city streets and out the main gate, the guard he had frightened with threats of leprosy again waving him by.

When he arrived home, he tied Shanaz's horse to the produce cart, placed more blankets inside to absorb the bumps, and ferried her toward the orchards. She would use the trees as cover until reaching the Rud-e Barik. And with Queen Vira's assurance that a cordon only blocked Zad from, she hoped to be in the clear.

A short while later, Xani lifted the tailgate and helped Shanaz slide out. Whether from routine or the additional padding, the queen found the confined quarters more tolerable. But that was about the best of it. The sun was on the descent, leaving little time to find the alchemist.

Xani knew as much and directed Shanaz to her horse before she could thank him. "It's not every day an old man gets to have an adventure with a beautiful queen."

"Nor a queen with such a handsome gentleman."

Xani assisted Shanaz onto the steed and handed her the supply bag. "I know you'll find him," he said, his visage becoming serious. "I've prayed for it, as I've prayed for the boy all these years. Promise your next visit will be much sooner?"

"It had better be. I have to finish my bowl of ash-e anar." Shanaz patted Xani's hand. "Keep it warm, would you?" And with those words, she bade the old man farewell.

Before long, she came to the river, and with little effort, her horse trotted through its shallow waters and up a gully.

Shanaz veered off to the northwest. She had no idea of Adarbad's whereabouts despite past prisoners being subjected to the same torture. Her husband had been less inclined than his predecessors to support the practice, viewing it as barbaric and less effective than other methods of intelligence gathering.

Lilya, however, urged him to use it, believing that coercion was only effective when driven by fear.

The late king had recounted the experience to Shanaz: a prisoner would lie naked, slathered in honey, and pinned between two truncated boat hulls, one fixed atop the other, with only his extremities exposed. The intermittent process of being force-fed milk and honey induced severe diarrhea, which enticed spiders, ants, and other desert critters to explore the orifices of the condemned. Often, they would lay eggs in the accumulated feces.

Shanaz knew her window for finding Adarbad would not stay open long. The hour was getting late, and progress was slow. Her horse labored in the sand. The view at the top of a crescent-shaped dune revealed a vast expanse covered in windswept yardangs—bedrock formations shaped like boat keels. As the dry air howled over the unforgiving terrain, she needed no reminder of the vermin lurking below.

With Lilya and her stooges in Raydur, Shanaz was less hesitant than she otherwise might have been in calling out Adarbad's name. But it made no difference. The headwinds was merciless, drowning out her voice whenever she dared to raise it. The canniness of it all seemed conspiratorial, and she castigated the wind in colorful terms unbefitting her status.

For some time, she wandered the desert sea. The keel-shaped rocks rose and fell with the slopes, and Shanaz rose and fell with them, a castaway amid a fleet of earthen ghost ships. Making matters worse, her calls to the alchemist were answered only by the caws of two buzzards circling an isolated yardang. Indifference, she thought, would have been preferable to such a taunting.

Discouraged and distressed, Shanaz halted her horse so she could rearrange her headscarf. In the face of such relentless winds, she had an unbidden wish, however fleeting, to be riding a winged beast high above the stinging sands. The envious thought unconsciously led her attention back to the scavengers. She didn't see them. The birds, in the brief interlude, had disappeared.

"Could it be?" she thought.

The queen headed in the direction they had been. As she rounded an outcropping, she was stunned to see a wooden structure and two hands dangling from its sides. A sand drift blocked the alchemist's head, so Shanaz had few clues to determine his condition. She lashed her horse to move apace. The buzzards, their inquiry into a meal thwarted, took to the sky, flying past a Zadian banner blowing in the wind.

Shanaz called out to Adarbad.

His fingers fluttered.

Nearly falling off her horse, the queen rushed to him with her bag of provisions.

The alchemist's lips were cracked, and his head sunburnt. Various insects crawled on his wrists and head while others buzzed around him. "I thought this was my end."

Shanaz wiped his face. "Well, it's not. I'm here, and you are going to be fine. Do you hear me?"

"If you say so." Adarbad's face hinted at a smile. "You know, the king said that when he first laid eyes on you, you hit him like a vision. And now, just like that, you come to me."

Adarbad winced at a fresh wave of pain.

Shanaz hurried to both sides of the capsule-like structure and pulled out the metal bars clipping the hulls together. Using all her strength, she slid the top hull over the other. An abhorrent odor rose up. Below lay the naked alchemist, covered in his feces while fanged and pincered irritants explored his body. She pulled him out by his arms and onto a silken cloth.

"Here, drink," she said, tilting one of the waterskins into the alchemist's mouth.

As Adarbad sipped the tepid water, the queen poured more over his body and wiped him as clean as she could. Red bite marks covered his skin, but it seemed she had staved off the worst by getting to him when she did.

From the supply bag, Shanaz retrieved a container, removed the lid, and handed it to the alchemist. "Apply this salve to your groin area."

Adarbad wore a bashful look. "Thank you, my lady."

"Thank Vira."

"Vira? What do you mean?"

"I evaded all others in the citadel except her. She told me what they had done to you."

Adarbad was surprised. He had always considered Vira a pleasant woman but blindly obedient to her husband. "I never would have guessed. She isn't just the dutiful wife after all."

"Lucky for us. But I fear for the young queen. She took a great risk telling me this and bringing me these supplies. When Lilya learns of your escape, she'll leave no stone unturned in finding out how."

Shanaz helped the alchemist into a pair of linen trousers before returning to rummage through the bag. "Let's see what we have here. There's some bread, some dates—"

"Don't mention food."

"Your appetite will return. Once it does, it'll be wise for you to eat. You need to stabilize your insides."

"Anything else?"

Shanaz smiled as she unfolded a square pattern of red silk embroidered with golden leaves.

"My amulet! This is most wonderful." The alchemist examined it, discarding the fabric, which tumbled away in a gust of wind. "I searched everywhere for this. How'd you find it?"

"Vira again, bless her soul. She overheard Sarvin telling Lilya that he'd snuck it out of your laboratory."

"The damn thief. I should have guessed."

"Anyway," Shanaz said, packing away the supplies. "Our concern now is finding Yaya."

Using the overturned hull as a step stool, the queen helped Adarbad mount the horse. Dehydrated, exhausted, and in pain, it took all of their combined efforts to get him on.

Shanaz saddled behind him lest he faint and fall. She also withheld what she knew about Yaya and the jackals, at least for the time being. Given the alchemist's fragile state, she didn't have the heart to worry him.

"We must cross the river and take a back route to Raydur," she said. "It'll be safer."

Adarbad grasped the reins. "Safer from what? Traversing the plain will delay our arrival by a half day, maybe more."

"Because the sky has eyes. I saw four winged figures ascend above the citadel and head west."

"Lion or bird? Sarvin has been collecting cellular specimens from both."

"I couldn't tell. Does it even matter? As we speak, Lilya and Kamran are meeting with King Delawar. They'll most likely return before dark, and trust me, they'll first look to question you. If we follow the road, they'll see us."

"So he has done it. Sarvin has cracked the mystery of genetic hybridization. I was a fool to have been so trusting of him."

Shanaz put a date in the alchemist's mouth. "Just as I had been of Lilya. They're mistakes we won't make twice."

As they slogged away from the yardangs, Adarbad began to feel queasy. Sometimes, he felt the urge to vomit, a sensation made worse by his inability to keep his eyes from scanning upward. The sky had taken on new meaning, and every flying animal—whether a distant hawk or vulture—invited justifiable scrutiny. But his and Shanaz's spirits, which had nearly been broken by despair and torture, were nevertheless high. Their faith was restored. They were together and away from Zad's confines.

"Faith," Adarbad once told Yaya, "is the elixir of fools."

As they headed over rock and sand, faith was all he had.

WINDS OF WAR

With Ruh in tow, Yaya strolled toward the gates of Raydur. At first glance, he was struck by the kingdom's seemingly pristine condition. The sewer drains and culverts were well maintained, and the outer wall showed few chips or cracks. Even bird droppings were conspicuously absent—unlike in his kingdom. With masons conscripted for the war effort against Danzardan, the joke in Zad was that they had become so short-handed, birds had been contracted to fill in structural defects with feces.

To the north of Raydur, and extending to Zad's burial grounds, lay a ridge of hills that sheltered the city-state from the brutal desert winds. As a result, Raydur's climate felt more temperate than its neighbor's. Rare were *wind catchers,* found only on the roofs of the citadel and bathhouses. Vegetation and trees were also more abundant, especially toward the high, plush Kuhha-ye Sabz, their foothills a short distance away.

Yaya led Ruh over the drawbridge that spanned the moat, an offshoot fed by the Rud-e Barik. They passed through the barbican—a narrow defensive passageway—into a small adjoining courtyard decorated with fountains, statues, and planters. At the inner wall, they followed other citizens through open gates of alder wood and into the city proper, where the aroma of roasted vegetables and baked bread greeted them.

The thought of a vegetable kebab tickled the prince's fancy. "What do you say, Ruh? Should we try the local fare?"

"You'll hear no complaint from me nor my stomach, but I don't go much for those orange squishy things."

"Don't worry," Yaya said, taking notice of a couple of curious passersby. "I'll spare you the *khormahloo*." Yaya adjusted his banded collar and dipped his head. "Hey, let's not talk if we don't have to. People are looking at me funny. The last thing I need is attention."

Ruh snorted.

The prince purchased food from a vendor and found a low retaining wall in the plaza where he could sit and eat. As his horse fed on a double portion of rice, he opened his kebab and took a seat. Having gone without a square meal since the rain festival, no sooner had he started eating than he found himself licking his fingers. He sighed contentedly and felt the urge to rest. But he knew he couldn't—not yet, anyway. He was told to wait at the fire temple should he and the others fail to regroup.

So the two travelers headed east along an avenue that gave way to palm-laden grounds. A footpath led them through shrubs and trees to a large pool. Behind it, secluded and peaceful, stood the temple, marked by the engraved winged *Faravahar* on the facade. A few steps brought parishioners to a portico that ran the full length of the perimeter.

Yaya walked up the stairs and entered the temple. In an otherwise vacant room, he noticed a bald man with his hands turned toward the ceiling. Nearby were several copper basins, each filled with sand and burning candles. At the center, a smoldering log of sandalwood rested on a higher basin, its wisps of smoke rising through a vent in the ceiling.

The relieved boy approached the man, who was busy in prayer. "Ada?" he whispered. "Ada, it's me."

The man snapped his head around. "Do you mind?"

Yaya recoiled. "I'm sorry. I thought you were someone else."

The man scowled and returned to his prayers.

Yaya stepped outside and spotted Ruh munching on sunflowers in the temple gardens. Shade was beginning to blanket the city. He considered a stone bench under the portico a suitable place to wait for Adarbad and Shanaz but moved to the bottom of the stairs where he would be more visible. Nevertheless, he began to worry. Having arrived nearly a day late, he wondered if his friends had backtracked toward Zad to find him.

Yaya tried convincing himself they would wait at the temple until he arrived. But why would they? If he hadn't shown up on schedule, of course they would think something had gone wrong.

The prince began to fret. The old man he had disturbed brushed past him on the stairs, a frown still etched on his face. Yaya found it odd that the serenity of prayer had not relieved him of his bad temper.

⸻ ◆ ⸻

Inside the citadel, King Delawar sat across from King Kamran, the table strewn with half-drunken goblets of wine and the remains of lamb, rice, and fruits. Servants entered the council chamber, removing large platters and replacing them with sweets, cups of tea, and rose water. Known for his love of the arts, the king of Raydur didn't disappoint. Musicians enthralled the guests with their melodies and skill, and Rayduri courtiers in attendance were as charming as their reputation alleged.

For the final act, the king's poet stepped to the center of the room for a recital:

> The night is hard for me.
> The day hides your shadows
> in the busyness of living.
> Meetings and state affairs
> kill Time and its spawn, Memory.
> But the night is hard for me
> when, in my routine before bedtime, you reappear
> and draw me back to yours.
> I see you brush your graying hair.
> I smell the scented oils on your skin.
> I hear you hum sweet melodies.
> I see you slip into silken gowns and
> I see you lying next to me.
> A depression still holds your form,
> yet when I touch it, you are not there.
> The night is so hard for me.
> When will morning come?

King Delawar struggled to rein in his emotions. His wife had succumbed to disease and passed away four months earlier—a loss the kingdom was still mourning. Despite his suspicions of Lilya, Delawar sympathized with her for the losses she had endured.

Princess Mahzarin, seated to his right, reached over and took him by the hand, her affection for her father evident by the lump in her throat.

Lilya felt a moment of sadness that turned to self-pity. In her mind, she had never been fully appreciated by her husband. So as she watched the king shed tears of love, the shred of empathy she felt gave way to envy for a queen she had known only superficially. She also wondered if this show of emotion was a deliberate ploy to dull the sharpness of the negotiations to come. With that, she nudged Kamran to give his toast.

The king of Zad rose from his seat, causing a hush to sweep through the room.

"My late father trusted few men like King Delawar. That trust is why our relationship continues to thrive. And thrive it must, for today, we face an insidious threat, the scourge of drought and the drying of our rivers. It is my hope that we can come together once again for the benefit of our peoples." Kamran raised his goblet, a gesture the others reciprocated. "To the great King Delawar and a friendship for the ages."

With the formal proceedings concluded, everyone left the council chamber except the principals. These included Princess Mahzarin and General Jangi of the Rayduri military. Jangi was a bear of a man. His exploits in battle against the Samjari of the northern territories were legendary, and his loyalty to Raydur was unwavering. Never deterred nor discouraged, he was an immovable force upon whom the aging king had come to rely.

"I want to express my gratitude, King Kamran, for your kind words," Delawar said. "I share your aspirations for cooperation and look forward to our conversation. Please, after you."

"Well, as you learned during your recent visit to Zad, the drought has been merciless to our people. The Rud-e Barik barely flows, and our qanats are bone dry. But we don't suffer alone. Danzardan and Jarak are suffering, too. We have received reports of such." Kamran leaned forward, palms on the table. "They'll come where there is water, and there is water here in Raydur. We are prepared to use our savaran to repel any advance onto your kingdom. Friends, after all, stand by friends."

"I appreciate the offer," Delawar said. "I do not, however, share your analysis regarding Jarak. We've been in contact with them. And though your observation is true—that the drought has spared no kingdom—they have rationed supplies and stored copious amounts of water. King Mazad is confident they can manage through the summer."

"That may be," Kamran said, "but you'd agree that the ties between our two kingdoms run much deeper than those between Raydur and Jarak. They are a people predisposed to isolation shaped, of course, by the mountains' constraints. No matter the state of your current relationship with them, it belies historical tendencies. And what if Jarak runs out of water? New friends can become foes when precious resources are at stake."

"Wisely spoken," Delawar said. "But those same mountains that impose isolation also deter imperial ambition. A Jaraki offensive against Raydur would be unsustainable, even more so given the conditions. Besides, King Mazad is a man ruled by caution, just like his father."

"But Danzardan has become a different sort of kingdom—erratic, immoral, predatory. That I'm sure we both could agree on."

"I will accord you that."

"We don't ask for much," Kamran said. "In exchange for our security guarantees, we only ask that you limit what you siphon from the Rud-e Barik so the rest of the water can flow downstream. Our kingdoms thrive when the other is strong—it has always been so. You might call it protection for water. We'll rub your back, and you rub ours."

King Delawar was growing irritated as he listened to the neophyte. Having only just returned following Kamran's inauguration, he was justifiably exhausted. Hosting guests and engaging in diplomacy so soon afterward only made it worse. In his mind, it was selfish behavior, so he decided to raise the temperature of the discussion.

"You might call it 'protection,' but I disagree with your overall premise. In regard to Danzardan, let's not forget that *you* share a border with them. Any predatory impulse they may have will be pointed at Zad—not at Raydur."

"Are you telling me that you wouldn't come to our defense? Have our years of friendship been in vain?"

"King Kamran, I have borne witness to your remarkable feats of strength. Unfortunately, General Jangi here, being on state business, had to hear about them secondhand. Moreover, you have cracked mysteries of alchemy long pursued. Tell me, under what conditions would you possibly need our help? If anything, Zad has fared best among the four kingdoms."

Lilya smacked the table. "I beg your pardon. Our people are suffering. We are prepared to sacrifice lives and treasure for a commodity that should be free."

"A commodity's value," Delawar countered, "increases in proportion to its scarcity. Offer a dying man in the desert a cup of water or all of your treasure—you'll see what is more valued."

"Your granaries and cisterns are full. The vegetation between here and the Kuhha-ye Sabz is lush. The evidence does not suggest scarcity."

"The evidence suggests planning," Jangi said. "King Delawar ordered contingencies months ago. Based on the limited snow cap and arid spring, we had reason to believe this year would be harsh."

"Yes, indeed," Delawar said. "I'm grateful to my alchemist for his prescient work in meteorology for the warning."

"My lord," Jangi said, "Farzan is a worthy recipient of your praise, but we wouldn't have been prepared for the drought were it not for your wisdom. We owe our good fortune to your stewardship."

Lilya's temper was on edge at the perceived slight, for there was truth to it.

King Delawar decided to play his trump card. "Perhaps we can reach a mutually beneficial agreement."

"And how is that?" Lilya asked.

"Your manticore beasts show that your military capabilities have surpassed those of all other kingdoms. We are prepared to share water in exchange for the alchemic knowledge that produced them."

General Baraz wasn't having it. "Never—that's asking too much. What about metallurgy? We can share the techniques that produced Prince Afshad's armor."

"The Rayduri are experts in metallurgy," Delawar said. "I see no need to improve our stock of weapons and armor."

"Sharing our alchemic knowledge is out of the question," Lilya said. "Instead, we can trade you manticores in exchange for water and other commodities."

"Other commodities? It seems you have moved the bar."

Lilya disagreed with the king's assertion. "If the river here is as shallow as you claim, it certainly wasn't months ago when you chose to siphon it for your sole purposes. This selfishness has put Zad in the predicament that it's in. To ask for surplus grain, in addition to water, is not asking for too much."

"Should a king not first look after his own people?"

"The foundation of trust between our kingdoms is shaken. In a matter of weeks, you have cast doubt on what had taken years to build. We'll have to consider other options."

"What might those options be?" Delawar asked, folding his arms.

Lilya stood, followed by the rest of her contingent.

"I asked you a question, Queen Lilya."

"And she doesn't need to answer," Kamran said, leaning forward, his hands on the table.

Jangi rose from his seat. "When you are in Raydur, Your Majesty, you will show respect."

Kamran ignored the general, his gaze fixed on Delawar.

Lilya pulled her son by the elbow, calling him off. "Let's not ruin this lovely gathering with quarreling. The hospitality we've been shown deserves to be met with an equal measure of gratitude. We owe the king of Raydur *at least* that much."

Tired of the talks, King Delawar summoned guards to escort his guests to their manticores.

As Kamran led the group from the council chamber, Lilya turned to the Rayduri king. "Could I impose upon you one small favor, Delawar?"

Taken aback by the woman's nerve, Delawar's brow furrowed, and he replied ironically, even if couched in the niceties his diplomatic nature had long since perfected. "Of course, you can. What can I do for an old friend?"

"We've somehow lost Prince Yaya. You remember the boy, don't you?"

"Why, yes, of course. I may be getting old, but I still retain most of my faculties."

"As you know, he lost his father, my dear son, not too long ago, and I'm afraid he hasn't been coping too well with the situation. We believe he's run away. And with Raydur being our dearest ally, we suspect he might come here."

Delawar found it odd the woman before him would refer to her own son's death as anything but a tragedy. "I'll put my guards on notice and alert the gatehouses."

"Would you?" Lilya said, using her most grateful tone.

"It's the least I can do."

"I don't know how I'd fare with losing such a wonderful boy." Lilya brought her hand to her chest, feigning sadness. "Farewell, King of Raydur."

As Delawar watched her walk down the corridor, his mind went on high alert. He was already aware of the improbable string of deaths in the Zadian royal family, but his suspicions only deepened with a potential heir on the run. He returned to the council chamber, took his seat on his throne, and contemplated his next move.

◈

After leaving the Rayduri citadel, Kamran and the others were escorted to the public stable, a safety precaution ordered by King Delawar to keep the manticores separate from the royal steeds. Just the arrival of the beasts, having swooped over the barbican, had sent the gatehouse guards and those on the ramparts into a near panic. Lilya was still seething at Delawar's slight. And there was no offense she ever forgot.

The Zadians saddled their manticores and led them to the center of the stable. With a few deft flaps of their wings, the beasts lifted into the sky. They flew east, soaring over streets that were beginning to fill with people eager to enjoy the cool evening. Lilya deliberately kept a low altitude, hoping to terrorize any onlookers. As they passed over the cityscape, she noticed a figure curled up asleep on the stairs of the fire temple.

"Raydur is not without its share of the homeless," she mused with satisfaction. Little did she know her grandson was right beneath her nose.

TRAMP ON THE RUN

On the ramparts of Raydur, birds convened for their pre-dawn chatter. A shroud of darkness still clung to the city as the faint glow of sunlight emerged on the horizon. Though he had fallen asleep on the fire temple steps, Yaya later moved to the gardens to be closer to Ruh. There, he could only doze. But with morning breaking, his body finally gave in to fatigue, and he slumped over, slipping into a deep sleep among the foliage.

"Wake up."

Yaya felt a nudge and sat up. Before him stood a man with graying hair and a well-trimmed beard. He wore a rust-colored robe drawn in by a studded leather belt. Yaya recognized the man as Raydur's alchemist and one of Adarbad's closest friends.

"Where are the others?" Farzan asked, his tone urgent.

Yaya wasn't ready for direct questioning—his mind foggy and half asleep.

Farzan could tell. "You didn't leave with them as planned, did you?"

"I couldn't."

Yaya blurted out a brief account of evading the jackals and escaping the burial pit.

"Come then," Farzan said, extending his hand. "You haven't much time."

Yaya took it reluctantly. "But I'm supposed to wait for Ada and Queen Shanaz here."

"The time for waiting is over."

Farzan led Yaya and his horse from the grounds of the fire temple and toward his residence.

Seeing the boy's bothered face, the alchemist wasted no time filling him in. "On the morning of Jashn-e Tirgan, I received a note from Adarbad's falcon about his and Queen Shanaz's plan for departure. That's how I knew to look for you at the temple. Although I must say, you're lucky I found you, going off and hiding in the gardens like you did. I've lost count of how many times I've been here searching for you.

Yaya shrugged in apology, though he bristled at being accused of inconveniencing the alchemist, given all he had endured.

"Anyway, we know why you were delayed," Farzan said. "What we don't know is why the others were. Clearly, something has gone wrong."

"Wrong?" Yaya said, weary of bad news.

"There's no other explanation."

Yaya's shoulders drooped, and despair filled his eyes.

Farzan stopped before a nondescript door in an alley and lifted the boy's sunken chin. "'Wrong' doesn't mean *terribly* wrong. Whatever the reason, I'm sure they'll get here."

The alchemist welcomed Yaya into a small foyer and excused himself.

While waiting, the prince peeked into the adjacent room, where he saw a large table covered with beakers, bowls, and various tubes and implements. Against a wall stood an apothecary cabinet divided into numerous cubbies labeled alphabetically. The floors had been swept, and the counters were free of clutter. The order and cleanliness of the laboratory were such that he wondered whether any work was ever done.

Still sleepy, Yaya sat on a narrow bench and closed his eyes.

Farzan soon returned with a tray of food items. He instructed the prince to retrieve his bottle, then added several pinches of crushed haoma leaves. "These sacred leaves represent the earth. Once you add water from the springs of Anahita, you must travel to Kuh-e Sholeh and Kuh-e Zuze. At the temple ruins of the first is a sulfuric sinkhole that has been burning for eons. Collect some of the smoldering ash and add it to your bottle. At the ruins of the latter, you must capture some of the sacred wind that howls over the mountain."

"But Kuh-e Zuze is near Danzardan."

"At least it's accessible," Farzan said. "Better yet, it's beyond the *Visgari* settlements. Just don't forget to pray at each of the temple ruins. We owe it to the yazdan to honor them for the gifts they bestow."

The alchemist asked the prince to hold open his bag.

Yaya folded his arms instead. "I'm not leaving without Ada and Queen Shanaz."

"If you haven't figured it out already, your life is in danger. You need not worry about them. They'll catch up to you."

"Earlier you said they'll get here. Shouldn't I wait at least for a while?"

"Things have changed since your departure. War is coming between our kingdoms. Also, my king has been made aware that you are missing. Later this morning, he will assemble his advisors and issue a directive for all eyes to look for you."

"What does King Delawar want with me?"

"You're a prince of a potential adversary. He doesn't care about finding you for your grandmother's sake. He wants to speak with you to find out why Zad seems to be coming unhinged. And until he issues that directive, I'm not breaking orders. That's why you must leave. If you refuse, I'll have to turn you in."

At face value, Yaya thought it a reasonable idea. At least in Raydur, he would be protected and eventually reunited with his companions.

Farzan could see what the boy was thinking, so he quickly intervened. "You know you're being hunted. And while King Delawar is a noble man, don't think for a moment that he won't hand you over to your grandmother if it serves Raydur's interests. Is that what you want?"

Yaya shook his head.

"That's a wise decision, and a brave one."

"It's the *only* one," Yaya said, lifting the flap of his haversack. "So how do I find the springs of Anahita?"

"Take the road outside the city. Head south. It'll lead you to the foothills of the Kuhha-ye Sabz and a stone bridge that spans the Rud-e Barik. It'll be the second such bridge you encounter. Off the road, there should be a path. It leads to an old salt mine and will put you on the right course. The springs that feed the rivers are much deeper in the range, on the eastern base of Kuh-e Ab. Finding them will be up to you."

"Can't you come with me?" Yaya asked.

"The king has tasked me with other urgent duties related to your kingdom."

"Like what?"

"That's not important." Farzan dumped the contents of the tray into Yaya's haversack and handed him an old map and another water skin. "The dried fruits and nuts should last you a while."

"What if I don't find the springs?"

"Prophecy says you will."

"But Ada also said he saw himself with me. And he's not here. So how can I trust his visions?" Yaya covered his face in anguish. "This is never going to work out."

Although Farzan had never created an elixir of precognition—the minerals being exceedingly rare—he had the utmost confidence in his friend's abilities. "Adarbad has never let me down, and he won't let you down either. Anyway, you know what must be done. And it will work out. All things do."

"Why does every adult say that?"

Farzan stood. "You must leave for both our sakes."

Leading his horse by the reins, Yaya followed the alchemist down narrow streets and under arched domes. Before long, they reached the confluence of the main avenue and plaza where the prince and Ruh had eaten their kebab and rice. The memory made his empty stomach grumble, and he wondered if he would ever again have the chance to dine on such food. At the plaza's edge, he saw the inner wall and gates. They were already open, with a few weary guards standing by.

"It's time," Farzan said. "Don't concern yourself with the guards—they have yet to be issued any orders." The alchemist helped Yaya onto his horse. "Keep up a good clip; you should reach the foothills before you know it."

Yaya found little consolation in the thought of a hasty arrival, evident in his solemn expression.

Seeing the fear in his eyes, Farzan tried to shore up the boy's courage. "And don't worry about the others. You know Ada, nothing he does goes according to plan."

All Yaya could muster was a token smile.

Farzan patted him on the knee. "They'll find you, son."

And with those words, Yaya commanded Ruh forward.

From behind a statue, Farzan watched the prince approach the gate. The guards looked at him incuriously, and he passed without incident.

Satisfied he had done what had been asked of him, the alchemist's attention turned to much-needed sleep. He tightened the belt of his robe and headed home. Along the way, he pondered the idea of "things working out" and took umbrage at the boy's dismissal of his counsel as banal.

Babak

Yaya and Ruh emerged from the barbican into a stiff breeze. They crossed the moat and headed along the road parallel to the burgeoning Rud-e Barik. Beyond the foothills and a low-level massif rose Kuh-e Ab, a muscle of a mountain—young and jagged, its prominent peak less snowcapped than usual. Except for a few produce vendors eager to start the day, Yaya found the road empty and urged his horse to move apace.

After two hours of hard riding, the road bent again toward the river. In the distance, Yaya saw a waterfall spilling over a keel-shaped stone formation, its smooth surface a stark contrast to the rough-hewn range. A line on the slopes marked the change in vegetation: on the lower elevations lay dense forests dulled by drought; above, a rocky landscape of cliffs and crevices, dappled only with foliage.

Yaya dismounted before the second bridge, an arched structure built by brigand slaves. Like a concerned parent, he reminded Ruh of what they had discussed. "You're sure you remember how to get to Farzan's house? Just follow the main road of the plaza and take—"

"How many times do I have to tell you? I'm a horse. My spatial memory is second to none. I'm more interested in the accommodations."

"Farzan is a good man. He promised he'd take care of you until I return."

"Yeah, well, we'll see about that. I had it pretty good in Zad."

"Spoiled rotten, you were."

Yaya and Ruh moseyed along the path—if it could be called one. Disuse had allowed tufts of tall fescue to overrun it.

As with all impending goodbyes, the companions didn't speak much. Yaya fed Ruh some dried fruits from his stash, and for his part, the horse commented on the cloudless, azure sky.

Near the stone outcropping, the two stopped to watch the mist from the falls split the rays of sunlight into a full spectrum of colors. Yaya knew he could no longer delay the inevitable. And even if he had wanted to, the path ahead was uneven and ill-suited for a horse.

The prince adjusted his haversack and tightened his sheath. "This looks like the end of the line, my friend."

"They say 'every end has a new beginning.'"

Yaya smiled.

"Did I say something funny?" Ruh asked.

"Not really. It's just that I never would have pegged you as a philosopher. Move over *Zartosht*."

"I thought about telling you how 'everything will work out,' but it seems that truism has been used before."

"More than once," Yaya said. "Anyway, thanks for sparing me the disappointment."

"It was the least I could do."

As the conversation fizzled, Ruh glanced at the mountains. "Don't you think you had better get going? Nobody ever saved the world by being late."

Yaya felt a lump in his throat. "I can tell you don't believe that stuff about the blessed springs and collecting the elements of the water cycle."

"Either things are or they're not. Whether one believes in them is immaterial. Chew on that for a while."

Yaya's expression turned sullen. "It's a pity that after all these years, I'm only now getting to know you."

Ruh rested his head on Yaya's shoulder as if to embrace him. "I feel we've known each other all along."

The prince began to cry, hugging his horse in return.

After some time in silent regard, the two travelers parted ways. Yaya watched as Ruh retraced his steps through the tufts of bunchgrasses. Once on the dusty road, he began to canter toward Raydur. The prince kept a constant vigil in hopes that Ruh might look back. But the horse kept his sights ahead and soon vanished behind low-lying hills. With no choice but to press on, Yaya wiped away his tears and climbed up a rock-strewn slope.

Not since leaving Zad did the boy have any chance to wash. So when he reached the deep pool beneath the falls, he wasted no time washing his face and refilling his water supplies. Refreshed, the prince followed the bank to the other side, where he found the miners' path cutting through the dense understory. He took comfort in the sight of ribbons of fabric tied to the trees, concluding they must be guideposts.

But as he hiked under the shaded canopy, a foreboding came over him. It mattered little that he was in unfamiliar territory—a boy of the desert recast in the mountains. His senses detected something altogether alien. The winds began to howl. The branches creaked and popped. The air smelled musty. What had once been a path of dead leaves had been overrun by woody vines, their bark flayed open, the inner flesh bleeding a black, viscous sap.

Then came a sustained, storm-force gust, sweeping down the slopes and testing even the stoutest trees. Some toppled over. Others swayed to their limits. Yaya lowered his head and ran, knowing the salt mine ahead would offer safe harbor from the falling oaks. But as he shielded his eyes, he tripped and fell face-first into the decayed sheddings of the forest bed. Loose twigs and debris pelted his body.

Eventually, the microburst faded, and the forest fell silent save for Yaya's labored breathing. His heart pounded so hard against his chest that his sternum ached, making him wonder if his bones might crack apart and unleash a blood-soaked beast. After catching his breath, he heard a faint roar followed by a muted thud. The sounds came again, slightly louder than before.

The prince left the path in the direction of the noise. The trees thinned out, leading him to a steep hill. Below lay the salt mine—a space of terraced pools—just as Farzan had described. Halfway down was a way-station surrounded by tools and haulage baskets. Yaya had half expected to find Rayduri mine workers swinging their pickaxes. Instead, he saw the strangest sight: a large brown bear with a basket on its head, facing off against a mountain goat.

After delivering several head butts upon the befuddled bear, the ibex trotted triumphantly out of the mine and vanished into the forest.

The bear sat back on his haunches and began twisting and tugging at the wicker basket. Eventually, it popped off like a cork.

He looked up to where the ibex had run. "So that's how you're going to play it? Cheap shot me when I can't see you? This mine is my mineral lick, you stupid goat."

Yaya wanted nothing to do with a territorial dispute and figured it best he keep moving. But before he could sneak off, the bear caught his scent, its nostrils flaring as it gathered clues. In response, Yaya receded like a skulking thief after the heist, only to be betrayed by a scaly-bellied woodpecker in the tree beside him.

Annoyed by the trespasser, the bird began drumming his beak on the bark.

Yaya abandoned his attempts at a stealthy escape and took off running. He crossed the miners' path and headed into the denser forest. The grasses and saplings posed no obstacle, and the downward slope gave him some confidence that he had given the bear the slip—or at least showed his benign intentions. But at the bottom, he encountered a tangle of vines and briars that stopped him in his tracks.

Yaya turned around, hoping against hope, and saw the bear rounding the hill in full stride. The boy unsheathed his shamshir and prepared to defend himself against the charging animal. When the moment came, he raised his sword only to have it ensnared by Caspian ivy. The harder he pulled, the tighter the tendrils wove around blade and hilt. They appeared to be moving, like serpents constricting their prey.

That left Yaya with one option. With the bear nearly upon him, he dropped to his knees and began to cower. "Please don't kill me. I mean you no harm. I promise."

The bear extended his forearms and skidded to a stop, stunned that he understood the boy's plea. He had heard humans speak before during their shifts in the salt mine, but from where he spied on them, their words were a jarring collision of mumbo jumbo. This utterance had rhythm and meter—this he understood. Still wary of the trespasser, he bowled the prince over with his head and sniffed him.

Yaya lay in a fetal position, his head covered and eyes closed.

"You can stop with that trick," the bear said. "I know you're not dead."

"Am I going to be?" Yaya's body was trembling.

"I haven't quite decided. There's something odd about you. For one thing, you make sense when you speak."

"And the other?"

"You're not as foul-smelling as most *uprights* who come here. Don't get me wrong; you still stink, but it's less offensive somehow."

Indeed, being a vegetarian meant that Yaya's body odor differed from many other humans.

"So what are you doing here?" the bear asked. "Come to dig for salt?"

Yaya hesitated to answer.

In a calm yet commanding voice, the bear leaned forward and asked, "Who's with you?"

"Nobody is with me."

"It's not often that uprights travel alone. Worse than wolves, I tell you." The bear scanned the forest, worried of being duped into a trap. "Then you must be a hunter."

"I don't even eat meat."

"So why are you here? Are you lost or something?"

Yaya sat up. He reached into his haversack and pulled out his bottle. "I must fill this with some water from the springs of Anahita."

"Ana... who?"

"They're a collection of blessed springs that feed the rivers of our land. They're in this range next to some ancient temple ruins."

"But why fill the bottle?"

"I have to collect the elements of the water cycle and present them to the rain god."

"The rain god?"

"His name is Tishtrya, and he needs help defeating the demon of drought. And that's only the half of it. We also have to defeat Ahriman and his evil minions."

"Whoa, whoa, whoa, one thing at a time. I'm still stuck on the rain god."

Yaya sighed. "Never mind. None of this will make any sense to you. All I know is that there is wickedness in this world, and if left unchecked, it'll only fester."

The bear didn't know what 'fester' meant, but the rest made sense. In fact, it was the first thing the boy had said that made any sense. Things in his habitat had changed for the worse, from a scourge of invasive vines and small, carnivorous plants to an outbreak of tree lesions and other herbaceous diseases. The drought seemed the least of it.

Yaya put his bottle into his haversack. "Perhaps you can lead me to the temple ruins? You must know where they are."

"This all sounds a little hocus-pocus to me. Anyway, the day bears involve themselves with uprights will be our undoing. We've been doing fine knowing as little about you as possible. It's probably best if you go home."

"I understand why you have doubts, but you can't hide from what's happening. You can't retreat into these woods and wish it away. If the demon of drought is not defeated, all of us will eventually die. You, me, and that ibex that knocked you on the head."

"Hey, that's not fair. That goat cheap-shotted me."

"Listen, whether you like it or not, our worlds overlap. Please, I'm asking you. I need your help."

The bear mulled over the proposition.

"Besides," the boy confessed, "I can't go home. My grandmother wants to kill me."

The bear almost laughed.

Even Yaya knew it sounded absurd, but he knew it was true.

"By the way, my name is Babak, or 'Baba' if you're in a hurry. And I'll help you on one condition."

"Name it."

Baba motioned with his snout toward Yaya's haversack. "Perhaps you can share some of what's in that bag. I know I smell fruit. After all that salt licking, I could go for something a little sweet."

"Deal—but only after we make some progress."

Baba started padding through the forest. "Well, come on. Getting to these temple ruins is no stroll through the woods."

Yaya freed his shamshir from the vines and chased after Baba. They crossed a narrow stream bed and passed between shrubs and saplings of elm.

Strangers through the Flame

Lilya lounged on her settee, legs crossed, and cooled herself with a *baad-bezan*, or handheld fan. The evening air was so stifling and stagnant that it rendered the wind catchers on the citadel's roof useless. Gratuitous garments were shed in favor of loosely fitting gowns. Shoes were removed. Even the jackals, evolved to endure such temperatures, struggled against the oppressive heat and fared no better despite sprawling on the floor.

Her patience waning, Lilya pressed Kamran to respond to her accusation. "Well?"

The king stopped pacing and brought his hands to his face. With undue force, he rubbed his forehead as if battling his thoughts. "She wouldn't have done it, Mother."

"Adarbad had help to escape."

"And we agreed it was Shanaz who probably helped him."

Lilya walked to a window overlooking the bazaar, the marketplace nearly idle for lack of goods. Vendors no longer arrived early to jostle for space. Rare were the heated arguments; incidents of fisticuffs, rarer still. In every way, Zad's vitality seemed to be dissipating. The people were suffering by the day, and the queen wondered how long it would be before any unrest reached the royal family.

She turned and leaned against the sill. "But what about the missing amulet? Sarvin doesn't misplace things. It had to have been stolen. That means inside knowledge."

"Why?"

"Because Sarvin told me where he had put it. Finding it otherwise would have required a complete dismantling of his laboratory—which, of course, did not happen." Lilya approached her son. "Nobody reported seeing Shanaz. That she could have snuck in undetected and, by the grace of good fortune, stumble upon the amulet is beyond impossible. It's preposterous."

"And what you're insinuating is unacceptable. You mention 'inside knowledge'? Why are you so convinced Sarvin didn't help Adarbad? They were friends."

"They were colleagues. The fact that they worked together and were cordial means nothing. Look at how I kept up appearances with Shanaz. You know how I feel about her."

"But several guards reported seeing Vira in the citadel yesterday afternoon. Sarvin was with her much of the day, and when he wasn't, he told you he was in his lab or chamber. Are you telling me she found a way to intervene on Adarbad's behalf without being seen by anyone? Now *that's* impossible."

Lilya retrieved a piece of fabric from her pocket. In her outstretched palm lay the silken doily Adarbad had discarded after being rescued.

Kamran took the item, giving it an incurious glance. "What's this?"

"Part of a gift I gave Vira for her birthday. It was thirteen years ago."

"And you remember that?"

"Women remember these things, especially when the gift has never been used."

"This proves nothing."

"It proves everything. I found it half-buried in the sand when we checked on our alchemist friend."

Kamran examined the fabric more closely, buying time to wrap his head around the idea that Vira helped Adarbad escape. As his mind searched for a rationale to acquit his wife, he sensed his mother's eyes upon him, waiting expectantly for a response. He said nothing and handed the doily back.

"You're learning what it means to be king," she said.

"Which is what?"

"Survival. Knowing who your enemies are on the outside is easy—the inside is a different matter."

"You once said a person's incentive can predict their behavior. Vira has no incentive to help Shanaz or Adarbad."

"I also told you to beware the faint of heart." Lilya sat down on her settee. "The incentive to help Adarbad came from Shanaz, so it wouldn't surprise me in the least if she persuaded Vira to help. You know your wife. Her desire to please is a weakness."

Kamran's expression turned to resignation as he finished weighing the circumstantial evidence his mother had presented. He sank into a chair and stared at the jackals, the animals alert, their tongues hanging out.

"I can't do it. I won't do it." The absurdity of his dilemma—in marked contrast to the blank-eyed, worry-free expressions of the beasts—made him laugh. "Look at their faces—so serene." He reclined and crossed his arms. "I don't understand."

"There is no greater crime than betrayal. And by its very nature, it comes from those we least expect. That's why you don't understand. You haven't been betrayed by anyone you love. But don't forget, you too have betrayed those who held you dear. This is an important lesson."

It was a truth Kamran found hard to accept. If his wife were indeed culpable of the charge levied, then loyalty and love were meaningless. A hollowness filled his chest like a poisonous vapor, unseen yet expanding to every part of his being. The deepening sadness focused his mind on the arc of their life together. He traced its memories from the day he first kissed Vira to the nights she stayed by his bedside as he recovered from scorpion venom.

With tears in his eyes, he leaned forward, his head drooping. "How could she do this to me? She is my wife."

"Because she doesn't know what it means to be 'queen.' You need more than a wife."

"I will not kill her."

"You don't have to. That's why we have a dungeon. Now fix the situation so we can move on. This is not the time to get in touch with your father's emotional side. We have a kingdom to mobilize for war."

Kamran knew what he had to do, but not before confronting Vira himself. He rose to his feet and took the doily from Lilya. "She should be at the temple."

"And why is that not surprising?" Lilya said, fanning herself. "After all, prayer is the last refuge of the damned."

Barefoot and veiled, Vira walked through the fire temple and entered an anteroom. In the center stood a large bronze brazier with a burning fire, its flames fueled by sandalwood. She placed a piece in the basin, sending fragrant wisps of smoke upward, and swiped some ash with her finger to mark her forehead and eyelids. With her palms turned upward, she began to recite the *Yasna* liturgy in honor of Ohrmazd.

But the young queen never got far. Her thoughts drifted to the day Afshad was born. What should have been a day of joy was sullied by Lilya's veiled criticism of the newborn's appearance. "Look, Vira, he has your thin lips," she had said. Ever since, Vira could never celebrate her son's birthday without recalling the derisive comment. The happiest day of her life was forever tainted, and she had always resented Lilya for it.

Vira returned to prayer, but she had the unsettling sense of being watched.

"I'm sorry," Kamran said, leaning against the doorway. "I didn't mean to disturb you."

"That's all right. I was in the *Ab-Zohr*."

"May I join you?"

The queen was surprised by the request. Though Kamran espoused reverence to Ohrmazd, he never took the rituals seriously. To her, such work gave faith its meaning. A prerequisite to the priesthood was the ability to recite all seventy-two chapters, and apart from the magi, she was the only known adherent capable of such mastery.

Vira welcomed her husband to stand beside her, and together they prayed. When it finished, she opened her eyes and gazed at the dancing flames.

Kamran let his hands fall to his sides. "That felt nice. Maybe I should pray more."

"I think you should. Self-reflection is the mirror of our sins. Without it, we fail to control vice."

"I've always admired your wisdom. Your faith grounds you. But you know me—my eyes are always fixed on the horizon."

"They weren't when we met."

"A man must leave his mark on the world."

"You are the son of a king. Your birth was a mark."

Kamran walked to a bin, retrieved a few pieces of sandalwood, and stoked the flame. "I had nothing to do with my birth or my past. I now have a chance to forge a glorious future."

"Your future was supposed to be with me."

"And why can't it be?"

"Because you're no longer the person I married. You're consumed with ambition. I can't remember the last time you embraced me without your mind being somewhere else." The queen began to cry. "And when you look at me, you look right through me as if I were a mirage."

"It's always about Vira, isn't it?"

"How dare you say that."

Kamran added more wood to the fire. "The other day, I rode out to the villages. A woman approached my escort carrying her dead baby, his bones protruding through his skin. The woman begged me to save her other child. Do you know what it's like to carry such a burden—to have the fate of a kingdom on your shoulders?"

Vira remained silent, staring at him through the flames.

"Answer me."

"That's not my fault. You never cared to share your burdens with me."

"As if you wanted to hear them." Kamran tossed the last piece of wood into the urn.

"That's not fair. The day you became king, I was replaced by *madar shohar*."

"Don't bring my mother into this. You never wanted to be queen. I'm sure you realized that in all of your self-reflection."

Vira looked at her husband, his face glowing orange through the flames. She no longer recognized him. "Why did you come here, Kamran? It certainly wasn't to join me in prayer."

The king tossed the doily at Vira's feet. "Remember the day we got married?"

"It was raining."

"We thought we were blessed."

"We were blessed."

"Why did you do it?"

"It was the happiest day of my life."

"Why did you help Adarbad?"

"You were so handsome."

"Why did you betray me?"

Vira picked up the doily. "You chose Zad over me. I guess I chose God over you."

Kamran walked over and embraced his wife. "I will spare you death, but not the dungeon. Guards outside the temple await you."

Vira trembled, her body suddenly cold. "I need a moment alone. Please."

She didn't watch her husband leave. Instead, she stared into the fire that had grown from his ministrations. Thoughts of Afshad filled her mind as she prayed, bracing herself and gathering courage for what lay ahead. As if in a trance, she turned and slowly backed toward the brazier, her gold-threaded gown brushing against it. The fabric resisted the heat briefly before the flames raced up the shawl and into her headscarf.

Piercing screams followed.

Loitering on the temple stairs, Kamran raced through the congregation hall and into the anteroom. He found Vira on the floor, engulfed in flames. As her body contorted and writhed in agony, he tore off his tunic and desperately tried to extinguish the fire.

Several guards, hearing Kamran's cries for help, charged in with buckets of water from the outside pool and doused the burning body.

Vira lay face down on the floor, her charred body twitching from shock. All that remained of her hair were a few smoldering tufts clinging to her blistered scalp. Pieces of her gown had melted to her skin. The air stank of burnt flesh—acrid and awful.

With a mournful cry, Kamran collapsed to the floor. He whispered a few words into his wife's ear, to which she responded with a faint squeeze of his hand. A moment later her body went still. Kamran let go, and despite his newfound strength, he barely had enough to bring himself to his feet. Vira, who had been queen scarcely a week, was dead.

The grand magus was the first to approach. "I don't have the words to express my sorrow, my lord. How could this have happened?"

"We prayed. I waited for her outside and then..." Kamran motioned to the brazier.

"She must have caught her garments in the flames," Rustem said.

Kamran stood motionless, his eyes glazed and full of shock.

The grand magus touched the king's shoulder to comfort him. "Return to your chamber, my lord, and grieve with Prince Afshad. He must hear this from your lips before word reaches him. Leave your wife to us. You can be sure we will care for her as befits a queen."

Kamran acknowledged Rustem's kind words and exited the temple, the guards trailing behind. He neither spoke nor moved his arms as he descended the stairs, and those who saw him had the impression that he glided over the temple grounds like a ghost.

⚬

In the council chamber, Lilya had convened a meeting of the high command to discuss war plans. They had resolved to overwhelm Raydur with their armaments and follow with a blockade, if necessary.

To assuage her concern that King Delawar might have a few surprises up his sleeve, General Baraz had begun to offer his counsel when Kamran strode into the room. All present acknowledged him.

But the king said nothing. He shuffled to his throne and sat beside his mother, slouching against the armrest.

While the general waited for permission to continue, Lilya gave her son a studied look. She, who noticed everything, could read the tension in his face. "I assume all went according to plan?"

Kamran shook his head.

"What do you mean?" she whispered. "Was Vira not taken to the dungeon?"

The king turned to his mother, whose eyes searched his face for a clue. In a measured tone, he delivered the news: "Vira is dead."

Lilya gasped.

The king rose from his throne, his face etched with grief. In a weary voice, he told his advisors how tragedy had befallen the queen. During the stunned silence that followed, a ghastly thought crept into his mind: having been to the burial grounds so often of late, he began to wonder when his turn would come.

"You have suffered greatly, my lord," General Baraz said, sensing an opportunity to ingratiate himself. "You have lost a beloved father, two brothers, and a dear wife in the span of a few months. Few men can say they have endured such pain. In this time of hardship, I swear my allegiance to you, our rightful and blessed ruler."

"Hear, hear," the others said.

Kamran expressed his gratitude, then stepped from the dais to where his men had gathered. He looked at his war staff, who awaited his command.

With a stiff upper lip, he gave the orders: "We march to Raydur in five days and should arrive at its gates on the eve, four days hence. Notify your troops and begin assembling armor, weapons, and supplies. Increase food rations for elephants, horses, and manticores, and plan to reconvene here tomorrow evening to finalize plans."

After everyone but Lilya had filed out, the king inquired about his son. "Where's Afshad?"

"He's in the barracks training. Shall I have someone fetch him?"

"I'll wait for him in his room."

The king left the council chamber, making it clear by his abrupt departure that he no longer wished to speak of the tragedy. Nevertheless, Lilya followed after him.

When he entered his quarters, he went to a window overlooking the barracks.

Armed with a wooden sword, Afshad practice different maneuvers against a straw figure. Satisfied with his progress, the trainers replaced his weapon with a shield and a lighter shamshir.

Lilya stepped beside Kamran and evaluated her grandson. "He's turning into a true warrior, isn't he?"

"He's much better than I was at that age."

Lilya could barely contain her curiosity, and she had no intention of discussing Afshad's training regimen. "What exactly happened in that temple?"

"I have nothing to add to what you already know."

Afshad noticed his admirers and waved.

"Come on, Kamran," Lilya said, acknowledging her grandson. "Did she refute the accusation? Argue with you? Something else must have happened that you are not telling me."

"Let's just say she made a choice."

"What's that supposed to mean?"

Kamran could no longer hide his annoyance at his mother's petty persistence. "You're a smart woman. Figure it out. Now please—may I be alone to console my son?"

"I think I should be here as well."

"Of course you do."

As they watched Afshad speak with the trainers, Lilya turned to her son, whose bottom lip was quivering. Such a display of emotion was rare, and it took her by surprise.

"I'll check on Afshad later," she said, touching Kamran's hand affectionately.

"As you wish."

Lilya walked toward the doorway but hesitated. "Before you arrived at the meeting, we had discussed a plan to deal with

Delawar's scouts. You know he'll line the road from here to Raydur with them to warn of the invasion."

"Yes," Kamran said matter-of-factly.

"As our forces approach and his scouts retreat, we'll pick them off one by one with the manticores."

"Goodbye, Mother."

With one last look at her son, Lilya stepped into the corridor.

Kamran heard her calling for attendants as he entered Afshad's chamber and approached the bed. He sat down, placed his hands over his face, and softly wept.

A Much-Needed Rest

On all fours, with mucus dangling from his mouth, Adarbad took a few deep breaths and prayed his nausea had passed. Shanaz rubbed his back, sometimes humming a song she knew was his favorite. There was little else she could do besides hasten their arrival at Raydur, where medical assistance awaited. Fortunately for Adarbad, his urge to vomit waned, which meant his stomach was adjusting to the food Shanaz had been feeding him.

Since his escape, the queen had insisted that he drink from the water skins and take in nourishment, however small the portions. Despite his protestations that her "force-feeding" was worse than what he had braved in the dungeon, Adarbad complied, knowing full well he needed the calories. The problem was that his body, given the trauma to his internal organs, rejected whatever he ingested.

After wiping his face, Shanaz helped him onto the horse.

Within an hour, they reached the outer villages of Raydur, which at first glance seemed free of the despair hanging over those of Zad. The dirt streets converging near the barbican bustled with the familiar rhythms one might expect from a vibrant city. Yet a pall of gloom lingered in the air, evident in the wary eyes of some people scanning the sky for manticores.

Even so, a few residents couldn't help but notice the wayward travelers. For though Shanaz had retained much of her well-kempt appearance, Adarbad was half-naked, wearing only a pair of dirty linen trousers held up by a frayed drawstring. His collarbones jutted out from the neck, his eyes sunk deep into their sockets, and the skin of his hands and wrists was beet red.

When they crossed the drawbridge, two spear-wielding guards inquired about their business. Surprised by the request, they replied by giving their names and stating their desire to see the alchemist of Raydur. But the shabby and undignified appearance of the shirtless rider did little to convince the guards of their credentials.

Adarbad grew frustrated at the impasse and divulged details of his ordeal that he would have preferred to keep private.

The guards remained skeptical.

"Listen, young men," Adarbad said. "Do you think I'd invent such a fantastical story about being tortured, and even dress the part, if I weren't who I say I am? Do I have to show you the bug bites on my ass?"

Shanaz intervened. "Ada, please." The queen smiled at the guards, sensing a change in tact was necessary. "It's clear that you men won't let us proceed. You're doing your job, and for that, I commend you."

"We're under strict orders from King Delawar," one of the guards said. "We're not to let anyone pass who we deem suspicious." His face radiated pride at the responsibility bestowed upon him.

"I'm sure the king would be most grateful for your due diligence. Even so, I'd like to speak to your superior. It's only fair you grant us that request. We haven't ridden for two straight days without a moment's rest only to be refused a fair hearing. As you can see, my friend needs urgent medical attention. To deny him that would cast aspersions on the charitable reputation of Raydur itself."

The eloquence of Shanaz's voice, paired with her graceful charm, affected the two guards. One left to fetch his commanding officer. When he returned, he was accompanied by a stocky man who walked briskly with short strides.

"My name is Nadir, deputy to the pushtigban-salar. What business do you have here?"

Adarbad recognized the deputy and called him by his name.

The man squinted and approached the horse. He studied the alchemist and glanced at Shanaz. "Adarbad? What on earth has happened to you? You look like a vagrant."

"I wish I were a wandering beggar. But, ay..." Adarbad winced in pain. "Such is not my fate."

"Please—forgive my men. There is anxiety in the air."

Knowing that they had a friend in the deputy, Adarbad's tone became magnanimous. "Hard to fault men for following orders."

"By all means, pass through," Nadir said, motioning toward the barbican. "I don't know what brings you here in this condition, but it's clear you need help."

"Well, lucky for me, I know the resident doctor."

After passing through the barbican and the gates of the ancillary courtyard, they rode through city streets until they reached a small complex near the royal citadel's inner wall.

Shanaz helped Adarbad from the horse and draped his arm over her shoulder. Together, they hobbled to the front door. As the queen lifted her hand to knock, the door unexpectedly opened.

It was Farzan. His shoulders sank at the sight of the alchemist.

"That bad, huh?" Adarbad said.

"My dear friend, what has happened to you?" Farzan ushered the pair inside and helped Adarbad to a sofa covered with silken pillows. "Parendi, bring my medicines. Hurry."

Farzan's wife soon returned with a small chest and a bowl of water. A little girl, no more than four years old, followed close behind. "Is there anything else I can do?"

"Take Queen Shanaz and Nilu to the garden terrace. We'll need privacy. In the kitchen, you'll find some ground haoma leaves in my mortar. Add them to a bowl of yogurt and leave it on the table."

Parendi took her daughter's hand and had Shanaz follow her to the backdoor.

"You're really handsome when you play doctor," Adarbad said.

"And your sarcasm has no limits. Lie still."

"Where's Yaya? Tell me he made it."

Farzan began inspecting the various bite wounds on Adarbad's body. "What on God's earth have they done to you?"

"Let's just say they tried to get me to talk."

"Did you?"

"Only with the vultures skulking around my head. But enough about me—what about the boy?"

Farzan wrung out a washcloth and tended to the more inflamed-looking injuries. "I found Yaya asleep in the gardens of the fire temple. He set out on his own for Kuh-e Ab yesterday morning."

"Yesterday morning?" Adarbad stiffened with anxiety. "Why was he delayed?"

"Queen Lilya's jackals chased him to your burial grounds. He evaded them by jumping into the ossuary and only escaped after discovering a hidden staircase. Some kid, I tell you."

Adarbad rubbed his forehead, second-guessing the execution of their departure. "We've failed him."

"You've only failed me with all this moving about. Relax and let me work."

Reaching into his medicine chest, Farzan pulled out a container of salve made from oils and marigold leaves. After applying it to Adarbad's pus-filled wounds, he covered his patient with a blanket and fetched the yogurt mixture from the kitchen. He fed Adarbad small spoonfuls, tenderly dabbing his mouth with a cloth until the alchemist, his eyes heavy, drifted to sleep.

Soon, the others came in from the garden terrace, and Parendi, having learned from Shanaz what had happened, took her daughter and went to the kitchen.

Shanaz entered the living room and looked at her friend stretched out on the sofa. His color was so wan, it took the rise of his chest to dispel her fear that he had died.

Farzan, who was seated at the dining table and keeping vigil, offered a chair. "He'll sleep through the night."

Shanaz sat beside him. "Tell me. How serious are his injuries?"

"Fortunately, the external wounds are superficial and will heal accordingly. He's not dehydrated, which is somewhat surprising given what he's been through. My main concern is the trauma to his ribs. Hopefully, they're only bruised. I'll take him to the bath house in the morning for a good soaking in salt. From there, we'll have to wait and see."

"He's lucky to know you," Shanaz said.

"I remind him of that every time I see him. But lest we forget, my lady, it's because of you that he's alive."

The queen and alchemist sat in companionable silence until Farzan excused himself to check on dinner.

In his place came Nilu, who used her father's presence in the kitchen as a pretext to search for their new and intriguing guest.

At first, shy and guarded, the girl became a proverbial chatterbox after she and Shanaz swapped bracelets. Unfortunately for the queen, this only encouraged her to inquire about other pieces of jewelry.

Shanaz laughed at the girl's tenacity and was reminded of some wise words. "I had always been taught never to barter when exhausted. It seems I've forgotten the rule."

Indeed, Farzan was surprised by the queen's patience as he and his wife set the table. "That's enough, Nilu. This isn't the local bazaar."

Shanaz tousled Nilu's hair and looked at the wonderful array of steaming dishes.

"My wife is a most splendid cook," Farzan said, taking his seat at the head of the table. "And my ever-growing belly can attest to it."

Shanaz tried her barley soup. "Mmm—what a rich, delicious flavor."

"The secret," Parendi confided, "is to add chicken bones while you let it simmer."

Farzan leaned toward Shanaz. "Be careful what you're getting into, my lady. There's only one other thing my wife is more effusive about than cooking, and she won't show it in mixed company."

"What might that be?"

"Her affections for me," the alchemist said, a grin of mischief across his face.

Parendi scoffed. "How could that be? I rarely see you." She served Shanaz some rice and lentils. "Not that I'm complaining."

"I have my work to do for the king," Farzan said as he sipped a syrupy drink of mint, strawberry, and ginger. "What my precious wife fails to mention is that it was I who broached the idea to our beloved king of hiring another alchemist, precisely on account of her complaint. And his response? 'Work twice as hard.' And he says this even though I have two apprentices ready for hire. Somehow, the charitable reputation of Raydur has not been afforded to me."

"Kings have limited resources," Shanaz said. "Anyway, it shows you are needed."

"And that's fine with me," Parendi said. "Keeps him out of my hair. I wouldn't have any if he were always hanging around the house. It would be 'do this' or 'do that,' 'clean this,' or 'clean that.' My husband should be Raydur's general instead of Jangi." Parendi smiled at her husband before turning to her royal guest. "Would you like some rose water?"

"Please," Shanaz said, amused by the familiar, good-natured bickering.

Parendi excused herself and headed to the kitchen.

Nilu crawled into her father's lap, her black curls dangling in her eyes. "My *pedar* is a scientist," she proudly told her guest.

"I know," Shanaz said, "and a very good one."

"What are you?"

"Well, I used to rule my kingdom alongside my husband, the King of Zad."

"You're beautiful like my madar."

"And you are a little flatterer." Shanaz began to tickle the little girl's feet. "Trying to keep my bracelet, aren't you?"

Nilu giggled, and after a tussle pulled her legs away. "One time me and Madar were sick, and Pedar had to care for us."

"Really?" Shanaz said. "That must have been hard for your pedar. Children complain and fuss. Caring for them isn't easy."

"Nilu was the easy one," Farzan said as his wife returned to the room.

"I heard that." Parendi set the cups of rose water on the table. "Don't believe a word he says, my lady. All that wine drinking with Adarbad has caused a certain amount of brain damage. Every time your alchemist comes to visit, it's the same routine."

"My little *moosh moosh-am,*" Farzan said, "why must you spread such slanderous rumors?"

"Don't 'mousy mouse' me. And then my husband comes in from his laboratory and chases me around like a drooling brigand."

Shanaz could barely contain her laughter as Nilu, now in her lap, settled down.

"What can I say?" Farzan said. "You are a caster of spells, my dear. Such is my curse."

Parendi waved her hand dismissively as she sipped from her mug.

After the meal, which included melon salad and cardamom-flavored pistachio cakes, a collective silence indicated what everyone was surely thinking.

"It's time we get some sleep," Farzan said. "There's a lot to discuss with King Delawar tomorrow. I'll take Adarbad to the bathhouse first thing in the morning, so if you hear us rummaging around, pay no attention."

"Thank you for your kindness, both of you."

"The pleasure is ours," Farzan said, "and I insist you sleep in our room tonight."

"I wouldn't think of it."

"And I wouldn't have it any other way." Farzan rose from the table. "Now, if you'll excuse me, I have some work to do in the lab."

Parendi showed Shanaz to her quarters and provided her with a bowl of water and a clean washcloth.

After tucking Nilu into bed, Parendi sat beside her and thought of *Drakht-i Asurig*, an ancient tale in which a date palm and a goat debate the virtues of an agricultural versus pastoral way of life. Thinking of the two alchemists in her house and their decades-long work in metal transmutation and metallurgy, she couldn't help but feel a new age was upon them.

The next morning, Shanaz awoke from a nightmare, convinced bloodthirsty animals were attacking her. The cause was much more benign—little Nilu in her room dragging a wheeled toy shaped like a lion. Around and around she spun, all the while roaring.

Parendi hurried into the bedroom. "Nilu, get out of there. Our guest is sleeping."

"I'm awake," Shanaz said, holding the string of the toy. "I think I have this little beast under control." The queen smiled at Parendi, conveying she didn't mean the toy.

Through the doorway, Shanaz spotted the divan where Adarbad had been sleeping. The sheets hung over the side and onto the rug. "Have Ada and Farzan not yet returned?"

"They're having breakfast. If you want any fresh naan, you'd better hurry to the table. That alchemist of yours has vowed to devour every piece." Parendi patted her daughter on the rump. "Come, *bacheh*. It's time for you to eat, too. I'm sure the queen would like to dress without being watched by a hungry lion."

Shanaz soon emerged and approached everyone gathered around the table. She greeted Adarbad with a kiss on the cheek and was pleased to see him wearing new clothes and a robe of his favorite color—midnight blue. He also smelled of sweet, cedar-scented oil. Apart from a sunburnt face and scalp, the alchemist looked no worse for wear.

"How do you feel?" she asked.

"Just happy to see another sunrise. And you?"

"I'm famished."

Farzan pulled out a chair. "Then have a seat, my lady."

Shanaz sat down and looked at the food with anticipation. She accepted a piece of naan offered by Parendi and spread a spoonful of sour cherry jam on a corner. "Everything smells lovely."

"And tastes even better," Farzan said. "Please enjoy your breakfast and relax for the rest of the morning. King Delawar wants to see us this afternoon. I've briefed him on your travails and Prince Yaya's quest. But he's eager to hear more." The alchemist excused himself. "I must now tend to my falcons. There's nothing more irritating than hungry, squawking birds."

Farzan glanced at Parendi, a quip coming to mind, but knew better than to say it aloud. He took a cluster of red grapes from a bowl and headed to the garden.

After breakfast, Adarbad retired to the divan to lie down. He couldn't help but dwell on his time trapped in the *boats*, recalling when a blister beetle had crawled onto his skin and released its poison. The burning sensation was so intense, he had briefly considered spilling everything to Queen Lilya if afforded the chance. The memory of his possible betrayal made him shudder, and his thoughts turned to Yaya, for whom he imagined a number of dreadful scenarios.

Despite tossing, turning, and wrestling with his thoughts, the alchemist was soon dreaming.

Meanwhile, Parendi escorted Shanaz to a bathhouse, then took advantage of the nearby bazaar to restock her larders with fresh fruit, flour, and meats.

To the queen's displeasure, all six of the bathhouse's pools were packed, with many other women eagerly waiting in the wings. She wondered if the throngs were due to the unusual heat, or if word had begun to spread about the dwindling water supply.

Soon, a young woman left the pool, freeing some space. Shanaz moved deftly, slipping in before a dozen bystanders had their chance. One older woman scowled, but the queen was in no mood to be generous. She lowered herself into the tepid water and closed her eyes, resting her head against the warm stone. For the first time since escaping the citadel, she allowed herself to enjoy the sensation of stillness.

But it was fleeting.

Like Adarbad, Shanaz's thoughts turned to Yaya. She wondered how he would fare against the large predators lurking in the mountains. Uneasy about his well-being, the queen found it unseemly to linger in the bathhouse for too long. Guilt-ridden, she stepped out of the pool and let the breeze from the wind catcher dry her skin.

After donning a gold-colored kaftan and lavender cloak borrowed from Parendi—both falling short of her ankles—Shanaz walked outside.

Parendi was waiting for her, having just returned with a basket of groceries. "Done so soon?"

"I was too excited to try on the clothes you lent me. I must say you have impeccable style."

Parendi was too consumed with pride to notice the less-than-impeccable fit.

"Any sign of our wayward alchemists?" Shanaz asked.

"Farzan took Adarbad to the bazaar to buy some *koloocheh*. They'll meet us here shortly before you speak with the king."

The women sat on a shaded bench and watched Nilu chase birds in a nearby plaza.

"That means Ada's on the mend," Shanaz said. "Seems your culinary delights were the medicines he most needed."

"Perhaps—but at the expense of working myself to the bone. I can't handle it anymore. When he mentioned a desire for sweets, I told Farzan to buy him some. I'm done cooking." Parendi motioned toward the bazaar. "Speak of the devil."

Adarbad beamed as he held up two large cookies.

"Look at him," Parendi said. "No bigger than a desert shrew, but with an appetite like an elephant."

Shanaz stood and greeted the men. "Parendi was just telling me how eager she is to make you her world-famous rice pudding."

"Wonderful," Adarbad said. "I was beginning to worry that I was wearing out my welcome."

In a business-like tone, Farzan cut through the levity. "Shall we continue this conversation on our way to the citadel? We don't want the king to be left waiting."

"Then you should have moved into the citadel like I did," Adarbad said.

"So says the man without a family. Believe me, we are close enough."

As the two alchemists headed toward the citadel gatehouse, Shanaz lingered to reassure Parendi. "Don't worry, my friend. It would be my pleasure to make the rice pudding."

"Then I'll be sure to invite the relatives."

Shanaz smiled before hurrying off to catch the others.

———◆———

Royal guards at the citadel escorted Farzan and his guests to the council chamber. Seated at a large table beneath a gold and magenta tapestry were Princess Mahzarin and General Jangi, along with several military officials and advisors. Farzan greeted his compatriots and introduced Adarbad and Shanaz. Before they could take their seats, the king entered, prompting everyone else in the room to stand.

"Please, be seated," Delawar said, making his way to a chair between his daughter and Jangi. "I want to welcome Queen Shanaz and Zad's royal alchemist to Raydur. From what I've heard, it's no small miracle that you are even sitting here. I assume Farzan and his wife have provided you with typical Rayduri hospitality?"

"They have indeed," Shanaz said.

"Very well, but having your own guest accommodations near the citadel would be more appropriate."

"Not at all."

"Fresh linens have already been placed in your quarters. Last night, you were guests of Farzan and his family. Now you are mine—and I won't accept otherwise."

Shanaz nodded her appreciation.

"Well then," Delawar said, "the last time representatives from your kingdom sat here, the discussion was far from pleasant. Tell me, what do you know of their intentions?"

Shanaz and Adarbad exchanged a glance, surprised by the king's directness.

"I can only speak to what the astrological signs and elixir of precognition have revealed," the alchemist said.

"And what is that?"

"That war will come to the land—and fire."

"How certain are you?"

"Quite certain," Adarbad said. "All signs point to it, signs that the magi have corroborated through their readings of the holy texts."

"Before your house arrest, did you see any signs of war preparations?"

"No, nothing—but I do know they're sparing no effort in searching for Prince Yaya."

King Delawar toyed with his beard. "Yes, that seems to be the case. Queen Lilya hinted he had run away and asked if I could keep an eye out for him. Why does the boy threaten her so much that she needed to torture you?"

"Because I gave the prince a magical elixir to aid him on his quest. I trust Farzan has filled you in on the details?"

Delawar nodded. "He has."

"Queen Lilya doesn't know what the elixir can do."

"Did you also give one to King Kamran? His feats of sword bending do raise questions."

"At King Khavar's discretion, I crafted 'wish' elixirs for his sons. They were gifts, if you will, a dying man's bestowment. How they manifested depended on the individual desires of the recipients."

"Perhaps you could replicate such magic for the benefit of Raydur?"

"These elixirs take weeks to create and require the rarest of ingredients. I have it on good authority that many of those are in short supply here." Adarbad glanced at Farzan.

"What about the manticores?" Delawar asked. "Any idea how they came to be?"

"Queen Lilya's alchemist must have created them."

"Really? Farzan has always regarded him as rather pedestrian when it comes to alchemy."

"A valid assessment," Adarbad said, "but what Sarvin lacks in training, he has made up for in collusion with the queen and the dark arts. In the months before the coup, he spent time traveling to the Jabiri ruins. I suspect he uncovered ancient scrolls of knowledge long since forgotten."

"So it is true?"

"I beg your pardon?"

"This insurgency." Delawar leaned forward, resting his arms on the table. "I must admit, the way the succession unfolded seemed precarious. Care to share the details?"

Adarbad deferred to Shanaz, who took a deep breath and recounted the tragic events. When she described how brigand mercenaries had murdered Yaya's father, the king interrupted.

"But he was Lilya's eldest son."

"But not the most beloved," Shanaz said. "Lilya saw an opportunity—a pathway, if you will—to guide Kamran to the throne. It began with eliminating heirs and culminated with the murder of my husband, all because he had the temerity to defy his illness. Now that Lilya has succeeded, she won't rest until she consolidates power and removes all threats. That means—"

"Taking care of Prince Yaya," Delawar said, completing her thought.

The Rayduri king contemplated what he had heard. If true, then Zad's new regime was capable of the most unspeakable acts. He feared for his people and imagined swarms of manticores and scores of enemy soldiers laying siege upon the Rayduri walls. The troubling thought might have led him to despair, if not for one crucial detail.

Delawar trained his sights on Adarbad. "You'll forgive my skepticism, alchemist, but if Zad has considered waging war against me, surely good sense will prevail among its leaders. My confidence does not rest on the deluded musings of a vainglorious king. It comes from sound judgment. Your kingdom is at war with Danzardan. To take offensive action against Raydur now would be a strategic blunder."

"With all due respect—"

Delawar raised his hand. "Allow me to finish. For the sake of argument, let's say your visions of war turn out to be true. Then I ask: how will Zad maintain the morale required for siege warfare when their forces are already stretched thin?"

"But they are not," Adarbad said. "Queen Lilya negotiated a peace settlement with Danzardan a week ago, which means that Zadian troops are returning from the front lines as we speak."

The king leaned back in his chair, the sudden revelation forcing him to pause and gather his thoughts. "It's clear, then, she has turned her gaze to Raydur."

Delawar began tapping his chin, the gears turning in his head. "What do you know about your kingdom's food and water supplies?"

"I'm not sure about the granaries," Shanaz said, "but the water won't last a month."

"So war will come to Raydur—and it will come fast." The king turned to address his military officials and advisors. "I want scouts positioned all the way to the Zadian burial grounds. Begin assembling armor and weapons. Prepare for war." He looked across the table at Shanaz and Adarbad. "Never in the deepest confines of my imagination did I dream this day would come."

Delawar dismissed his team, except for his daughter and General Jangi. "I have another mission for you two. I want you to depart for Jarak. It's high time King Mazad takes a stand."

"But what are we to tell him?" Mahzarin asked.

"Impress upon him that if Raydur falls, and God help us if it does, Lilya will turn her gaze toward Jarak. The question you'll pose to His Majesty comes down to a choice: preemption and victory, or inaction and defeat. Gather a sufficient escort and prepare to leave before dawn."

Delawar escorted the princess and general to the council chamber doorway, warmly embracing Mahzarin before bidding her safe travels. When he turned to rejoin the others, Shanaz was standing in front of him.

"King Delawar, you have been most kind in offering us accommodations, but Adarbad and I must find Yaya, who, as we speak, is wandering the Kuhha-ye Sabz looking for the springs of Anahita."

"And you think you can find him?" The king walked past Shanaz and took his seat on the throne. "I understand your desire to help the boy, but searching for him in such vast terrain is a fool's errand."

"With all due respect, there is no other option." Shanaz turned to her alchemist. "Ada, we must prepare to leave."

But Adarbad demurred, refusing to meet her gaze.

"Ada? What's wrong?"

"Forgive me, my lady, but King Delawar is correct."

Shanaz was stunned. "I can't believe what I'm hearing. That boy is like a son to you, and you're going to abandon him? Just like that?"

"I'm not abandoning him. I gave him the gift of speaking with animals. If the elixir is working, the animals will guide him to the springs."

"You have doubts?"

"I don't know if it'll work with *all* animals."

Shanaz's eyes welled up with tears, then hardened with anger at the betrayal. "Then I travel alone. We still have to bring him the amulet."

"I'm sorry, my lady," Farzan said. "But the amulet is gone."

The queen looked to Adarbad for an explanation.

Before he could answer, Farzan intervened. "If I may, Adarbad and I spoke about Yaya's quest and how best to assist him. Given the difficulty of such an endeavor, I advised that both of you forsake trying to find the boy. King Delawar has said as much. Regarding the amulet, let's just say we thought of a more practical way to get it to him."

"And what could that be?" Shanaz asked, her frustration evident.

"My best falcon, Minoo. He's most excellently trained, and finding Yaya will be far easier from the sky than from the ground. I secured the amulet around his neck this morning. As we speak, he's scouring the mountainside for the prince."

Shanaz felt deceived. "So that's why you checked on your falcons after breakfast."

Farzan nodded. "In a manner of speaking."

"And to think this decision was made without my say."

"Please forgive me," Adarbad said. "I knew you'd insist on taking the amulet to Yaya yourself."

King Delawar had been listening patiently to the exchange. "If I may ask—what's so important about this amulet?"

"It has four compartments," Adarbad said, "each filled with magical properties and substances representing the four elements. A one-word incantation activates the various spells. I owe its creation to what I learned from a cache of ancient scrolls my team unearthed in the Jabiri ruins."

"Let's assume the boy finds the temple ruins of Anahita," Delawar said. "What makes you so sure that he'll be able to take some water? Legend holds that the goddess protects her springs. There have even been purported eyewitness accounts, mostly from miners, of a giant monster roaming the foothills."

"So, it's true," Adarbad said. "I had always assumed those rumors were mere fantasy."

"And even if he collects the water, if I understand Farzan correctly, he's to travel to Kuh-e Sholehand Kuh-e Zuze to retrieve the remaining elements and present them to Tishtrya? Perhaps your Prince Yaya is the chosen one. But even if true, that's a mighty tall order. What concerns me more is Zad's aggression and the growing number of manticores. What say you, alchemist of Zad? Can you and Farzan counter this emerging threat?"

"We would have to begin working immediately."

The king clapped his hands together. "So be it. Consider this meeting adjourned."

"Your Majesty," Shanaz said, dissatisfied with how abruptly the discourse concluded. "With all due respect, victory over Zad means nothing if the drought is not ended."

"You may be right, but a victory over your kingdom will buy Raydur time. Defeat will not."

"The day I laid my husband to rest was the day it ceased being *my* kingdom. It won't be mine again so long as his killer sits on the throne."

"I can respect that," Delawar said. "Attendants will escort the two of you to your chambers."

The king excused himself. As he headed for the doors, he summoned Farzan to follow.

Shanaz wandered to the outside terrace overlooking the city. Beyond the villages lay grasslands and forests stretching all the way to the Kuhha-ye Sabz. As she took in the view, she knew Adarbad was right—the chances of finding Yaya on the massif were hopelessly slim.

The queen turned to her alchemist, who had joined her at the balustrade. "Is he going to make it? And don't tell me what you think I want to hear."

"I trust he won't be alone."

"How can you be so sure?"

"I gave the boy a gift," Adarbad said. "He's also quite bright and very willful, qualities which should serve him well on his quest. In many ways, he reminds me of myself. Strange, huh?"

Shanaz looked away as her eyes filled with tears. "Not so strange."

"But to answer your question, I don't know if he'll make it. What I do know is that he is the best chance we have to end this drought. And the best way we can help him is to stay here and help Raydur defeat Lilya."

"I agree he's the best chance we have. But you're mistaken otherwise." The queen's tone was resolute.

"I know that look, my lady. What do you mean?"

"You can help Raydur by working with Farzan. But staying here for me is useless."

"I don't understand."

"I'm going to Jarak with Princess Mahzarin. I've known King Mazad since he was born—and Lilya even longer. If anyone can convince him of her threat, it's me."

"But the road to Jarak can be treacherous," the alchemist said. "There have been reports of brigand forays into the hinterlands."

"King Delawar would not send his only surviving child if he thought it too dangerous. And you heard him—many will be traveling, including General Jangi."

Adarbad was not persuaded, as evinced by his furrowed brow and woeful expression. "What if we never..."

Shanaz placed her hand on Adarbad's. "Stop right there. No, 'what ifs.' Do you understand? We'll be back before you know it."

"Promise, Shanu?"

"You doubt the word of your queen?"

"I know better."

"As you should."

Shanaz patted Adarbad on the arm and walked toward the council chamber. "I suggest you stop dawdling and get to work. Don't you and Farzan have some conjuring to do?"

The alchemist watched her go, then turned to the balustrade. He looked far into the distance at Kuh-e Ab. As he took in the mountain's sublime presence, a wave of fear overcame him, and he began to doubt Yaya's safety.

His only recourse was action. As he headed inside, he recalled Shanaz's enjoinder. "You heard your cousin—get to work."

THE GUARDIAN

In the two days since Yaya and Baba had set out in search of the temple ruins, the prince had tried to engage his guide in chit-chat. But his efforts yielded little more than "mmhms," "nuh-uhs," and the occasional grunt. He owed it to the bear's solitary nature, unaware that they sleep most of the day and hunt or forage at night. Baba was no different. Forced to adjust to the boy's sleep schedule, he was simply too tired to talk.

Yaya's concern over his companion's reticence eventually gave way to a more pressing and recurring problem: his struggle to see in the dark. Another long summer day had faded to dusk. And though a crescent moon had risen, it offered scant illumination in such a desolate landscape. So rather than fumble through the foliage as he had done before, Yaya fell in behind Baba and let the bear's broad shoulders clear a path through the briars, switches, and shoots.

Soon, the travelers encountered a rise in elevation. The air became cooler and less humid. They left the last of the oaks and maples and wandered into terrain adorned with cushion plants, thorny shrubs, and tufts of grasses. To the northwest, the summit of Kuh-e Ab rose high above its smaller brethren. The moon was positioned in the sky as if fixed to the mountaintop, which, to Yaya, resembled some sort of primordial lighthouse.

On the first tract of level ground, Baba came to a halt. "It's best we rest here and pick things up in the morning."

Yaya found the idea reasonable enough. He sat on a small mound and wrapped his arms around his knees.

Baba could sense he was cold. "Aren't those things you're wearing supposed to keep you warm?"

"We're not really suited for the mountains, clothed or otherwise."

Baba snorted. "The problem with you uprights is that you hardly have any fur—just that scruffy patch on your head."

"Well, it's in a few other places, too."

"What do you mean?"

"Uhh," Yaya said, his teeth chattering. "I'd rather not show you."

"Oh, I get it. Boy, you sure are ugly creatures—a little fur here, a little fur there."

Yaya chuckled, amused by the bear's candor and imprecise terminology.

Baba circled a few times to smooth out his bedding, then eased down his massive frame and rested his chin on a pillow of primrose. "I suggest we get to sleep straight away. We'll rise with the sun."

Yaya lay downwind from Baba, using the bear as a buffer. He rested his head on his haversack and longed for the cloak he had forgotten in his kingdom's burial pit. As he observed the stars, he took comfort in their brief conversation. It reminded him of his grandfather, who couldn't walk and talk at the same time either. Much to the dismay of his advisors, the king would halt mid-stride and hold court in the corridors of the citadel. Yaya figured his guide must be similar.

As Baba's breathing grew heavy, Yaya's thoughts drifted to his father. He remembered the time he had defied him and gone swimming with friends in the Rud-e Barik. Later that afternoon, his father had been waiting in his room. Zahan told the boy that a child's greatest obligation was to respect and obey his parents. Yaya could still picture the disappointment on his face. The thought made him sad and long for second chances.

The prince scooted closer to Baba and turned onto his side. Despite his reflective mood, the bear's light snoring soothed him to sleep.

⸻◆⸻

The following day, Baba had a rude awakening. A hooded crow had landed on his head and was busy pecking at his skull. Unable to shake it off, he swatted the pest away with his paw. The incident got him thinking: never in his six years of living had he been so brazenly assaulted. He had endured his fair share of avian harassment—most bears do. Rarely are they welcomed guests into birds' territories. But this was different. And to Baba, it *felt* different.

Yaya mumbled something but remained on his side, facing away from his companion.

Of more interest to Baba than the prince's stirrings was his haversack. He knew better than to pilfer but convinced himself he was owed at least a few rations for his services. So, with the boy still asleep, he carefully unfurled the bag's loose leather straps with his claws and opened the flap. A medley of aromas burst forth. Pleased by the smells, Baba took a bite of the first thing he could find.

Yaya rolled over and searched for his makeshift pillow. When he couldn't find it, he opened his eyes. "What are you doing?"

Baba stopped chewing what turned out to be a date. "Nothing."

The prince sat up and stretched, scratching his head as he gathered his haversack. "You were stealing my pillow, weren't you?"

Baba swallowed the evidence and fessed up. "You caught me. Guilty as charged. So, um, how'd you sleep?"

"Fine... I guess."

"Well, that makes one of us."

"What do you mean?"

"You've got my sleeping schedule topsy-turvy and inside out. I was up half the night. Normally, I'd be nodding off right about now after a night of foraging, but instead, I have to guide you to the springs of Anita. And did I mention a bird just attacked me?"

"Her name is Anahita."

"Whatever—are you even hearing me?"

Yaya was caught off guard. "Looks like somebody woke up on the wrong side of the bed."

"You could say that again."

Yaya stood up. "All right, Babak, what are we waiting for? The faster we get to the springs, the sooner you can go back to doing what bears do. Does that suit you?"

"I can't go faster on an empty stomach."

Yaya shook his head. "I'm beginning to wonder which of us is the real burden." He took a few edibles from his haversack and tossed them to Baba. "Well, there you go. Be my guest."

"What about you?"

Yaya looked at the morsels on the ground. His stomach grumbled. "No, you go ahead. I'm not that hungry."

Baba was skeptical, believing the boy was trying to ration his supplies—which made sense in the colder parts. But where they were, in the subalpine zone of Kuh-e Ab, there were still grasses, grubs, berries, and bugs to be found. And if fortune favored them, one might even stumble upon a honeycomb or a forsaken carcass. No animal ever ate later than it had to, least of all a scrawny upright.

Unsure, Baba tilted his head.

"Well," Yaya said, "what are you waiting for?"

Baba wanted Yaya to join him. He felt bad enough for nosing around his haversack, and the boy's going hungry only made him feel worse.

Despite all the fussing, Baba could only bring himself to eat a couple of pistachios. "That should tide me over."

Yaya knew better. No animal the size of Baba would be content with just a few nuts, and the bear's slack-jawed, dejected face belied his words.

Nevertheless, Yaya was touched by the gesture. So, rather than call him out, he sat down and invited his guide to join him. They shared a few dates and a handful of pistachios. Baba even made off with a pomegranate, something he had never eaten before.

"Shall we get going?" Yaya asked.

"First things first," Baba said, relieving himself. "By the way, what did you say your name was again?"

Yaya was tying the straps of his haversack. "It's Yazdegerd, but call me 'Yaya'... if you're in a hurry."

"Funny. Where have I heard that before?"

The prince smiled.

"All right then, Yaya, let me give you a survival tip. If you want to find something to eat, look for the streams. I can't stress that enough. Find them, and I guarantee you'll find food—nuts, berries, you name it. And if you're lucky, you might even be able to ambush a deer, fox, or some other rodent. They come to the streams for the same reason."

Yaya wasn't listening; his eyes were fixed on a large figure lurking on the edge of the forest. "Baba," he said quietly. "There's something huge standing in the trees. Do you see it?"

Baba looked at the creature, then noticed the boy's hand on the hilt of his shamshir. "You're not going to need that thing. It won't hurt you."

"What is it?"

"We call it the 'guardian' of the mountain. It's been here forever, so they say."

The creature looked humanoid, with a discernible jawline but no mouth. It had sockets but no eyes, and a straight ridge for a nose. The color of its earthen skin was two parts clay, one part amber. Alchemists would recognize the oddity as a golem.

"Well?" Baba said. "Shall we get going? You are ready, aren't you?"

"Do I have a choice?"

Baba wasn't sure how to reply, so he started walking.

——◆——

Throughout much of the day, the travelers wandered the foothills of Kuh-e Ab. Every so often, they descended ravines, slopes, and other topographical undulations. However, with expansive views of the surrounding valley and forests, the overall trend was an evident rise in elevation. Yaya knew that their "ups" had surpassed their "downs," which fit Baba's description of the temple ruins' location.

When they had reached a confluence of mountain streams, Baba stopped for a much-needed drink. "We're almost there."

The two trudged on. Yaya even saw remnants of a footpath marked by lines of rocks, a relic of a bygone age used by his Jabiri ancestors for pilgrimage.

They wound around a bend and came to an overhang with sheer cliffs. Baba recalled the ruins being on the edge and overlooking the valley. What he saw instead was a billowing green fog as dense as smoke. Of equal concern was the murder of hooded crows circling overhead. Just the sight of them made his head throb. Nor did he like the foul, unfamiliar smell of sulfur. Something wasn't right, and he knew it.

Once in the haze, Yaya's eyes and throat began to burn. He coughed and retched, stopping twice to spit out phlegm. During these fits, he lost sight of Baba, who had wandered ahead and disappeared into the murk. Determined, the prince quickened his pace, hoping to catch his wayward guide. After a reasonable distance, he called out Baba's name—but there was no answer, only the caw-caw of crows above.

Yaya tried circling back but could barely see beyond his outstretched arm. The fog had thickened so much that he had lost his bearings and didn't know where to go. Frustrated, he yelled for Baba again. What answered him were muffled roars and hideous shrieking—sounds unlike any animal he had ever heard, real or imagined. Fearful, the prince unsheathed his shamshir and fled from the jarring, discordant noise.

Yaya soon stumbled over hewn stones, the first tangible signs he had reached the temple ruins. He fumbled his way up a few stairs and over the remains of a crumbled arch. After rounding a pillar shrouded in fog, he ran straight into the saggy-breasted chest of an Al—a demon of the underworld. Stunned by its sudden appearance, the prince froze in terror, unable to even breathe. When he finally did, the hag reeked of old, sweaty shoes.

The demon seized Yaya's arm, digging her claws into his flesh and forcing him to drop his sword. A struggle ensued. Though wily when wrestling the likes of his cousin, the prince was no match for the brute strength of Ahriman's minion. He was fast overpowered and dragged along the ground by a tuft of his hair. All he could do to keep it ripping from his scalp was hold onto the crone's gnarled wrist.

Yaya kicked and screamed and sometimes called for Baba. He even prayed to the goddess Anahita, something he had never done before. He imagined all sorts of gruesome fates: skewered and roasted alive; hoisted on an altar and sacrificed to Ahriman; torn to shreds to satiate the sordid pleasures of some dreadful demonic witch.

The demon stopped beside a metallic-colored disc rippling on the ground. With its prey in hand, it descended into a gaseous portal composed of water, ammonia, and methane.

Yaya knew he was on the threshold of hell. He braced himself, then was sucked into the rift.

But his brush with the underworld was short-lived. Some unseen entity of great power plucked him from the icy vapor by his ankle and gently rolled him away from the opening. He ended up on his side, marveling at the sight of his savior—the golem itself. The moniker Baba and the other animals had used was neither misplaced nor exaggerated. It was a "guardian" indeed, or so it seemed.

The golem squatted and peered into the rift with its eyeless sockets. It looked poised to pounce.

Yaya had enough of a bad feeling to scoot farther away—and it was a good thing he did.

The demon sprang from the gaseous portal, landing her torso at the rift's edge. As she reached for Yaya with her sinewy arms, the golem delivered three hammering blows to her head. Satisfied that he had rendered the demon unconscious, the guardian pushed the limp, haggard hag back into the rift. She sank slowly at first, like a stick in the mud. When the last of her body had gone under, the fissure sealed shut and vanished.

As the action subsided, Yaya pushed himself to his feet. He wanted to thank the golem, but it had already bounded away through the ruins.

With the fog fading fast, the boy ran off in search for Baba. Along the way, he discovered his shamshir lying in a creeper plant and scooped it up. But when he found neither hide nor hair of his companion, he feared the worst, that some hellspawn had dragged Baba into another rift.

"You looking for me?"

Yaya turned around, hopeful the mumbling voice belonged to Baba.

And there he was—alive and afoot on heavenly earth. Clenched between his bloody jaws was the prince's haversack, which he promptly dropped. "Boy, you look awful."

Yaya felt even worse. He sat on a dilapidated stone wall and buried his face in his hands.

Baba ambled on over, sensing something was terribly wrong. "Hey, I was only kidding. You seem to have come out of this better than me."

"I don't know about that. Have you been to hell?"

"I don't understand."

"Yeah, I guess you wouldn't." Yaya described the metaphysics behind the cosmic abyss and his fight with the witch. "Then the demon pulled me into some sort of gateway to hell itself."

"So what'd you see?"

"I saw nothing. It's what I felt."

"And?"

Yaya shuddered at the memory. He folded his arms and stared at one of the natural springs bubbling up from the ground. "You want to know what it felt like, Baba? Imagine having all your insides scooped out. Nothing is left but a cold, internal wasteland. Then you learn the reason why: it's because all you ever loved was taken away."

"Sounds like a place I'd rather not visit."

"Wise words."

The prince knelt by the spring and washed his hands and face—a ritual of ablution. He faced south, closed his eyes, and made a solemn, heartfelt prayer to Anahita just as he had been instructed.

A voice replied, as if tethered to the wind: "O champion of Ohrmazd, blessed be thy name. He who honors me shall himself be honored. Behold, the healing waters of Anahita."

Yaya opened his eyes to see an apparition hovering before him. It was Anahita herself. In her outstretched hands, she held a tiny, crystalline vial.

But the prince was too stunned by its bright translucence to realize it was an offering.

Baba had more sense. "Well, take it, silly. I didn't kill an enormous bird for nothing."

This time, Yaya didn't hesitate. He placed the vial in his haversack and then took out his bottle, adding a few scoops of sacred water. As he finished twisting in the cork, the apparition had dissipated.

"Can we leave now?" Baba said. "I've had enough of ghosts and demons for one day."

"This bird you killed… where is it?"

Baba led Yaya through the ruins to the spot where he had been ambushed. On the ground next to a limestone base lay a ghastly sight: a winged beast of both bird and human aspect, including feathers and hair, talons and fingers, and a tail and arms. Its open beak, from which seeped a viscous black liquid, even had teeth. Fortunately, this patron of crows was dead—its long, thin neck broken courtesy of an eight-hundred-pound brown bear.

Yaya's expression turned rueful. "I have a confession, Baba. I heard you fight, but I was too afraid to help."

"A bit lily-livered, were you?"

The prince nodded.

"It happens, kid. What do you say we get out of here and forget all about it?"

Yaya started walking. "You don't have to ask me twice."

"I already have."

"Yeah? Well, who's counting?"

Baba caught up. "So where to?"

Yaya stopped. "You mean you're coming with me? All the way?"

"Somebody has to. Besides, it's not like I have anything better to do."

"I guess this makes us fast friends, Baba." Yaya patted the bear's head and strode off with renewed vigor. "And to answer your question, we're off to find Kuh-e Sholeh and the temple ruins of Atar."

"You're kidding, right? More temple ruins? This Trishtya guy had better appreciate the effort."

"For one thing, he's a god. And his name is pronounced 'Tishtrya.'"

"Yeah, yeah—whatever."

EYES ON THE GOLDEN MOON

In the foyer of Kamran's living quarters, a copper basin filled with a cloudy liquid rested on a pedestal table. Gazing at it were the king and General Baraz. Curious about its properties, Kamran bent to the rim and took an ill-advised sniff. The odor reeked of sulfur, but worse were the acidic vapors that stung his eyes.

"Damn it," he said, wincing. "Where's Sarvin? How long does it take to collect some hair?"

"Shall I find him, my lord?"

"What do you think?"

The general gave a slight bow and strode off.

Since Vira's death, Kamran's complexion had grown pale and his face gaunt. Were it not for the magical properties of the elixir, he would have grown weak as well. To avoid confronting his tangled emotions, he immersed himself in preparing for war and exacting justice on those he blamed for his despair: the triumvirate of traitors from Zad and the king of Raydur, whom he felt was using the drought as a bludgeon.

Whether wargaming with his advisors into the wee hours or overseeing the assembly of siege armaments outside the city walls, Kamran dispelled any doubts about his commitment to the affairs of the state. But it came not without a price. With Lilya buried in books and Jabiri scrolls on alchemy and the dark arts, Afshad had been left to cope alone with the tragic loss of his mother.

Kamran walked down the hallway and into his bedroom. Afshad lay on the bed, his feet crossed, casually tossing a chogan ball in the air.

"Get your feet off the bed," Kamran said, slapping the soles of his sandals. "Those sheets are made of mulberry silk."

Afshad smirked and only rearranged his legs.

"What did I say?"

"I'm on Mother's side of the bed, not yours."

Kamran snatched the ball out of the air.

Not in the mood to deal with his father, Afshad covered his face with a pillow—but quickly reconsidered. "Probably not the wisest to do with *you* hovering over me."

Kamran bit his tongue at the gruesome reference. "Why were you late to the briefing this morning?"

"It's not as if I missed anything."

"But you're habitually late. Must I hire new attendants to tend to your morning routine—someone to brush your hair? If I'd known the elixir would make you even more vain, I wouldn't have permitted you to drink it."

"Must I remind you I've finished training with manticores and melee weapons? All that's left is ranged combat. If you doubt me, ask my instructors." Afshad turned away. "Maybe if you weren't pretending to be so busy all the time, you would know that."

"That's what you think I do? Play at being a king?"

"Those are your words, not mine."

"Look at me when I'm talking to you."

Afshad rolled back over.

"Lest you've forgotten, you missed yesterday's meeting of the high council. I made an excuse to your grandmother on your behalf, something I'm not inclined to do again. You need more self-discipline."

Afshad scoffed. "I told you I wasn't feeling well."

"That's because your priorities are out of order. A little less of this running around would be a good start."

"Running around? You're one to talk." Afshad rose from the bed, brushed by his father, and wandered over to an ornamental shamshir mounted on the wall. He unhooked it and began parrying and thrusting.

Kamran watched intently.

"Didn't Pedar bozorg give you this sword?" Afshad asked, drawing closer with each swing. "I've come of age, too, you know. Do you not have a gift for me?"

Kamran donned one of his specially forged gauntlets lying on a chest at the foot of his bed.

"Going somewhere?" Afshad said. "I hope I'm not running you off."

Kamran held his composure despite the taunting words and reckless behavior. What irked him most was the smug grin on his son's face, the kind most fathers wouldn't hesitate to remove. Not convinced of Afshad's self-professed skill with the blade, the king raised his hand and caught it dead stop. Metal clanged against metal. A different sort of battle ensued.

Afshad blinked first and released the hilt. He stormed off to the bed, this time letting his feet hang over the edge. Reminded of his place in the order of things, he settled in for a good pout and resigned himself to observing his father inspect the shamshir for any nicks. The attention paid to the blade struck him as odd, considering his father murdered the man who had given it.

The prince's silent brooding ended when he heard voices in the foyer.

Lilya entered, followed by Sarvin and General Baraz, and the three convened around the copper basin. "Let's first see what our renegade prince is up to," the queen said.

Giddy with excitement, the alchemist laid down three silken bags, opening one and dumping a small amount of Yaya's hair into the sulfuric liquid. Bubbles formed and popped on the surface, releasing an even fouler stench. Soon, both the bubbles and residual cloudy film disappeared. The mixture turned translucent, save for the strands of hair floating around the edge.

The party, including Kamran and Afshad, leaned in over the basin, waiting anxiously for any images to appear.

"It's not working," Sarvin said, his voice full of disappointment.

"Do you not trust what I have learned?" Lilya asked. "Be patient."

A sliver of light appeared.

"That looks like the moon," Sarvin said. "And mountains."

The images drew sharper into focus.

"And what do we have here?" Lilya pointed to a lump beneath a tree. "Might this be our precious Yaya?"

Confirmation came when the "lump" lifted his head and shifted to his side, eyes closed. Though the prince's hair was disheveled and his face dim in the evening light, there was no doubt about his identity.

"Where do you think he is, Madar bozorg?" Afshad asked, his voice low, as if Yaya might hear him and awake.

Lilya couldn't name a plausible location. "If 'nowhere' is a place, he's in the middle of it."

"Which suggests he ran away," Kamran said.

A blur appeared off-center, slowly moving. What came into focus was a large brown bear.

Everyone gasped, convinced they were about to see a mauling. But then, much to their collective befuddlement, the bear lay down beside Yaya and closed its eyes.

"What's the meaning of this?" Lilya said, feeling duped. "Why isn't the beast savaging him?"

Sarvin was quick to deduce an explanation. "Well, you wondered if Adarbad had given Yaya an elixir. I think you have your answer."

"An elixir for what?" Kamran said. "To cavort with animals? If this is the best Adarbad can do, I think Yaya is the least of our worries."

The king began to laugh.

"Is there something funny you'd like to share with us?" Lilya asked.

"Don't you see the absurdity of our gifts? I bend shamshirs, and Yaya befriends bears."

The vision in the pool slowly dissolved, and the liquid returned to its opaque disposition.

"All right, all right," Lilya said, returning to the business at hand. She straightened and folded her arms. "There must be a plan for this boy, yet I don't see it." Her eyes shifted side to side as her mind sifted through all possibilities.

"Perhaps the others hold the key to this riddle," the general said.

Lilya motioned for Sarvin to proceed.

The alchemist opened a pouch and dumped a few strands of Adarbad's hair into the basin. The pool frothed again, but this time remained cloudy.

"What happened, Sarvin?"

"I don't know—"

"Did you add all the hair?" Lilya snatched the bag and shook it over the pool. Nothing but a piece of lint fell out.

"There wasn't much hair in Adarbad's room to begin with," Sarvin said. "He is, after all, nearly bald."

"Damn him and his bald head. Then add Shanaz's. Surely, there was enough on her brush to see something useful."

Sarvin emptied the bag containing Shanaz's hair.

Like before, the pool popped and gurgled, sending sulfur droplets into the air.

When it became calm and clear, flickering lights appeared. They were torches. As the pool brightened, illuminating a large chamber, Shanaz came into view, followed by General Jangi and Princess Mahzarin. All were seated at a table covered with platters of food and glittering chalices. Sitting with them were King Mazad and two of his trusted advisors. The king could be seen mouthing words to his guests.

"What's he saying, Madar bozorg?" Afshad asked.

Kamran bristled, convinced his son's repeated questions were an attempt to undermine him.

"I wish I knew," Lilya said. "Still, we might be able to gather the tenor of this meeting through observation. Pay attention."

King Mazad set down his chalice of wine and dabbed his mouth. For the better part of dinner, he had heard a litany of arguments for intervention from his guests. Yet the crafty leader of Jarak remained unconvinced.

"Let me begin by saying I've been duly impressed with the conviction and sincerity with which you all speak. I must say, Princess Mahzarin, your grasp of strategy will serve your father well in the years to come. Perhaps you'll give the general here a run for his money regarding his job security."

"I wouldn't even dare consider it." As with all things, charm comes from its discretion, and having already been introduced to King Mazad's way with words during King Kamran's inaugural, the princess was unmoved by his honeyed speech. "General Jangi is our most revered warrior. His reputation is one he has rightfully earned."

"There's more to being a leader than skill on the battlefield," Mazad said. "One must also master the spoken word, and from what I have seen this evening, you have a talent that positively belies your age."

Apart from a few heavy sighs, Jangi remained silent whilst their host laid on the charm.

Shanaz, however, had less patience for their host's digression. "King Mazad, if I may? Tempting as it is to indulge your hospitality, it's imperative we get down to business. The hour is late, and we must depart for Raydur first thing in the morning. I wish we were here under more palatable circumstances, but we are not. The sweet taste of victory will not come unless we stand together."

"And when you say 'victory,' whom do you speak of?"

"Victory for the people of Raydur and Jarak."

"My lady, we have not suffered any direct threat from Zad, nor do I think we will. The Green Mountains are a formidable barrier. And our water supplies are sufficient, with more in the Kaz-e Rhun basin." As an afterthought, Mazad shook his head and sneered. "Why anyone would choose to settle along the banks of a seasonal river is beyond me."

The comment struck a nerve with Shanaz. "I'm not here to debate the wisdom of Zad's location. But rest assured, the Rud-e Barik used to be much more expansive. Some geographic evidence suggests it once fed into the Rud-e Mah. I wouldn't question the historical motivations for where your kingdom chose to break ground. I would appreciate the same courtesy."

"My apologies. No offense was intended. Based on your earlier disavowal of Zad, I assumed you'd agree with my assessment. Perhaps there's still an allegiance after all." Mazad leaned back in his chair and surveyed his guests. "Let me pose a question to all of you, one that summarizes the predicament we face: would a lamb ever come to the aid of two jackals in battle?"

The question caught everyone off guard—except for Mahzarin. "That's just a clever metaphor. I'll let Queen Shanaz speak for Zad, but my kingdom is not predatory, nor has it ever been. And in the years since my last visit to Jarak, the scale of growth I've seen suggests anything but lamblike behavior. Jarak has nothing to fear by aiding Raydur."

Mazad appreciated the compliment but even more so the guile behind it. In his mind, Zad was a declining power fraught with military overreach and inept rule. He was keen to hasten its demise but not at the elevation of Raydur.

Requesting privacy to consult with his advisors, the king invited his guests to enjoy the stunning views of his city.

Led by two sentries, the visiting dignitaries made their way to a wide balcony overlooking Jarak, its circular grid fashioned like spokes on a wheel. In Jangi's estimation, the kingdom had already surpassed Raydur in size and now rivaled Zad. With a fertile plain fed by the *Rud-e Hayat*, its potential for growth seemed limitless.

"He won't commit," Jangi said, leaning his arms on the balustrade. "And why would he? He has nothing to gain by involving himself in our conflict. We'll have to take down Zad on our own." He glanced at Mahzarin, who was observing the stars. "We'll need your archers most of all, Princess. I can go toe-to-toe with Zad's infantry, but I have nothing to counter the manticores."

"No matter King Mazad's decision, I know we'll prevail. We always have."

Mahzarin's certainty moved Jangi, but he knew the number of archers needed to stave off a breach of the walls exceeded what Raydur had available.

The sentries soon summoned the guests to the king's council chamber. When they entered, Mazad was staring at a bronze bust of his late father, perched on a side table of wrought iron and oak. He turned and invited them all to an informal sitting area inside the balcony.

As everyone took a seat, Mazad grew pensive, his eyes distant. "A father never leaves his son, even after death. I look at his likeness and hear his voice as if it were yesterday, though it's been a few years since his passing. I only hope I have made him proud."

"I'm sure you have," Shanaz said, adjusting her garments. "We were admiring how beautiful and impressive your city has become."

"I appreciate your kind words," Mazad said. "But as I've mentioned, a father's voice is never far, and the late king would be aghast if I sent aid to Raydur and left our own lands vulnerable." He turned to Jangi. "In terms of troops, what exactly are your needs?"

"Three hundred archers and three hundred cavalry. I'm confident in our infantry numbers."

"That's an impressive request, General. I'll give you a third."

"A third. I could've trained that many in the time it took us to get here."

Shanaz placed a hand on Jangi's arm. "It does not serve our purpose to debate the level of assistance. We must be grateful for what the good king is willing to offer. We've heard his concerns, and they are valid."

Jangi tried to temper his frustration. "Your Majesty, I beg your pardon, but as you can imagine, we are under considerable duress. For all we know, Zad's forces are already marching to our gates. At a minimum, we need two hundred of both forces. I implore you to reconsider."

"I will agree to one hundred and fifty of each."

"With all due respect, you're splitting hairs."

"General, as a leader of men, I assumed you—more than anyone here—would appreciate the weight of a warrior's sacrifice. Yet you haggle with me as if we were in the local bazaar. I don't think of my forces as mere 'hair,' to borrow your word. They are citizens. Many have families. A decision to send you aid is a decision to send a certain number of my men to death. This is not something I take lightly. I consider the well-being of my troops my highest responsibility. Do you not feel the same?"

Jangi leaned back in his chair, jaw clenched. "I love my men."

"I will send the two hundred you ask for, but they will fight under one condition." The king motioned to an advisor, who handed him a wooden scroll casing.

"I suppose your terms are contained in that?" Mahzarin asked.

"Please give this to your father upon your return. It's nothing for any of you to concern yourselves with. It's the sort of thing only another king can truly appreciate."

"Of course. So do we then have a deal?"

"We have an arrangement." Mazad rose from his chair, followed by the others. Handshakes were exchanged. "I will send word for the troops to assemble. They'll be ready to depart in two mornings hence. Given the uncertainty in the air, I advise you accompany them."

"We don't have time," Mahzarin said. "My father awaits your decision. The sooner we deliver it, the easier he can plan. We'll leave at daybreak."

"So be it. I'll escort you to your quarters."

The king stood by the doorway as the emissaries filed out, Mahzarin leaving last. As she exited, Mazad walked beside her and engaged her in conversation.

⸺◆⸺

The images in the copper basin faded away.

"Sarvin?" Kamran said, rubbing his eyes, which again burned from the acidic vapors. "Get this damn cesspool away from here. I don't care who you hand it to, but I'd better not catch another whiff."

Sarvin lifted the basin only to slosh some liquid onto the floor.

"For heaven's sake," Lilya said. "Afshad, help him."

As the two carried the basin out of the chamber, the queen caught sight of one of her jackals licking the spillage. She kicked the animal away. "Stop that, you idiot."

"It would seem a deal has been struck," Kamran said. "What do you think, Mother?"

"Handshakes aren't made over disagreements, but there is an old maxim in negotiation: nothing is agreed until everything is agreed."

"I don't follow."

General Baraz chimed in. "I believe the queen is referring to the scroll casing."

Lilya walked over to the jackal she had scolded and scratched its head. "The parameters of a deal were struck—there's no doubt about that. I'm also confident that Mazad will send aid, however limited."

"Then what do you think the message is about?" Kamran asked.

"I'm not sure, but I did notice something as hot as the air on your inaugural day."

"What was that?"

"King Mazad's blood, every time he looked at Delawar's daughter."

"One can't blame the man," Baraz said.

Kamran smiled and nodded, for the princess's physical charms had not gone unnoticed.

"Stop acting like a couple of rutting elephants," Lilya said. "Her beauty will fade, just like it does for all of us." Her eyes locked onto Baraz. "Why don't you make yourself useful and fetch my grandson."

Knowing he had overstepped, the general dutifully left the room.

Kamran watched as his mother walked over to a copper mirror and studied her face. She ran her fingers through her thinning hair, then made a cursory attempt to prop up her sagging neck. Unsatisfied, her sunken eyes reflected a rare glumness. She pitied herself—and Kamran pitied her for it. What was more, ever since Khavar's passing, her slender frame continued to diminish despite her increased appetite, a strange side effect of her newfound strength.

Kamran recalled her once lamenting that she had no daughters to care for her in her old age, stating that "boys are conditioned to need their mothers, not to tend to them." And though her relationship with Vira had been complex, he knew she missed Vira's presence. The one common bond they shared was their interest in their appearance. Lilya trusted Vira's taste and opinions in matters of beauty, however loath she was to admit it. Such was her way.

One of the jackals lifted its head and barked as Afshad and the others returned. "You wanted to see me, Madar bozorg?"

"You and the general."

Baraz followed Afshad a little sheepishly, anxious to return to the queen's good graces.

Lilya pointed to a location on an unfurled map spread across the table. "I suspect Shanaz and her cohorts will return to Raydur in the morning. I want you and General Baraz to intercept them in the valley of the Rud-e Hayat. You'll fly manticores and take one other warrior. Who's your best archer, General?"

"That would be Daryush. But there are four manticores. Why not take two archers?"

"Because I'll be taking the other manticore to go after Yaya."

"But Mother," Kamran said, "we don't know where he is. He could be anywhere."

"All evidence suggests he headed toward Raydur. We also know that he's on foot and in the mountains. If all that is true, how far could he be from here?" Lilya pointed to a spot on the map near Kuh-e Ab.

"I don't advise you to go alone," Kamran said. "Maybe I should accompany you—use the manticore you had in mind for Daryush."

"I won't be alone. My jackals will follow from the ground. Tonight, they'll sleep in Yaya's room to gather his scent. After all, nothing smells quite like a jackal."

"That goes both ways," Sarvin said.

Lilya smiled, appreciating the joke. "Let me put it this way: their sense of smell will lead me to him. By the time I return tomorrow, our Prince Yaya will be no more."

"And what is our charge once we meet the group in the river valley?" Baraz asked.

"Very simple. I want the 'beauty' of Raydur alive."

"For what purpose?"

"Leverage."

"And the others?"

The queen tilted her head. "What do you think, General? Kill them."

Lilya embraced her grandson before he took his leave. She noticed the way he clung to her and realized he was likely grateful for any kind of physical contact since his mother's death. Vira had openly displayed her love for Afshad through tender looks and caresses. This had never been Kamran's way—nor had it needed to be while Vira lived.

Lilya knew her son loved Afshad and worried for him, but grief had dulled his ability to give the boy what he needed. That failing had only widened the chasm between them, one that seemed to grow with each passing day. Lilya resolved to work harder to rebuild the bridge between father and son, once the affairs of the state afforded some time.

Alone with Kamran, she addressed the issue. "I know you're worried about Afshad."

"I don't think he's ready for this."

"You seem to be forgetting he'll be with General Baraz and Daryush, our two most capable warriors. And he'll be wearing impenetrable armor. He'll be safe."

Unconvinced, Kamran shook his head, his eyes focused on the map.

"Listen," Lilya said, "he wants nothing more than to make you proud. His first real test had to come sometime, just as it did for you at his age. Have you forgotten the northern incursions and how you and General Baraz led our forces into battle against the brigands? This mission is the perfect chance for him to prove his mettle."

Kamran sighed. "I suppose you're right."

"Of course I'm right. Besides, who would run Zad if tragedy befell all of us? Sarvin? General Baraz?" Lilya moved toward the doorway. "What this kingdom lacks are heirs. And what you lack is a wife. It's something you need to be thinking about."

Kamran watched his mother leave his foyer. It was getting late, and he was exhausted from the hours of meetings since his return from talks with King Delawar. He walked down the hall to his chamber and lay on his bed, thinking about what she had told him. As he pondered his mother's words, he imagined Vira telling him to take his feet off the bed. The king smiled ruefully and kicked off his sandals.

Up a Tree

Baba had been right about the odds of finding food along the stream beds, but he was sorely disappointed in the bounty. The farther he and Yaya traveled from the springs, the hotter and drier the air became. Even with a sniffer like his, finding plump and juicy berries posed a challenge. Still, as he had told the boy, there isn't much for a bear to do *but* search for food. Beyond the obvious need for nourishment, it was simply habit.

Much to Yaya's amusement, his furry companion poked his snout into every bush he suspected of having fruit. On top of that was Baba's need to stop walking when he desired to speak. Yaya wasn't sure what had caused the once-reserved animal to turn into an incessant chatterbox, but he wasn't complaining, even if their progress had been halting. He shared tidbits of food from his haversack to keep them moving.

Though the morning sun had yet to rise above the tree line, its rays diffracted through the dust-filled air, turning the eastern sky crimson. Waves of scorching heat already beat down upon the weary travelers. No less merciless were the winds, which had shifted west, bringing the dry, dusty, and unmistakable flavor of the Dasht-e Marg.

The stream they had been following widened along its banks, if not in volume. What should have been a torrent had diminished to a gentle flow. Here and there, isolated pools dappled the bed, providing sanctuary to the forest congregants. Two squirrels and a raccoon drank alongside a few birds. Further ahead and around a bend, the travelers came upon a babbling brook feeding into the stream.

Yaya stopped to survey the landscape, taking a moment to eat a few pistachios.

Baba paid heed. Having grown used to handouts, he waited patiently for an offering but was duly ignored by a boy lost in thought. Offended by the lack of consideration, the bear grunted and lumbered down the banks of the stream bed. He lapped at some stale water, then noticed a cluster of berries hanging from a spindly shrub. As he meandered toward it, he let loose a trickle of scat.

The prince chuckled at the "plopping" sounds hitting the water.

"What?" Baba said. "Is there a problem?"

"You pooped in the water."

"I did?"

"Good thing you drank first."

Baba frowned.

Still sleepy, Yaya stretched his hands to the sky, closed his eyes, and yawned. As he curled his wrists, he heard a rustling noise on his side of the stream. Unnerved, the prince ducked behind a tree and saw several young bucks, does, and fawns bounding over bushes and fallen limbs. One after another, they rushed by until a few stragglers rounded out nature's parade.

Yaya felt overwhelmed by the spectacle. "Baba, did you see that? A whole herd of red deer came out of nowhere."

"I smelled them before I heard them, and heard them before I saw them."

"It's not every day you get to see nature in action."

"Have you forgotten who you're talking to?"

"I was speaking rhetorically, Baba."

"Rhetor-a-what?"

"I'm only saying it was pretty neat."

"If you say so." Baba's tone was circumspect. "So which way are we going? Should we keep following this stream?"

Yaya looked at the feeder brook, its waters cascading over rocks and boulders covered in fern moss. Tired of traversing the dense, uneven terrain surrounding the creeks, the prince opted to push into the forest.

Soon, the travelers found themselves strolling through a meadow brimming with yellow, white, and lavender wild-flowers. Yaya had plucked a few stems when Baba suddenly stopped and rose up on his haunches.

The bear peered into the distance and sniffed the air. "I knew I smelled something else back at that river. If you were wondering why those deer were running, your answer is across the field."

Standing on the far side of the meadow, almost indis-cernible amid the dark hues of the forest, were three gray wolves. The one in the center was more robust than the oth-ers, presumably the alpha. His coat was also lighter, flecked with specks of white. He stepped forward and assessed the two figures standing in the distance.

Baba realized the larger wolf, after sizing them up, was hatching a plan of attack. "Listen to me, boy, and listen well. You see that snag in the middle of the field?"

"Standing among the saplings?"

"When I drop to all fours, run there and climb that old tree as fast as you can."

"What about you?"

"They're not concerned about me. It's you they want."

Baba took off running through the flowers.

Yaya followed as best he could. Over a knoll, he glanced back to where the wolves had been. Not surprisingly, they were gone—the hunt had commenced. He scanned the meadow and spotted them tunneling through the tall grasses, making a bee-line in his and Baba's direction. Even facing what promised to be a life-or-death struggle, the prince couldn't help but question what canines had against him—jackals or otherwise.

With the cluster of maples before him, Yaya realized he was still carrying the petal-less flower stems. He tossed them aside and raced to the gnarly snag, home to a large bird's nest at the top. Nicks, notches, and knobs on the bark provided easy holds and steps for his hands and feet. But Yaya made the mistake of looking for Baba, who the wily alpha had lured away. His misplaced focus caused him to slip and slide down the trunk.

One of the other wolves was poised to attack.

Yaya cried out for help. "Baba!"

As the wolf prepared to lunge, a brown eagle—none too happy with the threat to her fledglings—swooped down and raked the trespasser's head. The wolf recoiled and backed away from the tree.

Before it could recover, Baba barreled into it, sending the wolf sprawling onto the ragged, broken limbs of a decayed branch.

The sharpest impaled it through the chest. The wolf struggled briefly and then fell still, its eyes open.

Enraged at the loss of their companion, the alpha and his kin squared off before the bear.

But Baba was in no mood to negotiate, not with Yaya safely up in the tree. "It's high time you look elsewhere for your meal. This boy is off limits."

The alpha began to circle the snag from a safe distance. "Well now, are my eyes deceiving me, or is a bear sheltering an upright?"

With his butt against the tree, Baba kept a wary eye on the wolf, circling with it as if in a synchronous orbit. "Your eyes aren't deceiving you. I'd suggest not letting your self-confidence do the same."

"Spare me your attempts at insight, juvenile. The lack of white on your snout shows your inexperience. In the skills that truly matter, your kind is inferior to the wolf. I'll take slim and swift over big and dumb any day."

Baba's anger reached a fever pitch, but as he tracked the alpha's movements, he had unwittingly left himself vulnerable. The other wolf darted in and nipped his hind leg.

To a degree, the alpha had assessed his opponent correctly. "I rest my case," he said.

While there was truth in those words, Baba had been around long enough to know that the two wolves who stood before him were no match for his brute strength. What he feared more were reinforcements and the wolves' orchestrated skill to kill. He had seen it before with other bears. Should such a fate befall him, Baba knew full well they would wait for the boy to tumble from the tree, either from starvation or exhaustion.

Yaya grew more and more incensed by the scene below. Since the wolves worked in tandem, he figured he and Baba should do the same.

From his perch, he hurled a dead limb at the alpha. "Chew on that, *madar be khata*."

Surprised by the human's sudden aggression, the wolf leader retreated a few steps.

Yaya felt emboldened. He inched farther out onto the limb—only for it to give way, sending him crashing to the ground. With Baba briefly distracted and harassed by the other wolf, the prince found himself all alone and face-to-face with the alpha. As the big wolf lunged, snarling and eyes full of rage, his only recourse was to shield himself with his haversack.

That primal focus gave Baba his chance. He ignored the other wolf nipping at his heels and caught the alpha unawares, charging into it like a landslide. He pinned the animal down and bit into its back.

With the alpha paralyzed from a spinal injury, Baba turned to see Yaya fending off the lone remaining wolf with his shamshir. He rushed to the boy's defense.

But the wolf, seeing that he was outnumbered, sublimated his desire for food in favor of survival and fled into the forest.

Baba checked in with his companion. "Are you all right?"

The prince was trembling, his heart pounding against his chest. "I'm not sure. How about you? That smaller wolf got you pretty good."

"Are you kidding? Those nips felt like mosquito bites."

Yaya sheathed his shamshir. "Is this going to be a regular thing?"

"You're in the forest. Were you expecting something else?"

Yaya knew the dangers, but somehow they seemed less real in the confines of his imagination.

"Listen," Baba said. "Anything can happen in the woods. And while wolves are nasty little creatures, there's one animal we don't want to run into."

"I'm afraid to ask. What's that?"

"A bear, especially a hungry one."

Yaya contemplated Baba's words and knew he was right. Were it not for his ability to communicate with animals, his life would likely have ended when he first met Baba in the foothills of the Kuhha-ye Sabz.

"Then I'd better share more of my food with you."

"Wise words," Baba said. "If you and I run out of food... well, let's just say it'll get pretty ugly around here."

Yaya looked uneasy.

"I had you going there, didn't I?" Baba let out a big slobbery laugh. "Don't worry, kid. I've been around you long enough to know there isn't enough meat on your bones for the smallest weasel."

"Weasels are the least of my worries." The prince glanced at the alpha and noticed he was still breathing.

"Don't mind him. He's not going anywhere."

Indeed, the wolf lay on his side, seemingly resigned to his impending doom.

Baba pointed to Yaya's haversack lying on the ground. "I think you might want that."

Yaya slung it over his shoulder and ran his fingers over the holes left by the alpha's fangs. The memory of his close call was evident in his somber expression.

"You're alive," Baba said, sensing the boy's thoughts. "There's no reason to dwell on what might have been, just as there's no reason to dwell here any longer. The scent of death travels fast. Others will come. Unless you want to tempt fate, I suggest we leave now."

Yaya wasn't going to argue.

No sooner had the two companions left the meadow for a forest of oaks than Baba's thoughts shifted from battle to food. Such was the mind of a bear.

When the Wood is Gone

For much of the day, the two travelers crossed the wild-flowered glens and forests that filled the emerging Rud-e Hayat river valley. They made good time, too, as going downhill helped. But as the sun reached its zenith, the tailwinds shifted, bringing an unusual odor. Baba's senses perked up at the anomaly. Though unfamiliar with this region of the Kuhha-ye Sabz, he still felt something was amiss.

Stretching his neck high, the bear pointed his dry nose into the air. "Do you smell that?" he asked, his tone foreboding.

Questions asked in such a way always put one on edge. It had been only hours since Baba pulled the same stunt and alerted the prince to the presence of the wolves. Despite the small sample size, the bear's hyperactive nose was quick to portend danger. After all, he was a bear—his olfactory system had evolved over eons to detect trouble.

Since his sense of smell was far less refined, Yaya replied in the only logical way he knew. "Smell what?"

Baba didn't answer.

Yaya headed toward a nearby outcropping to take a gander. On the way, he passed a passel of wild pigs, a covey of pheasants, and other small critters, including a red fox, all heading the direction he and Baba had come from. Once he reached the top of the rock formation, it didn't take long to see what they were fleeing: smoke plumes rising in the distance.

Yaya scampered back down to where Baba was waiting. "We can't go this way. What you were smelling was smoke. The forest is on fire."

Any lingering doubts Yaya had about Adarbad's visions of war and fire vanished.

"So what do we do?" Baba asked.

"We'll go around the flames and pick up the river where it turns south. Once we do, we stay the course all the way to Kuh-e Sholeh."

The two companions had trekked a few miles when they came upon a stretch of forest dotted with small, sporadic fires. The air was thick with smoke and humidity. Even so, Yaya could still make out the day moon through the trees. Waves of heat distorted its shape, giving the impression it was melting. He went along with the idea, imagining globs of yellow moon mud dripping onto the earth.

With his gaze skyward, the prince stepped on a loose rock and twisted his ankle. A few choice words escaped his mouth.

"Are you hurt?" Baba asked.

Yaya grasped his lower shin and winced. "This is what I get for daydreaming."

Baba was confused. "Daydreaming?"

"Nothing—just talking to myself. I'll be all right." Yaya tried to walk but a noticeable hobble gave him away.

Baba was not in the least convinced. "'All right,' my foot. Look at you—you can barely stand. Now, sit down and rest. We've been pushing hard for most of the day, and this bear is tired. And I'm not too proud to say it."

Yaya acquiesced to his better judgment, voiced his agreement, and gratefully reclined on a gentle slope covered in cushion moss. Behind them lay a cluster of charred foliage under a limestone shelf. Some of it still smoldered.

For his part, Baba stretched out flat on his belly, his chin on the ground. "If I fall asleep...," he began to say.

"Yeah?"

"Don't wake me."

Yaya looked at the bear, bemused by his demand, until a crackling sound drew his attention to a few small flames dancing from twig to twig. Wisps of smoke wafted his way. Upon catching a whiff, he recognized the scent of the hallucinogenic plant used in *Booz-Rooz*, the pagan ritual of communal bonding. He recalled being with his father on a diplomatic mission to Raydur and taking part in the rite.

The prince nudged Baba and pointed to the smoldering cluster. "Hey, do you smell that?"

"Do I? With a snout like mine, it's hard *not* to smell everything." Baba adjusted his head on his forearms.

Yaya put his hands behind his head and watched a few birds soaring above. They circled slowly, sometimes holding still against the stiff winds. The prince felt still, too. How could he not? Just as he had remembered from his trip to King Delawar's kingdom, a feeling of calm drifted over him. His mind began to wander. He thought of Gulzar and wondered if she had accepted Afshad's courtship.

In his altered state, Yaya didn't care. He rolled onto his side and looked at Baba, whose eyes were half open and glazed over like a drunkard's.

"Why are you looking at me?" Baba asked. "Can't you see I was sleeping?"

"No, you weren't. Who sleeps with their eyes open?"

"An animal knows when he's asleep, and I'm telling you, I was sleeping. I even dreamed you were staring at the sky."

"I *was* staring at the sky," Yaya said, raising his voice.

Baba grunted, not convinced. "Why don't you pipe down a bit? You're going to draw attention to us. Want another tussle with some wolves?"

Yaya came to his knees and held out his hand. "How big is your paw?"

Baba sat up and pressed his paw against the boy's outstretched fingers. It was twice the size, counting claws.

Yaya pushed against it, switching to two hands for leverage.

Baba held firm, then suddenly shoved him to the ground, where he landed beside the sharp blade of his shamshir. "Oops."

Yaya glared at the bear for his insufficient concern while bringing himself to his feet, sword in hand.

"I'd put that down if I were you. You wouldn't stand a chance in these woods without me."

"I don't know about that. I'm pretty good with a sword. If I'd wanted to, I could've taken out those wolves all by myself." Yaya began slashing and stabbing at imaginary foes. "One down, two down."

His *coup de grâce* was a pirouette into a counterattack. But on the thrust, he slipped and landed squarely on his behind. Fortunately, the moss cushioned his fall.

Baba cracked up at the boy's failed bravado. "Yep. Those wolves wouldn't have known what hit them."

Yaya tossed his shamshir aside. The smoke he'd been inhaling made him feel too good to take the ribbing seriously.

His mind bounced from the death of his father to the royal guard he'd evaded in the date palm orchards. The image of the billhook lodged through Piruz's neck was still vivid—as was his blood. With dying everywhere, Yaya was certain *Death* itself was after him. Were it not for the hallucinogen, he might have fallen into despair.

Instead, the prince did what anyone under such conditions would do: he waxed philosophic. "What do you think happens when we die?"

"Oh, I don't know," Baba said. "I suspect not much. Probably not too different from before we were born. Why?"

Yaya pointed to the one remaining flame burning the Booz-Rooz plant. "You see that little flame over there? See how it's struggling to stay lit? It's fighting to stay alive. It needs wood to keep going, and if it doesn't..."

The flame petered out, releasing a thin wisp of smoke.

"You see," he continued, "we need wood to stay alive—wood for the fire. And when we can't find any or give up looking, we release something like smoke, which fills the air and gets absorbed by everything else. Some smoke we remember. Some we forget. Some smoke makes us laugh. Some makes us cry. It's neither good nor bad—just smoke when the wood is gone."

Baba nodded at the boy's musings, though he wasn't sure what to make of them.

Meanwhile, a lone bird circling above seemed to show a keen interest in the terrestrial travelers. With each pass, it descended lower and lower, until taking up residence on the limestone shelf. It was a large falcon with something tied around its neck.

The bird let out a few loud screeches to announce its arrival, then fluttered in Yaya's direction, landing at his feet. "I didn't think I'd ever find you. Now take this thing off my neck—it's killing me. If it's not meant for you, give it back so I can be on my way."

Yaya removed a leather pouch from around the falcon's neck. He loosened the drawstring and pulled out a lusterless object about the size of his palm. It was the magical amulet. Also inside was a folded note.

It read: "Dearest Yaya, what you're holding is the amulet of elements. You'll recall what it can do from our conversations. Just remember to recite the incantation that matches the inscribed symbol. Disregard the earth compartment—those contents were stolen by Sarvin to create Lilya's jackals. The other three can each be used only once, so be judicious with your choices. Make haste. Your friend, Ada. P.S. I'm sorry I didn't join you in time. I got a bit... tied up."

Yaya choked up. He hadn't been forgotten, a sentiment he had all too often considered. While he wished his dear friends were with him, he took solace that Adarbad had likely made it to Raydur.

The prince stuck the note in his haversack and hung the amulet around his neck.

To the falcon, that meant mission accomplished. "All right then, I'll be on my way."

"Hold on," Yaya said, his eyes scouring the ground. "Baba, help me find a piece of bark."

With the effects of the hallucinogenic plant beginning to wear off, Baba was amenable to the request.

Yet in no time, the falcon had dropped a piece of burnt wood at Yaya's feet. "Anything to get this show on the road. What do you need it for?"

Yaya retrieved his shamshir and held the wood steady with his foot. Using the point of the sword, he carved a short message. Then he snapped the piece off and placed it in the empty leather pouch. "Take this with you and see that your owner gets it."

"Are you kidding me? I'm no beast of burden."

"It hardly weighs anything. You'll see." Yaya slipped the drawstring over the bird's neck. "There. I think you can handle that, don't you?"

"I usually get a tip for this kind of work, especially a round-tripper. You wouldn't want me to get weak with hunger and fail to return, would you? Besides, I might have to contend with bigger things in this sky than me. Come to think of it, I'd watch out if I were you. I'm talking about *big* things."

Yaya obliged and tossed a few pistachios on the ground.

The falcon duly snatched them up, then with a loud "chup, chup, chup," took off flying.

Yaya watched until the bird vanished over the trees. "What do you think he meant about bigger things in the sky?"

"Nothing," Baba said through a yawn. "Just a bunch of yapping." He gave his coat a good shake. "Say, you think you're up for walking?"

"I'm fine enough."

The two encountered a drop on the other side of the limestone shelf. Yaya sat down and scooted over the edge. Baba took a more casual approach, walking the whole length of the rock until it leveled with the ground.

The display of delicacy was something to behold, and Yaya had trouble squaring it with the power and speed the bear had shown in his fight with the wolves.

When Baba came back around, he had a curious thought. "You mind telling me what you inscribed on that burnt wood?"

Yaya smiled. "An 'O' and a 'K.'"

SHADOWS IN THE SKY

Yaya and Baba walked several miles through forests untouched by the fires. The winds had died down, bringing a welcome reprieve from the sooty air they had been breathing. Alder trees, standing shoulder to shoulder, provided almost complete cover from the sky. Nearly as uniform was the forest floor, still brown with debris from last year's shedding. Splotches of green moss, clinging to roots like lily pads on a murky pond, were all that stood out.

Since receiving the amulet, Yaya had been preoccupied with thoughts of home: his father, Shanaz and Adarbad, and his place in the order of things. He wondered what events might be unfolding in his absence. Not knowing troubled him, made all the worse by imagined scenarios too unpleasant to ponder. His mood darkened, and he soon found himself despairing, which only forced his pace.

None of this was lost on Baba. Mostly, he stayed quiet and let Yaya lead the way.

The companions crossed through a thick patch of bushes and brambles. A light breeze stirred the air, rustling leaves and swaying branches overhead. The movements cast a ballet of shadows that danced around them as they stepped over a hollowed tree shorn of its bark. On the other side lay a clearing. Mixed among the tall grasses were shrubs of firethorn whose white flowers masked a prickly defense.

In short order, a briar snagged Yaya's haversack and sleeve, stopping him in his tracks.

Baba thought it was a good time to probe. "You've been keeping to yourself since talking with that bird. You want to share what's been on your mind?"

"Swimming."

"Hmm?" Baba was not expecting such a precise reply.

"I was thinking about this river back home. It's called the Rud-e Barik. I learned to swim there."

Baba was much more interested in a cluster of yellow berries than swimming, but figured he owed the boy a show of interest. "Sounds nice."

"My father taught me. Later, I found out that he might have done so because of a tragedy."

"Tragedy?"

"Two twin boys drowned in that river. He was supposed to be watching them. Or my Uncle Kamran was—I'm not sure exactly. All I know is, he was adamant I learn how to swim early on."

Yaya freed himself from the briar but pricked his finger. A dot of blood pooled on his skin, which he sucked away. "And now he's dead."

Baba could sense sadness and tried to feel empathy—at least to the degree he was able. His earliest memories were of his mother, but only until his second spring, when he and his sibling struck out on their own. Never had he met his father, nor did he care. The ways of nature excluded such bonds. Still, the bear knew he needed to say something. As he searched for words of compassion, a shadow swept over the clearing.

Yaya noticed. "Did you see that?"

"See what?"

"That shadow. It passed right over us."

"Wasn't paying any attention. Probably a flock of birds."

Baba stuck out his snout but couldn't gather the scent of any imminent threats.

Yaya scanned the skies. "I have a strange feeling… almost like we're being watched. Let's get moving."

The prince led the way across the clearing. On the other side, beyond a stretch of dense bushes and woody shrubs, they encountered a ridge of limestone, its sides jagged and sharp as if hewn by a dull blade. While Baba searched for a way around the rocky formation, Yaya happened to glance upwards. What he saw—two animals peering at him over the edge—sent a shiver down his spine.

"Not you again. I told you, Baba. I knew something wasn't right."

"You've run into these things before?"

"They're my grandmother's jackals."

Having found their prey, the jackals darted along the ridge toward level ground.

Baba turned to face where he knew they would come. He widened his stance and readied himself for a fight. "Get out of here. Find a tree. I'll hold them off."

"But I can—"

"Go!"

Yaya made a mad dash to the clearing with his shamshir in hand. By the time he reached its tall grasses, he could hear the horrible, discordant sounds of beasts in battle. He spotted a mulberry tree where he could take refuge. But as he moved to sheathe his sword and prepare to climb, a shadowy figure clad in a black hauberk stepped out from behind the trunk.

Yaya came to an abrupt halt. "Madar bozorg."

Lilya had her hands behind her back, her disposition oddly casual. "You seem surprised to see me. Should I not be looking for my wayward grandson?"

"But how did you find me?"

"That's neither here nor there. What's important is that you be home, where you belong." Lilya stepped forward and extended one of her hands. "Shall we?"

The prince was hardly convinced by his grandmother's overt appeals to family. He turned his head and glanced across the clearing.

"Don't even think of running," she said. "I didn't come all this way to lose you again. I know that I've been tough on you—but understand that it comes from a place of love."

"Love? You sure have a strange way of showing it. Why have you been hunting me with your jackals?"

"My dear boy, they've only been trying to find you."

"You're a liar."

Rankled by the insult, Lilya saw no further utility in the charade. Her visage grew stern, and her eyes filled with rage.

It was a look all too familiar to Yaya, who put forth his shamshir. "I can only imagine how much it pains you that I got away from them."

"You won't get away from me." Lilya drew the sword she had been hiding behind her. "Behold the queen of Zad."

Down came the blade.

Yaya could only muster a defensive maneuver. Though he managed to parry the attack, the force of the blow dislodged his shamshir from his hands and sent him sprawling to the ground. He scooted backward, trying to flee. But before he could scramble to his feet, a boot struck his back, knocking him face-down onto a burgeoning ant colony.

Lilya reached for his collar.

As in any battle, one must use the resources at hand. So Yaya spun around and tossed two handfuls of ant-infested dirt into the queen's eyes. But the desperate act proved of little use against a foe bent on punishment. Likewise, his kicking and flailing did nothing to thwart his grandmother's advance. She batted away his legs and bashed him on the head, leaving him dazed.

Lilya pulled the prince to his feet by the nape of his neck. "Such a silly boy... thinking he could escape his madar bozorg. Have you not learned anything about me in your fourteen years?"

"Fifteen."

Ever so slyly, Yaya began to toy with his amulet.

"Tell me where you're going," she said. "I know you didn't come out here to cavort with animals. Does it have anything to do with an elixir? What gift did you receive from Adarbad?"

Despite his beating, Yaya held his silence.

"Answer me, you bastard."

Yaya heard a mournful yelp—the death knell of the last surviving jackal. "You'll see my gift soon enough."

Alarmed by the ominous warning, Lilya called out to her manticore, left in a nearby glade.

Yaya knew he had no time to spare. With his arms restrained, he resorted to his only viable option—his head. He snapped it sharply, striking his grandmother square on her nose.

Dazed, Lilya let go and staggered back a couple of steps.

The momentary lull gave the prince time to reach for a gelatinous ball stored in the water compartment of his amulet. He tossed it into his mouth and recalled the word that would activate the spell.

"*Ab!*"

Yaya's gut and gullet gurgled. A liquid filled his mouth, ballooning his cheeks like a puffer fish. As Lilya lunged forward, reaching for his throat, he puked a frothy green substance onto her face.

The queen recoiled and wailed in pain. Her screams echoed through the trees as she retreated, hunched over and careening through the grass.

Her manticore, hearing its mistress's distress, flew to her.

Meanwhile, Baba barreled through the brush to Yaya's defense, wide-eyed and madder than a desert viper.

Lilya struggled to mount, only to collapse after straddling the saddle. In shock, her body reeling from the acid, it took everything she had to command her manticore to flee. After several successive flaps, the beast ascended over the mulberry tree and banked sharply, flying just above the canopy. Such was the tumult of its wake that the treetops swayed.

Baba padded through the tall grasses and joined Yaya in watching the manticore fade into the haze. He was panting, his jowls were sodden with a red-hued slobber. Tufts of fur had been ripped from his coat, and his left ear had been gnawed on. Save for his vanity, none of his injuries were of the sort to cause undue suffering.

"You won't have to worry about those jackals anymore. Remember when I told you there was nothing worse than a hungry bear? I was wrong. There's nothing worse than an angry Baba." The bear chuckled at his joke when the prince embraced him out of the blue. "Whoa, whoa, easy there."

Yaya was crying—and with good reason. He understood his grandmother's hatred for him with newfound certainty. Attempted murder will do that. He had suspected as much when the jackals chased him into Sarzamin-e Mordegan. But the hatred he just saw in her eyes and heard in her voice was manifestly different than at home, as if her contempt for him had been freed from the shackles of family and polite society.

When at last he had gathered himself, he turned his face to wipe his tears. "Well, that was embarrassing."

"Nah. It happens to the best of us."

Yaya smiled. As he regarded his companion fondly, he noticed the extent of the bear's injuries. "Your ear, Baba. Part of it is missing."

"Oh, that's nothing. I can still hear. Those jackal bites don't compare to hornet stings. Trust me."

Yaya looked at the bear tenderly. "I'm lucky to know you, Babak, even if you sneak food from my bag when I'm sleeping."

Baba was baffled. "What? How did you...?"

Yaya began walking through the grass. "Because I'm not stupid, that's how."

"Where are you going?"

Yaya stopped to pick up his shamshir. "To check on the jackals. I need confirmation."

Embarrassed that his food heisting had been exposed, Baba mumbled to himself as he lagged behind. He wondered if somehow he was going soft. After all, his existence was one where might makes right. To the victor go the spoils. Yet the more the bear pondered the ways of his world, the more he questioned why he hadn't used his physical advantages to take from Yaya whatever he wanted.

Under the limestone ridge, they came upon the dead jackals, their heads bloodied and flies inspecting their wounds.

Baba sniffed one. "Your hunters are dead."

"Only two of them. I told you my grandmother wanted to kill me."

"That's who that was, flying on that strange animal?"

"I have a feeling we'll see many strange things, Baba. Anyway, she knows where we are. We have to go back."

"Back? Back to what? I'm not heading into those forest fires."

"We'll head west, over the other side of the mountains. From there, we'll circle around and pick up the Rud-e Hayat near Jarak."

"All I caught is, '...over the other side of the mountains.' Just so you know, it won't be an easy route."

As the travelers embarked on their return journey, Yaya looked at Baba strolling beside him. The earth beneath their feet—the land of mountains, streams, and trees—was the world he lived in. There were no guard rails, no neutral zones, no hiding places. It was kill or be killed, fight or flight. Every day, without fail, the play went on. Top billing changed, but the cast of characters remained mostly the same. Yaya didn't know his or his grandmother's role, but he had a sneaky suspicion who would be playing the part of the hunted.

BATTLE AT RUD-E HAYAT

General Jangi drove the party hard as they neared the river valley north of Jarak. The air was cooler, and the morning sun had barely breached the Green Mountains, their peaks shimmering like diamonds. Despite the drought, the bucolic plain they traversed was still lush with grass and groves of green ash. On the banks of the Rud-e Hayat, swaying in the breeze, were cattails as far as the eye could see. They reminded Jangi of skewers of minced meat.

Soon they came upon a bend in the river, revealing a familiar way station and garrison outpost. Princess Mahzarin waved to the guards as they trotted past, but no friendly gesture was returned. Instead, the guards looked upon the party with dull expressions. Mahz thought it rude, but not out of character—after all, the Jaraki people were well known among the four kingdoms for being cold and insular.

To give both the riders and the horses a breather, Jangi slowed the pace to a walk.

Shanaz was amused by the exchange. "Don't take it personally, Princess. Were you confined to this hapless position, I suspect you might exhibit an equal dearth of hospitality."

"I don't think I would," Mahz said, a hint of wistfulness in her voice. "One does tire of the obsolete duties and inane rituals of royalty. Besides, there is something to be said for an honest day's work. I'm sure you can understand the urge to get away from it all."

"Well, when I want to 'get away from it all,' the last thing I think of is work. A good soaking in the bathhouse comes to mind. Anyway, don't you think you're a bit young for such an attitude?"

"Not when it's all I've known. You have memories of a life before you were queen."

Shanaz reflected for a moment. "I hope you'll forgive my candor, but you're romanticizing what you don't know. Those rituals and duties you speak of so harshly, whether entertaining foreign dignitaries or overseeing the cadre of citadel staff, are a small price we pay for the trappings of the court."

Mahz, though self-possessed and confident beyond her years, was still only seventeen, which meant she hadn't outgrown the overwrought theatrics of adolescence. "Trappings? More like 'trapped' if you ask me."

Shanaz was irritated by what she considered pampered behavior. Nonetheless, she checked any urge to chide the royal, suspecting the recent death of Mahzarin's mother, the late Queen Meher, was the reason behind her rebellion. "I've known you all of your life, Princess. Never have I suspected you of being unhappy."

Mahz looked away, embarrassed. "I'm not unhappy. It's... I don't know. It's hard to explain."

"Have you spoken to your father?"

"I wouldn't dare."

"Why?"

"Let's just say he hasn't been the same since Mother passed. He's weary and burdened, sometimes even distant. He has enough to worry about, least of all a daughter who has never had any real problems to complain about."

"You're a young woman who's lost her mother. You have every right to feel adrift. Don't let anyone tell you differently."

Mahz fought to swallow the lump in her throat. "I'm afraid I'll never be able to fill her shoes."

"You don't have to. You walk your own path, in your own shoes, and Raydur will be better for it. Besides, you're gifted with the bow and, from what I hear, a newly named leader of the savaran archers. That speaks to your father's trust in you."

"Except I never wanted to be an archer. I had my sights set on the heavy cavalry."

"Why didn't you pursue it?"

"I did, but my father was adamantly opposed. He'd say, 'You are my only heir. I will not sacrifice Raydur's future for your desire to prove yourself.' Then he would go on and on about how awful war is and how I don't understand it. But he's wrong, and much too protective of me. I'm not afraid."

Jangi yelled back, urging the women to stop lagging.

With a dismissive wave, Shanaz acknowledged the general but otherwise ignored the order, given how grouchy he had been since breakfast. As it happened, she had nixed his third helping of Jaraki cheese and jam to hasten their return. His sour mood was in response to her questioning his judgment.

The queen continued her conversation with the princess. "The burdens and expectations placed upon youth can be the cruelest of a parent's bestowment, at least from the child's perspective. But I think your father is protective of you to ensure your destiny. Planning is left up to the parents, not the children."

"I understand what you're saying, but sometimes a parent's concern can stifle a child's potential."

Shanaz saw little reason to belabor the point. "I have no doubt you'll find your way, Princess. Just remember, there are worse things in this world than being kept from battle."

"Maybe I'll get kidnapped by brigands and won't have to worry about it."

"My dear, let's hope not." Shanaz tightened her hold on the reins. "Come. I think your general has lost patience with our loitering."

At a narrow stretch in the river, the lead riders crossed a bridge to the flatter terrain on the valley's western side.

Once the queen and princess had caught up, Jangi pushed the pace. "We won't take a break until we clear the valley. With reports of Visgari incursions, we're better off putting it behind us."

The party pressed on, their horses' hooves echoing like rolling thunder. After a mile, the valley walls closed in, the ivory-colored granite cliffs rising higher in steep, vertical swoops. Shade enveloped the land, and a headwind funneled the scent of wild caraway.

Jangi rode at the head of the phalanx, the rest fanning out behind him. As he brooded over what he thought was gossipy collusion by the women, an arrow swooshed through the air over his head. The general quickly glanced back to check his flanks—three of his savaran had fallen.

Any notion that this was a brigand ambush was dispelled by the sight of three large beasts banking through the air—two to the east, one to the west. After completing turns, they leveled out, gliding like falcons chasing a desert shrew. As they descended, their riders readied another volley.

Mahzarin called out to Shanaz. "Are those what I think they are?"

"They're not ground jays."

As Jangi implored the women to take cover, an arrow struck his lone surviving horseman. The rider lurched and nearly slipped off his saddle, saved only by his iron grip on the bridle. But the wound was fatal. In a final act of soldierly charity, knowing his death was nigh, he waved the others on as another arrow struck his horse. The steed staggered and convulsed, dropping the rider to the ground.

Duty-bound to save his own, Jangi drew his sword and rode toward his fallen compatriot. An arrow whistled overhead; another screamed past his ear. While two of the manticores veered off, the third set its sights on the general, its razor-sharp claws extended and primed for the feasting. Jangi braced for a collision with a soldier's fatalism, when a fortuitous gully allowed him and his horse to duck out of harm's way.

Meanwhile, as Shanaz rode off seeking shelter, Mahz turned to face the enemy. The princess recognized Afshad's gold armor and remembered the smug expression he had worn during his last visit to Raydur. She pulled her bow taut—aiming for his chest—and released.

"This should wipe that smug look clean," she thought.

The iron-tipped arrow, feathered with handcrafted fletching, spun through the air and struck Afshad in the shoulder. Rather than piercing the metal, the arrow bounced off with a hollow "ping."

Mahz was dumbfounded, believing that no armor could withstand the arrows in Raydur's quivers.

Still determined to inflict some pain, she took aim at another rider. Arrows crossed paths. The one marking the princess barely missed, ripping through the ornamental tassel atop her helm. Hers found its target flush, felling the great archer Daryush, whose body plummeted to the valley floor.

Mahz reached for her shamshir but was too late—Afshad's manticore slammed into her, knocking her from her horse.

Seeing his soldier was dead, Jangi spurred his mount toward the fallen princess.

But General Baraz cut him off, landing his manticore in his path. Jangi's horse recoiled. As it rose up on its hind legs, the manticore turned and swung its barbed tail into the gelding's belly. The horse crumpled to the ground, forcing Jangi to toss his sword and tumble off lest he be crushed. And tumble he did, with all the grace of a blind drunkard.

Baraz urged his manticore to attack. "For Daryush."

Jangi quickly retrieved his sword and engaged his foes. As he parried blows, he caught a glimpse of Shanaz, the queen armed with a fallen soldier's sword and sneaking up behind the beast. To aid her ambush, he taunted Baraz with foul language and insults. The tactic worked to enrage the general, whose singular focus on his enemy left his manticore vulnerable to a shamshir plunged into the hip.

The beast roared in anguish. It spun, lashing out and swatting Shanaz to the ground.

At Baraz's urging, it prepared to pounce when Jangi levied a mortal wound, driving his sword deep into the manticore's neck. The beast collapsed onto its side, one wing extended toward the sky. The gash was deep, and the lifeblood poured forth unabated. With each waning breath, until the last, its wing slowly drew in like a baker's bellows.

Jangi spotted Baraz, forlorn and kneeling beside the corpse. More concerning was a band of riders half a mile to the south. They looked ragtag and bore no sign of Jarak's blue and green standards.

Afshad was the first to sound the alarm. "Brigands. Retreat."

General Baraz rushed toward Daryush's manticore, which was still mauling a horse.

As for Jangi, he barged through the tall grasses in a last-ditch effort to save the unconscious princess, her body belly down and secured atop Afshad's manticore.

Afshad took macabre pleasure in Jangi's desperate advance, drawing out his departure as long as possible. Only when Jangi was within striking distance did he nudge his manticore into the sky. It was an indignity the prince relished, as evinced by his exultant laughter.

He was joined in flight by Baraz. Their mission complete, the two Zadians turned east over the Rud-e Hayat and flew toward the Green Mountains.

Short of breath, Shanaz arrived at the scene. "General, we must get out of here. There's nothing we can do for the princess."

But Jangi's eyes were fixed on the sky, his expression vacuous as if in a fit of paralysis.

Shanaz tugged at his arm. "Now."

With all the horses either dead or out of reach, the two fled the flats and sought safety up the granite wall of the valley. They scaled a steep incline, pulling themselves up by the branches and roots of scrubby trees growing in the rock. This effort was especially hard for the queen, whose shoulder hurt from her tussle with the manticore.

Jangi helped where he could, even pushing against her lower back when she faltered. "You'll forgive my taking liberties, but they're on our heels."

Indeed they were, indicative of the jumble of voices urging their capture.

"Get 'em."

"Don't let 'em get away."

The two fugitives ascended along a narrow edge at the base of the rising cliffs. But the queen soon tired, the weight of exhaustion dragging her down.

With Jangi leading Shanaz by the hand, they rounded a bend and spotted a narrow gap between a large slab of stone and the mountain. Hiding was a risk—but with the brigands gaining ground, it was their only choice.

Jangi guided Shanaz toward the opening. "That way. Hurry."

To their surprise, the cleft opened to a cavern deeper than it first appeared in the dim light.

A steep downward slope led them to an underground river, its surface dappled with calcium deposits that reached the ceiling. On the ground, lay remains of charred wood, encircled by rings of stones. There were also broken jars and a few scattered utensils. Two small skiffs nestled on the shore offered further proof of an encampment.

Jangi helped the queen into one of the boats, but the hull of the aged vessel was no match for his weight, its rotten planks splintering with his first step.

"To the other boat," he said.

The queen led the way, sloshing through murky water until reaching the other vessel. Wasting no time, she pulled on the bow.

"Forget that," the general said. "Get in."

But Shanaz was too deep in the water to step aboard. The best she could do was lean over the hull and pull herself in.

As she inched onto the only seat, Jangi heaved the skiff forward and jumped in the stern. The bow lurched upward. Despite the undue stress on the wood, the ashen frame held. The boat moved away from the shore, carried by the currents. And not a moment too soon, for voices could be heard entering the cave.

"After them!" the brigands yelled.

Hoots and catcalls followed the marauders' footsteps to the edge of the water, a subterranean offshoot of the Rud-e Hayat. A few waded to the other boat and piled in, ignoring that the vessel listed to port and had already taken in significant water. With the added weight, it sank like a stone.

Soaked and sputtering, the brigands stepped ashore and admonished one another while their fellow Visgari hurled rocks toward the wayward travelers. But to no avail.

The boat carrying Shanaz and Jangi drifted behind a cavern wall and into the darkness.

THE CAVERNS OF FOG

Jangi and Shanaz drifted for hours in the pitch black, sometimes bouncing off cave walls, other times off rocks that protruded from the water or lay submerged just below the surface. There were few sounds, no sense of direction, and time lost meaning in the underground hollow.

As the current slowed and the boat's momentum waned, Shanaz sensed the futility of leaving their fate to the water. "General, we have to do something. We simply can't float here, staring into nothing."

Jangi picked up the boat's lone oar. "Then brace yourself. I'm going to paddle until we hit a wall."

"Hit a wall? Shouldn't we avoid them?"

"Bear with me." The general began to paddle from his knees, alternating sides. "Once we reach a wall, we'll hew to its direction. It's the only physical marker we have to guide us."

Shanaz chastised herself for not supporting Jangi's efforts, but the positive character she was known for had receded under the duress of their misfortune. It didn't help that her shoulder throbbed with a dull pain, made worse by the interminable darkness that offered no visual distraction.

After a spell of vigorous paddling, Jangi relented, his muscles too exhausted to persist. Sweating and short of breath, he set the oar over his thighs. "What on earth is this place, an underground sea?"

"Let me paddle. From the sound of your wheezing, I think your lungs need a rest."

"I only need to catch my breath."

"I don't need you to keel over and fall into the water, General. I think I know the routine: three strokes on the left, three on the right."

Jangi sighed but didn't protest. He realized there was nothing skillful about what he was doing. So they continued, alternating turns.

After many rotations with nothing to show for their efforts, Jangi let out a yawp of frustration. "I've had it. Where's the damn wall?"

His outburst startled and annoyed Shanaz. "Yelling doesn't help."

"I'm going to be yelling more if I don't get something to eat."

"Don't even talk about food. I had much less than you this morning."

"What can I say? I'm a big man. Let's not forget I didn't even finish my breakfast."

"You give new meaning to the word 'finish,' considering you'd already finished your second helping."

"But not the third. It takes a lot to keep this body moving."

"That's been evident since we left Raydur. We weren't even halfway to Jarak when you'd already eaten your rations. And don't get me started on dinner last night. Do you not hear yourself when you eat? I don't think I've ever heard as much muzzled belching and quiet purring in one sitting. Even brigands have better manners."

Jangi mumbled under his breath, convinced a little more gratitude from Shanaz was in order. After all, he was the one who had seen the cavern entrance. Had it not been for his quick thinking, he assured himself, his royal companion might be enjoying an up-close and personal view of the brigands and the "manners" she characterized with undue charity.

"All I'm suggesting, General, is that you show a little restraint. Even after breakfast, we were barely beyond Jarak's gates when your hands began pulling fruits from your supply bags. You'd probably eaten all of the rations King Mazad had given us when we were attacked."

"Not true. I had a few dates left and a handful of pistachios."

Though dismayed by his response, Shanaz realized the uselessness of continuing the childish back-and-forth. "Listen. We're both tired and hungry. If we intend to get out of here, we'll need to pull together. Yes?"

"Who's pulling us apart?"

"Seriously, General?"

"Look, if King Delawar didn't trust me, he wouldn't have put me in charge of this diplomatic mission."

Like a hammer striking an anvil, the absurdity of their quarrel ended with the general's inadvertent admission of failure. Both took refuge in the abundant silence that followed.

Shanaz felt pity for Jangi, for she knew what he must have been thinking. "You're worried about Princess Mahzarin, aren't you?"

"I can only imagine what she's going through. Tell me, Queen Shanaz—you're from Zad, you know your people. Is there any hope for her?"

"I could offer you hope for its own sake, but what does that do for us? I thought I knew Queen Lilya well. Thought I had her figured out. But the extent to which she usurped control of Zad and cleared away rivals far exceeded anything I believed she was capable of. Don't get me wrong, I've always been wary of her motives. After all, she is Danzardani by birth. But this? The takeover of Zad? I didn't see it coming."

"So you're telling me that anything is possible?"

"I'm telling you, her ambition and cruelty have no limits, and the window to save Princess Mahzarin will soon shut."

Jangi began to paddle with unbound, almost maniacal fury, flailing from one side to the other, and splashing water into the boat and onto Shanaz. He made no effort to stay on course.

Eventually, his panting and hoarse wheezing were such that the queen felt the need to intervene. "General, that's enough."

Heaving from exhaustion, he dropped to a seated position and folded his arms around his knees. Meanwhile, the boat slowed to an imperceptible drift. "King Delawar will never forgive me. His daughter has been in my charge ever since she came of age. Whether it was overseeing her training or keeping the ogling eyes away, it's been my duty to..." Jangi hung his head. "I have failed."

Shanaz felt the urge to comfort him when their skiff collided with something jarring.

Hopeful, the queen reached out into the dark. "Well, what do you know?"

Jangi scrambled to his knees, extended his arm, and touched the cool, moist surface of limestone. Overcome, he burst into joyful mirth. "That's the fastest answer to a prayer if I say so myself. Ohrmazd is most merciful."

With his spirits lifted, Jangi continued on course, using the wall as his guide. They pressed forward, zigged and zagged, and sometimes wound around bends that seemingly reversed course. Despite the convoluted path, Jangi and Shanaz tried to remain hopeful—for there was no alternative.

<hr>

Much time had passed, and much distance had been covered when Jangi began retching over the starboard side of the skiff.

Shanaz voiced her concern. "General, are you all right?"

"Let's just say if I want that third helping of breakfast, I can find it in the water. I think the air in this cave is getting to me. I'm feeling weak."

"You need to relax. Breathe with me—slow, long breaths."

The queen took a deep breath and slowly exhaled the stale air. The general followed her lead. Together, they repeated the exercise until, at length, his queasiness had abated.

Jangi resumed paddling when there was a splash not of his making. "Did you hear that?"

"Hear what?"

"Something jumped in the water."

Soon after, their boat, parked at the edge of the wall, began to rock gently on small waves.

Shanaz grew worried. "Any ideas?"

Jangi failed to come up with a benign explanation. Then came another splash—and another. Many more followed. "There's your answer. This water's come to life."

Shanaz then sneezed, startling a colony of bats clinging to the ceiling. She and Jangi ducked and covered their heads as the agitated mammals sought safety in the familiar recesses of the cavern. Eventually, they heard the bats' flapping and shrieking fade in the distance, and in their wake, amid the silence, came a rush of fresher air.

Shanaz sat up. "Do you feel that draft?"

"I do. I can finally breathe again."

"You know what this means, don't you?"

"That this boundless cave has another opening? You'd better believe it." Jangi dipped the oar in the water, but only briefly.

"What's the matter?" Shanaz said. "Why aren't you paddling?"

"I think I found a guide rope. Grab it."

"Where?"

"I've lifted it. It's right beside you."

Shanaz felt the rope brush against her. She reached out, expecting to grab hold, but instead touched something rough and scaly. "Ew."

The moment it shifted beneath her touch, she yanked her hand back, realizing too late what it was. The snake unwound itself, briefly dangled, then plopped squarely onto her feet. With a sharp shriek, the queen leapt up, rocking the boat from side to side.

"What are you doing?" Jangi said. "You're going to tip us over."

"I'm coming to you. That's what I'm doing." Shanaz felt her way across the seat until her hand found Jangi's beard and nose.

"Akh! That's my face."

"There's a snake in the bow. Switch places with me."

"And what makes you think I can? Is this the privilege I get for being a man?"

"It's the privilege I get for being a queen. Move it."

Switching positions was perilous, not least because of the pitch black and the presence of a cave-dwelling snake. Yet somehow, they managed it. With renewed vigor, they pulled themselves along the cavern wall. Every twenty feet, their hands came upon hollow pieces of wood that functioned as buoys for the knotted strands of rope. Whoever had built the line knew that navigating such a twisted maze would be nearly impossible, even with torches.

But just as they had found their rhythm, some unknown entity moving at great speed rammed the boat, sending Jangi halfway over the bow. Before he could get himself back in, a bone-crushing force clamped down on his arm. The pain was excruciating, even through his studded leather bracers. Far worse was that whatever had hold of him was trying to pull him into the murky depths of the mountain sump.

"I'm going in."

Shanaz leaned forward and snagged the belt around his hauberk, helping him stave off any mortal reckoning.

"My dagger," Jangi said, desperately trying to hold on. "It's inside my boot."

"Which boot?"

"The right one."

Shanaz groped down his leg and managed to find the three-inch gambler's knife. But in her haste to unsheathe it, the blade slipped from her grip.

Jangi let out a blood-curdling howl. "My lady, if you haven't noticed, I'm not enjoying myself."

Not a moment too soon, the queen located the dagger. She threw herself across Jangi and repeatedly stabbed. Again and again, she plunged the blade until the creature—whether from pain or resignation—released his arm and sank into the water, silent as a blade of eelgrass.

Shanaz helped Jangi sit up. "Are you hurt?"

"Never mind that," he said. "Can you find the rope?"

Before long, and with even more incentive to escape, both castaways pulled themselves forward with all the energy they could muster. The air became steadily warmer. Then there was a faint glow of light.

Jangi peered over the boat's edge. For the first time, the water's surface was visible, and just a few feet down, a bed of igneous rock sparkled in streaks of colors.

"Blessed is the believer. We're in shallow waters at last."

Shanaz patted Jangi, letting him know that she, too, was delighted in their good fortune.

After two more turns, the labyrinth opened to a vast cavernous dome that ran half the length of Zad's bazaar. Stalactites hung down from the ceiling. At the other end loomed the mouth of the cave.

They paddled forward, taken in by the wonderment, when Jangi tossed the rope aside and stepped into the thigh-deep water.

"What are you doing?" Shanaz asked.

Before he could explain, a hideous, pulsating shriek erupted from the darker recesses of the cavern.

"Get out," he said.

Shanaz extended her hand for help.

But there was no time to be dainty. Jangi grabbed the queen under her arms and plucked her from the boat.

In her place, the general caught a glimpse of their uninvited guest nestled and coiled near the stern. For being a stowaway that had just been exposed, the viper looked remarkably composed—certainly more at ease than its harried companions wading through the water.

After fifty yards, Shanaz and Jangi reached a mud-covered bed. The air became dry and hot, the familiar summer staleness to which both were accustomed. Trailing alongside them over the ground was their guide rope, moored to a stone formation at the cave's edge.

At last, they arrived in the outside world. The terrain was uneven, and the drought had not been kind to the vegetation and trees, their orange-tinged leaves singed by the searing heat. The sun sat low on the horizon above distant mountains. Alas, there was one problem. Below them lay a vertical drop of at least forty feet.

And coming for them, having nearly reached the boat, were the hungry beasts. As they slithered into the shallows, the abominations rose, their pinkish-hued bodies reptilian in form. Their heads had no perceptible faces except protruding jaws capped with serrated teeth.

The general felt hopeless. "We're trapped." He reached for his dagger in his boot, only to realize it was still in the boat.

Shanaz glanced down the cliff, then back toward the cave dwellers who, oddly enough, had halted their pursuit. "General, they've stopped."

"It must be the sun. They seem bothered by the light."

Even as Jangi spoke, the barrier of light receded. In equal measure, the creatures advanced.

Shanaz looked to the setting sun. "We don't have much time. What are we going to do?"

Panic set in.

The queen paced back and forth, then looked over the cliff's edge to consider the horrifying prospect of leaping. The choice seemed clear enough—and awful: eaten alive or broken on the ground below.

The beasts had stopped short of the boat when Jangi sprinted their way. As he waded into the shallows, the cave dwellers became more agitated. They snapped their tails and gnashed their teeth but refrained from moving closer. Jangi knew he had only seconds. He reached the skiff and looked in the boat for the knife.

Nothing.

With Shanaz urging him on, Jangi scanned the broader area of the stern, and this time, he saw the tip of the blade. But there was another unexpected problem: the olive-colored rat snake coiled around the hilt and none too eager to move from its makeshift nest.

Jangi couldn't believe his predicament: giant slimy salamanders ready to devour him, or his greatest phobia.

"Of all places to rest," he said, as if to scold the serpent.

He reached for the dagger but was rebuffed by a quick strike, the snake quite taken by its possession.

"Then this will have to do."

Jangi flipped over the skiff and pushed it toward the cave dwellers. Below the ripples, he saw the shimmering blade. Wasting no time, he retrieved it and began to wade back, at least to the degree he could. Drained of all endurance, the water felt as viscous as quicksand.

When the general reached the shallows, he could barely lift his boots above the surface. Twice he tripped, and twice he fell into the water. Once out, all he could do was plod along, his steps hampered by the suction between the soles of his boots and the muddy riverbed.

At a calculated distance, he knelt, sliced the rope, and carried the slack to the cliff's edge.

Only the sun's corona remained above the mountains.

Jangi handed the rope to Shanaz. "Wrap it around your wrists and hold tight."

The general helped the queen over the edge and lowered her down, sometimes letting the rope slip no matter how the fibrous material flayed his palms.

The moment Shanaz reached the base of the dried-up falls, the remaining light—the last bulwark against the flesh-eating salamanders—had vanished.

Jangi looked back into the dome. The beasts were nearly upon him, climbing over each other like waves crashing the shore. Before their bile-dripping jaws could find their target, he scooted over the edge and began rappelling down the cliff face.

Foiled in their pursuit, the creatures turned their collective ire upon the rope and gnawed it feverishly.

Jangi knew it wouldn't last long against their razor-sharp teeth, so he loosened his grip and began a controlled fall.

Snap! The rope gave way.

Jangi's frame buckled upon hitting the ground. He wound up on his side, grasping at his ankle.

Shanaz rushed to his aid and managed to get him to his feet.

Jangi leaned on her for support, wrapping his arm around her shoulder. "That's what I get for going second," he said.

Both looked to the cave opening, where the silhouettes of the salamanders could be seen sniffing at the air. Convinced they were at last safe, the battle-weary companions gazed into each other's eyes with the silent regard of soldiers who had lived through a battle.

Shanaz noticed the general favoring his left hand. "Your hand, Jangi—it's bleeding."

Jangi brushed it off. He didn't have the heart to tell the queen that his injury was due to her reckless stabbing. So instead, he smiled.

"What am I missing here?" she asked.

"That was the first time you called me by my name."

The queen nodded in recognition and slapped Jangi on the shoulder. "Well, don't get used to it, General."

Injured and battered, the two limped across the lakebed. With Jangi's sprained ankle, traversing the ground was arduous, and his imposing size made it difficult for Shanaz to offer much support. The terrain was also craggy and uneven, with pathways hard to come by in the dense foliage.

Before long, the general had to stop and rest. "At this rate, we won't see the walls of Raydur for a fortnight."

For once, since their odyssey began, Shanaz didn't argue. She knew he was right.

Bedside Manners

Sarvin entered Lilya's chamber carrying a shallow basin of black paste composed of oils and cotton ash. He set it down on a side table from which he gathered a few linens and a small bowl. The alchemist turned toward the queen, who was seated and looking out to her balcony. A gentle breeze ruffled the tips of the shawl draped over her shoulders. Her posture was stiff, her body still. She was none too thrilled to see him.

"What's in the bowl over there? It stinks to high heaven."

Sarvin walked over and knelt in front of her. "It's an ointment made from the Alghuzdeh plant. I need to apply it before we continue with the ash. I apologize for the odor, but it's for your own good."

Sarvin began to dab the mixture on Lilya's wounds.

The queen cringed as he touched her face, the right side dotted with blisters from her forehead to her throat. "What about my eye? I can't see anything."

"We have to give the drops time to work. Until then, we have to wait and see."

"You mean, *you'll* wait and see."

"You can still see with your other eye, my lady."

Sarvin returned to the side table to tend to his treatments and medicinal solutions. But from his expert diagnosis, he knew any recovery of sight was unlikely.

Lilya felt a cool, soothing effect from the ointment and remained still until a tingling numbness spread through her raw layers of skin. She sighed as the pain receded and briefly considered touching her face. Instead, she rose from her chair and walked onto the balcony. With evening setting in, the stars began to emerge like fireflies suspended in flight. She observed them in their shimmering brilliance while rearranging her rusari to cover her wounds.

Since her return, Lilya had not asked to see her face or, at least in Sarvin's presence, ventured over to her full-length mirror of pressed copper and tin. Despite her injury, her mood remained unsullied. Her capacity to endure pain was a quality the alchemist had seen in her before. Yet impermeable she was not. Her fragility resided in the deeper recesses of her mind, and Sarvin knew such was the reason she had not looked upon her visage.

The alchemist was offering a small prayer to Ohrmazd when Kamran barged into his mother's quarters.

"They're back," he said, his eyes searching the room. Seeing the queen on the balcony, he rushed to her. "Mother, they got her. They've captured the princess."

Lilya closed her eyes and exhaled, a small gesture of relief, as a clatter brought her attention to the room's entrance. Afshad strode in, followed by General Baraz. With her face half hidden in the rusari, the queen turned and walked down the two steps leading into her main chamber. She moved deliberately toward Afshad and embraced him.

"You have done well, my boy," she said, whispering into his ear. "My confidence in you will only grow."

With his helm in hand, Afshad beamed with pride at his father.

Kamran returned the smile, yet felt guilt-ridden for not trusting enough in his son's capability.

General Baraz approached Lilya, his demeanor solemn. "The expedition was not flawless. Daryush fell, as did my Juju. The Princess of Raydur is most skilled with a bow."

"A loss that will not go in vain. I can assure you of that." Lilya brushed Afshad's hair away from his eyes. "And what of the others, General? I assume they've been, shall we say, properly incapacitated?"

"We took out the savaran, but General Jangi and Queen Shanaz managed to escape."

"Escape? What did they do—vanish into the aether?"

"They escaped from us. But I dare say they hardly vanished."

"I don't like riddles, Baraz."

"Brigands, my lady. During the battle, a band of Visgari, perhaps a dozen or more, came upon the scene. Faced with such numbers, and with Princess Mahzarin secured, the prince ordered a retreat."

Afshad confirmed. "It would have been too risky to give pursuit."

Lilya pulled at her arthritic fingers. Fatigued by a mix of pain and emotions, she wandered to the settee and sat down, crossing her legs and leaning on the armrest.

Afshad took a seat next to her. "I hope my prudence does not disappoint you."

Lilya kept her face lowered. Her expression was pensive but not critical.

"My lady," the general said. "The others fled on foot, with the brigands in hot pursuit. I'm confident they didn't escape—even if they somehow found the entrance to the Caverns of Fog."

"But that collapsed from an earthquake several years ago."

"Precisely my point. There was no escape."

Lilya turned her gaze to Kamran. "Bring this girl to me. Let's see if her wit is as sharp as her aim."

"She was rendered unconscious after landing."

"Feisty thing, huh?"

"But no match for the hilt of my sword," Afshad said.

Kamran chuckled. "The princess is resting in Shanaz's chamber, with royal guards standing by."

"Very well," Lilya said. "When she wakes, I want to be the first to know."

The queen settled into the nook of the settee and folded her arms around a silken pillow. She grimaced, turning her face away from her grandson.

Basking in his triumph, Afshad had momentarily forgotten his grandmother's role in the larger plan—eliminating Yaya—until her look of discomfort reminded him.

He excitedly sat up. "Madar bozorg, what about Yaya? Did you find him?"

"Indeed, I did," she said, her countenance glum.

When Lilya offered no further details, Afshad looked to his father, then around the chamber for her canine companions. "What happened? Where are the jackals?"

To her grandson's horror, Lilya pulled away her headscarf. Her right eye was translucent, with pus seeping from the socket. Blisters ran the length of her face. Where they had burst, the underlayers of dermis were red and raw.

"Your cousin is more capable than I ever gave him credit for. He seems to have befriended a large bear, the one we saw in the sulfuric pool. It killed my precious jackals. As for Shotor himself, he vomited acid onto my face. There must have been magic involved, no doubt given to him by our good friend Adarbad." Lilya's one working eye grew distant as she stared at the floor. "That man has been a bone in my throat longer than I care to remember."

Afshad held his grandmother's hand. "I will avenge you. I will kill Yaya. I promise you, whether by sword or by hand, I will end him."

Lilya wanted to smile, but the pain was too much. "I know you will."

Kamran tapped Afshad on the shoulder and motioned to the general. "Let us leave Mother to rest. In the meantime, I'll see how our guest is faring."

All alone with the queen, Sarvin readied the next application of the ashen mixture.

"Do we have to do this now?" Lilya said, yanking the rusari over her face. "I don't feel any pain at the moment."

"Your skin is in shock. I assure you the throbbing will return, and when it does—"

"Okay, okay, you're like a recurring nightmare. Hurry and be done with it."

The alchemist moved Lilya's headscarf and looked her in the eyes. His expression was sullen.

"What's the matter with you?" Lilya asked. "I was only joking."

"Do you have any regrets?"

"Regrets? About what?"

"Coming here. Becoming a queen of Zad."

"As you know, it was my father's wish… for political reasons. For me to thrive and have any semblance of a normal life, I had to not look back."

Sarvin nodded ruefully. "If only Manija had been able to do the same."

Lilya patted her alchemist's hand. "You aren't to blame for your wife's death. What afflicted her was much deeper than homesickness. And you know that."

"If you have no regrets, tell me—what do you miss most from home. There must be something."

Lilya thought for a moment. "Stomachaches."

"I beg your pardon?"

"When ripe, my brothers and I would collect basketfuls of sour cherries from the citadel gardens. After washing them, we'd sprinkle them with salt and eat until our bellies burst."

"Sounds like home."

"Maybe if you hurry and finish this treatment, I'll have the servants fetch us some. They won't be Danzardani, but they'll do."

Sarvin dutifully applied the ointment, careful not to let any get under the queen's eyelids. When he finished, an amused look crossed his face.

"What is it now?" Lilya asked.

"I was thinking about Queen Shanaz and how much she must be enjoying herself."

"What do you mean?"

"Well, being a brigand gets terribly lonely—all that roaming around. And to have a regal presence like Shanaz in their midst, I can only imagine the festive time they must be having together."

Despite the pain, Lilya couldn't help but smile, wallowing in her sadistic thoughts.

K amran walked into what used to be Shanaz's private living quarters, passing two royal guards who stood at attention.

Upon seeing the king, a couple of nurses outside the bedroom finished gathering cleaning cloths and bowls of water and hurried to the doorway.

"Not so fast," Kamran said.

The women stopped.

"Tell me. How is she?"

"She is asleep, my lord," the elder said. "We gave her an herbal sedative."

"Any serious injuries?"

"Nothing too noticeable. Besides a few bruises and minor scratches, the young lady appears to be in good condition, though I suspect she'll have a headache once she wakes."

Kamran entered the bedroom and looked at the princess, who lay on her side facing the wall. She was covered by an embroidered bedspread of floral patterns, her shoulders exposed.

The king sat in a chair at the edge of the bed and studied her, noticing the gentle rise and fall of her bosom as she breathed. He was struck by how the bronze skin of her neck met the shimmering whiteness of her collarbone and upper bosom.

Used to taking liberties, Kamran reached out to touch her.

But Mahz awoke, turning toward her trespasser with eyes fully open. "What are you doing?" she said, pulling the bedspread tightly around herself.

The king drew back into his chair. "You looked cold. I was going to pull the blanket around you."

The princess sat up and tried to get her bearings, her eyes darting around the unfamiliar room. She rubbed the side of her head, still pounding from her tussle with Afshad.

Kamran took note. "My nurses inform me that you'll endure some prolonged discomfort. It seems you suffered quite a fall."

"What am I doing here? And where are the others I was traveling with?"

Kamran leaned forward. "The others don't concern me. My only concern is you and seeing to your recovery."

"If you truly cared, you'd see to my safe return to Raydur. And I asked you a question. Where I come from, it's considered rude not to respond. So I'll ask again—where are the others?"

Kamran snorted. "I find it peculiar that here you are, in my kingdom—half-dressed, no less—yet still full of demands. Perhaps your beauty, Princess, has blinded you to the necessity of humility."

Mahz softened her tone. "Please, King Kamran. I implore you. Tell me where my people are."

"All of your escorts were killed. As for General Jangi and Queen Shanaz, by all accounts, they were taken by a band of brigands."

"I don't believe you."

"Whether you do is immaterial. Their eternal absence will confirm it."

Mahz's eyes filled with tears of rage. "My father will not rest until I'm home. You know he will come for me."

The king shrugged.

"Do you not realize that my being here against my will is an act of war?"

"Then I'll have to change your will."

Mahz watched Kamran walk around to the other side of the bed and fill a small cup with water from a golden-rimmed chalice. She debated whether to accept what appeared to be a gesture of hospitality. But instead, the king took a few sips himself and sat down on the edge of the bed.

Unnerved by his proximity, Mahz pulled her knees to her chest and wrapped her arms around her legs.

Kamran ran a finger down the princess's cheek. "I do know your father will come for you. If you were my daughter... let's just say I wouldn't hesitate to come. But I doubt my kingdom has anything to worry about."

"You underestimate my father."

Kamran rose from the bedside and tossed Mahzarin the linen dress and shawl that servants had laid out. "Put these on and meet me on the balcony."

The princess dressed behind a folding screen and joined the king near a stone-pillared balustrade. From the perch, she could see a caravan of wagons beyond Zad's western wall, many loaded with iron-hooped casks affixed to wooden chocks. Elephants imported from the eastern lands, fitted with leather and chain breeching, were harnessed to long traces attached to the wagons. Around their flanks, cavalry escorts busied themselves assembling.

"What is the meaning of this?" Mahz asked, her hands atop the railing. "Regarding water and food, we made it clear where we stand."

"Where *you* stand, Princess, is more relevant to how this unfolds. You should also know we're assembling the full arsenal of Zadian forces. To be blunt, my kingdom is running out of food and water. Given the historical ties between our peoples, we had hoped Raydur would offer aid. But as in any relationship, the give and take between kingdoms is rarely equal. In our case, we gave, and you took."

"What Zad suffers afflicts all kingdoms. It's unfair of you to accuse my father of unreasonableness."

"When the survival of my people is at stake, I have little interest in being even-handed. Why do you think we spared your life in the river valley?"

The princess pondered his words, turning over the possibilities—until it hit her. "I'm the ransom... to ensure my father complies."

"Well done. You are intelligent as well as beautiful. Perhaps I should consider making you my wife. After all, I am a widower."

Kamran's admission stunned Mahzarin. She had spoken with Vira at the rain festival and had always been fond of the late queen. Vira's youthful temperament had put her at ease during such gatherings, and in recent years, the princess often found herself seeking her company.

"It saddens me to hear that. May I ask how the queen died?"

Unnerved by the request, Kamran turned to leave—but hesitated. He clasped his hands behind his back, his head drooped. "There was an accident in the temple. Her gown caught fire. By the time anyone reached her, it was too late."

The hint of sadness in Kamran's voice led Mahz to believe his description of events. Yet, having learned from Shanaz and Adarbad the extent to which he had laid waste to his own family, the idea of the new king murdering his wife no longer seemed far-fetched.

Kamran turned around and surveyed the princess, who was still facing the western plain. Through the fabric of her dress, his eyes assessed the contours of her body. "You haven't responded to my offer."

"I would rather lie with carrion than take your hand in marriage. Surely, your late wife's death was less painful than the life she suffered with you."

Stung by the words, Kamran stepped forward, wrapped his arms around the princess, and rested his chin on her shoulder.

Mahz struggled in vain. "Let go of me."

Kamran pressed against her. "There's more to me than meets the eye, Princess. If you'd only give us a chance, I'm sure you would find my charms irresistible."

He released her and stepped back, spreading his arms with a smug grin.

Without thinking twice, Mahz swung around and slapped him.

Kamran rubbed his cheek, a gleam in his eye. "Now you're playing my kind of game. I, too, like it rough."

The king yanked the princess close, pressing his chest against her bosom. He forced her backward until her heels bumped against a vase of withering desert marigolds under the balustrade. "You will either fall or learn to embrace me."

Mahz glanced down at the stone-paved walkway some thirty feet below. Several marigold petals drifted in the air. Against Kamran's weight, she knew her hold on the railing wouldn't last long. When Kamran's tongue began to explore her neck—a vile sensation of wetness and whiskers—she recoiled, her fingers slipping. Just as she was about to fall, she screamed and wrapped her arms around his neck.

Kamran swung the princess around and set her down away from the balustrade. He appeared amused by his antics.

Having succeeded once already, Mahz tried to slap the king again.

This time, he caught her wrist and bent it sharply, forcing her to her knees in pain.

"You need to work on your manners, young lady. You're dealing with the King of Zad. I suggest you get some sleep to cool your temper and clear the bags under your eyes."

Kamran pushed the princess to the floor and headed for the chamber. Before reaching the archway, he stopped. "I have business to attend to. When I return, you'd better be in a more amenable disposition. Have I made myself—"

"What's going on?" Lilya stepped onto the balcony, the undraped half of her face barely visible in shadow.

Kamran moved toward her. "Mother, it's good to see you up and about. I was tending to Princess Mahzarin's needs."

"With her on the ground, one would suspect your bedside manners." Seeing that her son was fidgety and most likely guilty of the charge levied, Lilya provided him a way out. "Why don't you check on the status of the caravan? I want a few words with our guest."

After her son left, Lilya strolled over to where the princess lay. "Are you a dog or something? Get up."

As Mahz brought herself to her feet, Lilya looked her over, her face hard and unforgiving. Her good eye seemed void of compassion, almost reptilian in its coldness. Her blistered skin was visible at the edge of the rusari, prompting the princess to look away.

"There was an accident with my alchemist. It's nothing the body can't heal."

"Of course."

Lilya walked to the balustrade and observed the preparations in the distant fields. "I assume my son has informed you why you were brought here?"

"My father won't give in to blackmail. I can assure you of that."

Lilya sneered and turned back toward the princess. "Oh, he'll give in. Trust me. When he sees what might happen to you if he doesn't, he'll be more than ready to change his mind." The queen looked to the sky as if searching for something. "I can still hear their screams of mercy."

"Whose screams?"

"The fates of two Samjari spies. You know, I almost think the elephant enjoyed it—the sense of power when their skulls cracked open."

It then dawned on Mahzarin what Lilya was alluding to. She found herself beginning to tremble. "We outlawed such forms of execution before I was even born. It was understood that such practices had ceased in Zad as well."

"They've been reinstated. A society gets nowhere being soft on criminals, not to mention the cost of caring for prisoners. That's a luxury we don't have. There is a small problem, however."

"From my vantage point, it looks like a rather *large* one."

Lilya forced a slight grin. "It's good you can keep your sense of humor, Princess. But I'm referring to the fact that your father has no idea we even have you—such was the success of our raid. With no survivors to report to Raydur, sending word falls on me." She stepped closer. "Tomorrow morning, the caravan departs. Two days later, we'll join it at your city gates. I have no doubt your father will be relieved to see you... despite the lost sheen of innocence."

"Everyone here speaks in riddles. Say what you mean."

Lilya's temper flared at the rebuke. "Perhaps a night without food will help clarify my speech."

"Are you mad?"

Lilya stormed up to Mahz and seized her chin. "You'd better watch your mouth, young lady. The last thing you ever want to see is me mad."

"But I've not eaten all day."

"Then consider yourself fortunate to be alive." Lilya shoved Mahz's face aside and headed for the chamber. "You'll get food the night before we leave. I suggest you sleep away the time."

Mahzarin stood still until she heard Lilya's faint voice address the guards. She returned to the bedroom and sat on the edge of the bed, legs crossed. A lone tear fell down her cheek as her thoughts turned toward her father.

"Save me, Pedar. Save me."

Under Wedlock and Key

King Delawar signaled to his escort of two dozen savaran to slow their pace. Though the morning sun had not yet breached the horizon, a dust cloud was visible on the outskirts of Zad. The cavalry, among them Jangi's subordinate, General Hemog, had reached the Rud-e Barik bridge. They narrowed their formation and filed in behind their leader, the Rayduri king unsure what to make of the aberration.

"What do you do you think it is?" Hemog asked. "It's not windy enough to create a haboob."

Delawar glanced north toward Zad's burial pit. Above the dakhmeh, the usual patrons had already convened in the hopes of a chance morsel. With their wings stretched out and the color of their feathers dulled by the dim light, the buzzards looked like circling shamshirs descending for the scraps below.

"We're about to find out," he said. "Keep the flags held high. With suspicions between our kingdoms at a fever pitch, I don't want our presence to be misconstrued as adversarial."

When the clap-clap of hooves crossing the bridge had ended, the savaran thundered on. Soon the contours of the Zadian citadel and watchtower came into view, including the source of the dust cloud.

Delawar brought the riders to a halt. In the distance, they saw the faint vanguard of a caravan: wagons and elephants, trudging in their direction, a desert swirl of sand trailing behind.

"My lord," Hemog said. "It seems your strategy to bide time has been preempted. What do plan to do?"

Delawar shook his head. "This makes no sense. Zad knows I won't provide supplies. Our talks broke down because of it."

To Hemog, there was only one possible explanation. "The caravan represents the 'end.' The 'means' will be the Zadian forces that follow. It would be folly to organize and send something as logistically challenging as a caravan without the implicit threat of force."

"As usual, you're astute."

Hemog looked at his king, the old man's profile etched with worry. "My lord, how much time do the alchemists need to finish work on the griffins?"

"Farzan says days, not weeks."

"My knowledge of alchemy is limited, so forgive me if this question is steeped in ignorance. But what is their contingency plan if the Great Plains of *Namak* fail to provide what they need? And how long before they return to Raydur?"

"A couple of days at most. We need at least a week, Hemog." As if seeking solace from Ohrmazd, Delawar gazed into the orange hue of the morning sky. "This new sorcery of Zad unsettles me." The king sighed and looked at his general. "Regarding your other question—there is no contingency. With war, as with life, you must sometimes get on with it."

"Our archers are the finest in the land," Hemog said, trying to lift his king's spirits. "And when Princess Mahzarin and General

Jangi return with guarantees from Jarak, we'll be more than ready."

Delawar acknowledged the compliment but reserved his doubts about reinforcements from Jarak, given that kingdom's long-standing aversion to foreign entanglements.

The group rode on. As the full extent of the caravan became clear, Delawar counted at least a dozen wagons. Most were drays bearing water casks secured to chock blocks, while the rest were box wagons designed to hold grains.

Angered by what he deemed brashly unreasonable, the king's mood turned grim as his savaran passed row upon row of armaments and siege engines. Zadian soldiers loaded stones and gathered iron bolts for the ballistae. They adjusted the tension of the torsion springs. Others rigged makeshift reins onto the battering rams to accommodate the many horses needed to pull them.

Delawar no longer harbored doubts about Zad's intent: all-out war and the destruction of his kingdom.

———◆———

A saddled General Baraz happened to see the Rayduri savaran being escorted into the citadel stables. Despite the lethargy in his limbs, he swiftly dismounted and barreled through double doors. He sprinted down the corridor until he reached the council chamber. Stumbling and nearly breathless, he caught himself on the doorway's frame and peered inside. King Kamran, Afshad, and a few advisors stood around a large table.

"Thought you were heading to the fields," Kamran said. "Forget your supply ledgers?"

"My lord," Baraz said. "We have unexpected visitors."

"I'm a little busy. You deal with them." The king and his staff refocused their attention on a replica of Raydur and the surrounding landscape. He pointed to a berm near the southeastern wall. "If need be, we'll pull the infantry back to this area. It should be out of their archers' range—"

"It's King Delawar."

Kamran stood up straight, his face anxious. "I guess it's never too early for late entreaties." He placed a hand on Afshad's arm. "Fetch your madar bozorg. She should be finishing her morning treatment."

As Afshad hurried down the corridor toward the royal residence, Kamran moved to his throne and began to ponder the unwelcome intrusion. He had barely settled in when the pushtigban salar entered to announce the arrival of the King of Raydur.

Kamran motioned to Dadgar to bring in the visitors. Moments later, he returned with two guards, who took their posts on either side of the doorway and placed their spears across their chests. In walked King Delawar, followed by Hemog.

"Greetings, King Kamran. I hope I've found you in good health and heart."

"Indeed, you have. I've never felt better—nor more optimistic about the future."

"By all accounts, your activity on the fields suggests everything but optimism."

"Just the opposite, old friend. Now tell me, what do I owe the honor of your unexpected visit? At our last meeting, you had the temerity to rebuff our most reasonable offer. Is it possible you've had a change of heart?"

Lilya, already on her way to the strategy session, entered the chamber. She brushed past the unheralded visitors, ignoring their attempts at courtesy.

"Mother, we have guests." The tension in Kamran's body eased.

"It's a little early to call on people, isn't it, King of Raydur?" Lilya sat beside Kamran, carefully arranging the rusari to partially conceal her face.

"A pleasure to see you, too." Delawar pondered the perversion of the queen sitting on the throne beside her son. "Has the good lady developed a sudden aversion to light? Such a radiant smile as you possess should be celebrated, not tucked behind silken veils."

"Your attempts at flattery, Delawar, unnerve me."

"They are as sincere as the reason for our visit."

"And what might that be?"

"After considering the initial terms of your offer, and weighing them against the accord that has long bound our peoples, it would be nothing short of an abrogation of neighborliness not to come to Zad's aid, especially during its darkest hour. As we speak, a Rayduri caravan is in the final stages of being loaded with water and food rations to last your people at least a month. If the drought persists, this extension of our hand should see you through."

"That is most kind of you, Delawar. How soon will the caravan arrive?"

"Ten days."

"You said the caravan is nearly ready. If that's true, it could be here in a week."

"Such an undertaking carries logistical challenges, my lady. Surely, your people can manage a few more days."

Kamran was losing patience. "Few of our people have been spared the stitches in their necks from staring at the sky for clouds. Your caravan won't just arrive within a week, stocked to the hilt—you'll also be filling ours. You couldn't have missed it when you arrived."

"But that's impossible... and unnecessary. What am I to feed my people? Prayers can fill an empty soul, but they do little for empty stomachs."

Before Kamran could answer, Lilya placed her hand on his wrist. "I think we can bend a little to your will, Delawar. We will allow you a fortnight before sending the second caravan. That should be ample time to restock your supplies. And who knows, by then, the rains may return."

Delawar scratched his chin. "I need a moment to think this over."

"By all means, take your time. I know all too well that running a kingdom is often choosing between equally bad options."

"I would welcome a dilemma, but it seems I have only one choice. Allow me to consult with my men in the corridor."

"Of course, we are in no hurry. But before you step out, Delawar, I was wondering about your precocious daughter. How's Princess Mahzarin doing these days? It must be hard to lose a mother so young—even more so if the bonds run deep."

"She's doing quite well, thank you. She's a remarkable young woman with an enduring faith. I do not doubt that, in time, she'll overcome her grief."

"That she is remarkable, I agree. But whether she has the time to overcome her grief remains to be seen."

"What on earth are you speaking about?"

Afshad escorted a shackled Princess Mahzarin into the council chamber. Her cheeks were pale from a lack of food and water. Dark sunken eyes from a lack of sleep stared out beneath frizzy braided hair. The linen dress she wore, torn at the shoulder by the molester who sat before her, barely clung to her body.

So shocked was Delawar that he unwittingly brought a hand to his contracting chest. He rushed toward his daughter, only to be thwarted by the guards who crossed their weapons in his path. "Let me through, you barbarians." He attempted to pass again but the guards forced him back into Hemog's arms.

Mahz pleaded with her father. "Please, don't aggravate the situation."

Emboldened by the turn of events, Kamran grew more brash. "Your daughter speaks wisely, King Delawar. You would do well to heed her advice."

Delawar looked achingly at Mahzarin, his arms outstretched in disbelief. His paternal instinct was to wrap her in a protective embrace. "How did this happen?"

"We were ambushed by manticores." In her mind's eye, she returned to the battle, a sense of shame overcoming her. "I'm sorry, Pedar. They overpowered us. At some point, I was thrown from my horse."

"And what of the others?"

"Our savaran were killed. As for General Jangi and Queen Shanaz, I've been told they were captured by brigands." Mahz looked at Kamran in disgust. "But why should I trust what I hear in this place?"

Lilya called upon Afshad to escort the princess to the thrones.

With short steps, Mahz dragged the slack of the heavy chain over the floor. The clamps pressed against her rubbed-raw skin as she stepped onto the dais. The pain was excruciating. But for her father's sake, she remained expressionless, her pride forbidding even the slightest whimper.

Lilya took notice, recognizing a quality she held in esteem within herself. She turned to the visiting king. "You said you wanted a dilemma, Delawar? Well, you have one."

Delawar's shock gave way to rage. "Get to the point. Enough with the crooked insinuations."

Lilya scoffed at his futile demands. "My, my, what a temper we have." She tugged on Mahz's elbow, turning her around toward the room. "Very well, here's the deal: unless the caravans arrive exactly as we discussed, your lovely daughter will be executed. But if you find it in yourself to see they arrive on schedule, then well, her life will be spared."

Delawar glanced at his daughter's swollen ankles. He studied her face, her eyes on the verge of tears. His heart sank. "How have they been treating you, *khoshgele*?"

Fearful to speak honestly, Mahz demurred and looked down at the floor.

Delawar turned his searing gaze upon the thrones. "I need no time to decide. The last thing I'll do is abandon my daughter to this house of horrors. You'll get your caravans on time. But I have a demand of my own."

"For someone in a position I do not envy," Kamran said, "you certainly have no shortage of demands. By all means, spare us the suspense."

"That you treat my daughter with the respect and hospitality befitting her status."

Kamran smiled at Mahzarin. "But of course. In fact, I'll personally see to her well-being."

"Then we're through here. You'll have your caravan in a fortnight, and I'll have my daughter. You'll forgive us for not staying for the requisite emissary banquet, but my men and I have work to do."

The king brought his right hand over his chest, a gesture of encouragement to Mahz, then made for the doorway, Hemog close behind.

"Oh, Delawar," Lilya said. "There seems to be a slight misunderstanding."

The king turned around. "And what is that?"

"When I said we would spare your daughter's life, I was speaking strictly of that—provided the caravans arrive. I said nothing about setting her free."

"Your villainy knows no limits."

Lilya dismissed the accusation with a wave as she rose beside Mahzarin. "I don't necessarily agree with your characterization. There are no villains here, only opportunities. And I have a knack for seizing them. In the realm of politics, your aspersion is ill-conceived. Perhaps I held you in too high a regard, for I never took you for such a naïf."

Delawar stood listlessly, like a man who had wandered for days on foot through the Dasht-e Marg. "There's no reason for you to keep my daughter. Not a week has passed since you came to my kingdom to request food and water—and now you'll have it." The king's expression became forlorn. "In the name of Ohrmazd, show me the grace of setting Mahzarin free. Her place is in Raydur, among those who love her. I beg you."

"You grovel like a castrated dog. I preferred you better when you had a spine." Lilya squeezed the princess's hand. "Your request is denied. Besides, Mahzarin has grown on us, especially my son, who, as you know, is a king without a queen."

Kamran stood and put his arm around Mahz's waist. "How do we look?" he asked, beaming at Delawar. "Is this not the image of a perfect family?"

"Take your vile hands off my daughter, or I swear—"

"You'll swear what?" Kamran stepped down from the dais and sauntered arrogantly toward Delawar. "Was that a threat, King of Raydur?"

"Touch my daughter, and you'll never see a desert moon again. It's not a threat. It's a promise."

Kamran snickered. "If you want us to spare your daughter's life, I suggest you listen carefully. In one week, your caravan will arrive in Zad filled with water and rations. In a fortnight, our caravan will return, stocked as well. As added incentive, our forces will depart tomorrow and take position outside Raydur's walls. Any delay, either way, and you'll receive the full fury of Zad.

"On the eve of our caravan's return, your daughter and I will wed. Rest assured, I'll see that you have a good seat. After all, I will be your *damad*. And to prove I intend to be a good one, I give you my word that I won't touch the princess until the night of our nuptials. I know it may not appear as such, but I'm a man who holds fast to tradition." Kamran placed a hand on Delawar's shoulder. "Anyway, I want it to be a night she never forgets."

Delawar's knees nearly buckled at the thought. He was too stunned by the dilemma to utter any words.

Mahz intervened. "Pedar, listen to me. You must do what's best for Raydur. Do as they say. Save our people. You can't make this decision with only me in mind."

Delawar wrestled with his options. The drought was real, and potentially unyielding, and by agreeing to send two caravans of supplies, he would all but ensure the death of a certain number of his people. On the other hand, a head-to-head battle with Zad, even from a defensive posture, would be futile without a counterforce to the manticores. Slaughter and enslavement would come quickly.

The King of Raydur briefly regarded the replica of his kingdom used for Zad's war-gaming. But his thoughts came back to his daughter. As she stood before him, a flood of images retuned: her radiant smile, his late wife singing her to sleep, Farzan setting her broken finger, a tantrum in the fire temple, riding horses together, the day she received her first bow.

Kamran extended his hand. "Do we have a deal?"

Delawar reached out but hesitated. "Wait. I have one simple request."

"You must be kidding."

"I'd like a word in private—with your mother."

"Make it fast," Lilya said, "or you'll have to contend with my grumbling stomach." The queen shooed Mahz toward the doorway. "You go over there to your future husband."

As the princess shuffled across the floor, she stopped before her father. King Delawar embraced her and tenderly kissed her forehead.

Lilya's foot tapped on the floor. "Come, come. My time is precious. Let's get on with it."

Delawar stepped onto the dais. After a brief conversation, Lilya motioned to her son to join them.

Mahz tried to ascertain the nature of the discussion by their expressions, but only Kamran showed any hint of emotion—a slight annoyance and doubt at the Rayduri king's last-minute proposal.

In the end, Kamran and Lilya extended their hands. Delawar shook them, sealing his daughter's fate.

THE GREAT PLAINS OF NAMAK

Farzan had had it with Adarbad's choice of packhorse dropping their equipment. "Ada, this is the third time he's been spooked. First wild pigs, then a fox, and now pheasants flapping in the brush. We already lost one of my trowels."

"You have another."

"It was my oldest one." Farzan motioned toward the jittery horse. "He's all yours this time. And while you're at it, don't miss the chance to nudge him over that ledge."

"Don't be silly," Adarbad said. "Prepare to be dazzled by my natural affinity with animals."

The Zadian alchemist dismounted and crept toward the wayward gelding, the frightened steed standing next to a crevice.

The horse stomped and whinnied.

"Easy, boy," Adarbad said, slightly crouching.

The horse scooted back to the edge, its hooves kicking loose rock into the chasm below.

Adarbad extended his open hand. He and the horse locked eyes. "That's a good boy. You can trust me."

But as he reached for the reins, the horse jerked its head away, snorted, and casually trotted past the alchemist.

Farzan burst into laughter. "Affinity with animals, my foot."

"No offense, Ruh," Adarbad said, "but we'd have been better off with a mule. It's a good thing you're Yaya's horse; otherwise, I might have heeded Farzan's advice."

The alchemist retrieved a waterskin from the ground and remounted. Soon, the men and their horses headed down a deer path slicing through the undergrowth.

At times, they lost their way. Arguments ensued over which markings were hoof prints, as if the alchemists, learned though they were, had become experts in tracking. But humility rarely found safe harbor in their minds when it came to any endeavor. Both were leaders in their respective fields and resident know-it-alls. And when two of the same species argue, no one is ever wrong.

The alchemists and their horses meandered up and down hills, over fallen trees, and through dense brush. Often, they had to backtrack to find where they had gone off the path. The routine grew tiresome, and progress was slow.

To break the frustration and stop the bickering, Adarbad began to sing:

Copper and Tin,
How've you been?
Get together and have some kin.
Alloy, loy, loy, Alloy, loy, loy,
You can't break the bonds of my son, Bronze.
Copper and Zinc,
What do you think?
That's too much haoma for you to drink.

Alloy, loy, loy, Alloy, loy, loy,
You're such a pretty lass. We'll call you Brass.
Carbon and iron,
It's your turn,
Fire the smelter; watch it burn.
Alloy, loy, loy, Alloy, loy, loy,
Let's seal the deal with another son, Steel.

Ruh snorted and tugged on his tow rope.

"What's the matter?" Adarbad asked. "Don't like my singing? That goes for you and Queen Lilya. She couldn't stand to hear me croon, especially early in the morning. Said it made her hair stand on end."

For a few miles, Adarbad treated his companion to a litany of self-composed metallurgical melodies.

Farzan feigned exasperation, but he rather appreciated the catchy tunes, which were a homage to his profession.

As Adarbad sang a dirge about silver and gold, the path disappeared along with the tall oaks and grassy understory of broombush. The soil took on a more arid composition. Few grasses grew, and the travelers found themselves winding through a grove of tamarind trees.

On the other side, still at a considerable elevation, the alchemists came upon a vast expanse of salt, dappled with large clusters of rocks and shrubs. They looked like islands rising from a sea of white.

"Behold," Farzan said. "The Great Plains of Namak."

Adarbad marveled at the landscape, including the jagged peaks of the distant mountain range. "That tall one must be *Kuh-e Sang*. How far away is it?"

"King Delawar told me that once we see Kuh-e Sang, we're halfway between the mountain and Zad."

As the riders descended, the slope of the massif grew steeper. The trees vanished, giving way to reddish-brown soil covered in shrubs and sporadic cacti.

To contend with the severe incline, the horses moved in serpentine fashion. Near the bottom, the soil faded to white as salt replaced dirt.

"We'll need to dig farther out," Adarbad said. "It's unlikely we'll find lithium-infused brine on the edge of the flats. That's been my experience excavating for minerals north of Zad, beyond the yardangs. Besides, the horses could use something to eat. They can feed on the cacti fruits of one of those rock islands."

"Then let's hurry. We don't have much light left."

Despite Farzan's plea, the horses could barely muster the energy or will to trot through the ripples of heat rising off the flats. Soon, their mouths began to froth and drip with strings of saliva. The soaring temperatures were such that even the outcropping's shadow, once they had arrived, provided no more than a slight reprieve.

The alchemists dismounted and led the animals to the cacti. Determined to get his fill, Ruh staked out a succulent patch and nudged the two other trespassers away with his muzzle.

While the horses fed on the desert fruits, the men busied themselves with shovels and spades, digging until they were waist-deep in the earth.

Adarbad was the first to relent. He took a few swigs of rose water from his water skin and leaned wearily on his tools.

For his part, Farzan pulled a bundle of naan from his satchel and unfolded the cloth around it.

Adarbad's eyes widened. "If you ever get the urge to fly the coop, do me a favor and let me know. I'll show Parendi the appreciation she deserves."

As they nibbled on the bread, Farzan looked pensive.

"What's on your mind?" Adarbad asked. "You've never seen someone eat naan before?"

"No, no, I was just wondering why, in all your years, you never married. I know it's not because you don't fancy women. I've seen how you look at the fairer sex. I don't know, the way you joked about my wife made me wonder."

Adarbad tossed the last bite into his mouth and rubbed the crumbs from his hands. "I love my work, Farzan. And serving King Khavar was an honor I didn't take lightly. The demands of the job left no room for matrimony."

"I managed."

"That's because your life reflects your balanced nature. I'm anything but balanced—you know that. Besides, I'm not husband material. I'm untidy. I drink too much. No woman in her right mind would put up with me."

"Don't be absurd. Many men think the same before marriage, but they adapt."

Adarbad resumed his digging. "Well, I don't want to adapt. I don't want any part of marriage, and I'm selfish enough to admit it."

"I don't believe that. I've known you for years, and I've seen your heart. You have your faults, to be sure. You're stubborn like Prince Yaya's horse and sometimes a little secretive, especially with alchemy. But one thing you're not is selfish."

Adarbad wiped the sweat from his brow and peered at his friend. "Of all the times to be prying into my business."

"There's nothing like being waist-deep in salt, tools in hand, and searching for brine to bind men together."

"Be careful what you wish for."

Adarbad glanced at Farzan, who had returned to the task at hand with renewed focus. Had it not been for the circumstances—stuck in the desert under the cloud of war—he might have continued to guard his privacy. But, alas, his visions told him otherwise, and he understood the distance he had kept between himself and Farzan was getting in the way of their friendship.

"There was one."

Farzan stopped digging, bemused by the sudden disclosure.

"It was long before I knew you. In fact, I hadn't even started working for the king. How's that for being secretive?"

"Well, what happened?"

"Nothing," Adarbad said matter-of-factly. "She got married. My window shut, and that was it. I'm not interested anymore."

"Do you know who she married?"

"Know him? I knew him very well. She married the king."

Adarbad's shovel sliced through the salt. In the breach, a slushy, sea-smelling mixture percolated to the surface. "There's the brine."

The alchemists chipped away to widen the opening and began filling the bags with the lithium and salt mixture. By the time they loaded them onto the horses, twilight had set in. The thought of spending the night on the outcropping was tempting, but both men agreed they had better get going. Their horses were ready, having rested and eaten during the excavation. So even saddled with the extra brine, they crossed the salt flats with renewed vigor.

Farzan looked over at Adarbad and realized that his friend's daily proximity to Queen Shanaz must have been wearing on him in both spirit and body. It certainly explained his heavy drinking and lengthy absences from Zad, ostensibly for alchemical research. That he had remained King Khavar's alchemist all these years, despite his suffering, meant only one thing: Farzan understood that his friend still loved.

The alchemists returned to Raydur late the following evening. They dismounted in front of Farzan's house and began unloading the bags of brine.

Hearing the commotion, Parendi came outside. "Did you find what you needed?" she whispered, careful not to add to the bustle and risk waking Nilu.

Adarbad lifted two full bags for her to see.

"It's going to be a long night," Farzan said, hugging his wife. "We have to get right to work. I want to show the king the fruits of our labor by the time he returns."

"How is Queen Shanaz?" Adarbad asked. "Any word of their mission to Jarak?"

"I haven't seen hide nor hair of the queen."

"What about General Jangi or the princess?" Farzan asked.

Parendi opened her hands and shrugged.

"Well, that doesn't make any sense. They should have returned by now."

Adarbad set down the bags and hurried down the street toward the citadel gatehouse. In the manner accustomed to men his age, his shuffling limbs appeared to move much faster than they were. Eventually, he passed under the portcullis, crossed through a flower garden with hewn stone paths, and arrived at a large house reserved for foreign dignitaries.

Two sentries stood by the arched entrance. Adarbad climbed up a few stairs, his lungs heaving like bellows. "Queen Shanaz, is she here?"

The guards, at first unnerved by the intrusion, retracted their spears once they recognized Farzan trailing behind. "As far as we know," one said, "she hasn't returned from Jarak."

"But it's been several days. You must be mistaken."

The alchemist passed between the guards and ran down a torch-lit corridor toward Shanaz's chamber. He pounded on the door, waiting briefly for an answer. When no reply came, he opened the door and entered. The furniture was faintly visible in the moonlight. The queen's bed lay under silken drapes billowing in the warm breeze. It was empty and still made.

Farzan appeared in the doorway behind him. "I asked the guards about General Jangi and Princess Mahzarin. They haven't seen them either."

"This is not good. They should have returned yesterday at the very latest. Could it be that they were held up in Jarak?"

"Unlikely. The mission was urgent. General Jangi had direct orders from the king. He wouldn't have permitted any delay."

Adarbad's mood shifted from anxious to hopeless. "First, Yaya... and now Shanaz. I knew I should've gone with her."

"And what would that have accomplished? Then *you'd* be missing, too. I know this pains you, but we can only control what we can. And right now, that means getting into my laboratory and getting to work."

Adarbad began shaking his head. "She won't fall for it. She's not going to fall for it."

Farzan frowned. "What are you talking about?"

"King Delawar's ruse with the caravan. I've known Lilya for a long time, and I promise you, she has something up her sleeve. Everything is falling apart." Adarbad's eyes looked dazed and distant. "She won't fall for it. She won't—"

Farzan gripped his friend by the shoulders. "Ada, listen to me. You cannot give in to despair. Your people need you. Queen Shanaz, Prince Yaya—all of Zad depends on you. So snap out of it."

Like a reprimanded child, Adarbad followed Farzan out of the dignitary residence. For most of the way, his head hung low in contemplation, his feet dragging in the dirt. By the time he had arrived at the alley entrance to the laboratory, Farzan was already preparing the experiments.

Adarbad moped through the orderly space and leaned against a table near the cubbies of alphabetized minerals.

Noting that his friend needed direction, Farzan told him to get the brine Parendi had placed on the garden terrace. Meanwhile, he busied himself arranging cultures of eagle and feline cells in shallow bronze basins on the floor.

"Ada? What's taking so long?" Farzan stood and took notice of his friend. "What's the matter with you?"

Adarbad lingered just outside the doorway, his profile frozen as he held two bags of brine. "He's back."

"Who? The king?"

"No, your prized falcon. Didn't he have reddish-brown feathers on his head?"

Farzan brushed past him and rushed to his bird cages. Sure enough, through an open door and perched on a scaffolding of twine and sticks was Minoo. The bird stalked about, pecking at the sticks as if to remind his owner of his feeding duties. The leather pouch that carried Yaya's cargo dangled from his neck.

Farzan removed it, loosened the drawstring, and reached inside. "The amulet... it's gone."

Adarbad walked toward him. "That doesn't mean anything. It could have fallen out."

Farzan pulled out a small piece of wood.

"What's that?" Adarbad asked, setting the brine on the ground.

Farzan studied it briefly, then handed it over with a smile.

Adarbad saw some etching that read, "ɥo." Baffled, he looked at his friend and scratched his head. "I don't understand."

"It's upside down, genius."

The alchemist realized the meaning of the message as Farzan finished speaking, and it was all he could do to fight back tears.

Farzan placed a hand on Adarbad's shoulder. "Tonight, hope is still alive. Yaya is alive. And as long as he's still fighting, we must as well."

Adarbad pocketed the piece of wood and picked up the bags. "You're right, my friend. Let's get to work."

The alchemists returned to the lab and assembled several large terracotta pots housing copper cylinders and iron rods. Copper wires attached to the vessels ran into the basins and connected to the nickel cases of the cellular cultures. They began filling the basins with the brine mixture, whose elements would insulate and preserve the specimens as they underwent transformative hybridization. To one trial pot, they added vinegar, whose acidic properties would initiate the electrolysis process.

After checking to ensure all liquids were at the requisite levels, Farzan shook his head in doubt. "I don't see how you generate the necessary heat without damaging the cells."

"You have to get the heat out of the way," Adarbad said, heading to a table to retrieve a bowl containing white powder with blue hues. He brought it over along with several thin, malleable tubes.

"What's in the bowl?" Farzan asked.

"Alabaster."

"And the blue?"

"I've added a little cobalt and salt byproduct to help. And don't ask me how much because I don't remember."

Adarbad handed Farzan some of the tubes, which they duly connected to the cases.

As the alchemists waited for the brine to boil, Parendi brought a platter of rice and lentils, along with some tea. More anxious than they otherwise would have been, the men ate hurriedly. However, before they had a chance to taste the tea, the brine began to simmer.

Adarbad walked over to the bowl of powder and added water to make it soluble. He knelt by the basin and held the cup to the tube. "When I give the word, take out the case and set it on the ground." He handed Farzan a large pair of metal tongs. "You have to be fast."

"Then what?"

"Get out of the way. If all goes to plan, an embryo will become an adult faster than the blink of an eye."

Farzan gulped. "I sure hope you know what you're doing."

"Do I ever? Anyway, here we go. The brine is boiling." Adarbad noticed that the casing around the cellular culture was expanding from the heat. "Steady... steady. Get ready, Farzan." He poured the dihydrate down the tube. "Now."

Farzan retrieved the casing using the oversized tongs and set it on the floor. The lid popped off, and a yellow mucus frothed over the brim. It poured forth, leaving nothing but a large, viscous puddle on the floor.

The experiment had failed.

Farzan looked at Adarbad who was on his knees with his arms folded. "What do you think happened?"

"Let's review the process from the start. By the way, how many cultures do we have?"

"I don't know... two and a half, maybe three dozen."

Adarbad stood, walked over to the table, and took a few sips of his tepid tea. "I have a feeling this will be a long night."

TIT FOR TAT

Throughout the night and well into the morning, the alchemists had tried but failed to create a griffin. They re-tied tubes, re-measured liquids, substituted powders, and changed their execution of each step in the process. Even Adarbad, a lapsed follower of his faith, found himself asking Ohrmazd for guidance.

By midday, both men were exhausted and cranky.

Parendi came to the laboratory to see if they wanted lunch—roasted meat and rice—but Adarbad, much to her surprise, declined.

Farzan thought differently. "If you don't mind, Ada, I'm famished."

"No, no, go ahead. I'm going to tinker a bit."

As Farzan headed outside into the garden terrace, Adarbad walked over to a basin and removed the casing containing the cellular culture. He ran his finger around the seams, then opened and closed the lid.

"Too much heat is escaping," he speculated to himself. "That has to be it."

The alchemist went to his colleagues's orderly supply cabinets and measured out quantities of silk filaments, ground animal bone, and pine sap. After collecting them onto a tray, he returned to the table and mixed the ingredients into a gooey, gelatinous substance which he proceeded to rub along the seams of the casing. Once applied, the caulking solidified almost instantly.

"That should do it."

He had placed the case back in the basin when Farzan returned with a plate of raisin and saffron cookies, one of which he was already chewing.

"Feel better?" Adarbad asked.

"MmHmm." Farzan set the plate down. "Have you figured anything out?"

"We'll know soon enough. Go ahead and add the vinegar to the pot. I'll get ready with the dihydrate."

The briny mixture came to a high simmer. As both men nestled closer to the basin, they exchanges glances filled with renewed optimism.

Soon the cellular culture began to roil in the bubbling brine. It was time. Like they had done on twelve previous attempts, Adarbad poured the dihydrate into the tube while Farzan retrieved the casing with the tongs and placed it on the floor. The lid popped open, spewing a cloud of mist that evaporated almost instantly from the intense heat.

In some ways, the alchemists had grown accustomed to failure, having seen their repeated efforts thwarted at every turn. But this time, they were in luck.

There before them, dripping with solution, stood a creature that was half eagle, half lion. It extended its wings and clawed at the wet floor with its talons.

So triumphant were the alchemists, they let out blithe-some whoops and embraced, exchanging the obligatory pats on the back for a job well done. After composing themselves, they gazed in wonder at their creation.

Ever so slowly, Adarbad stepped toward the animal, his hand extended. As his fingers made contact, he half expected the griffin to nip at him or, at the very least, shy away. But unlike Ruh on their way to the salt flats, this creature was amenable to the alchemist's advance.

He caressed the moist white feathers around the griffin's head, letting his hand explore the bony frame of the wings. The front half was all eagle. Beyond the shoulders, the body and hind legs were that of a lion, tail included.

In response to his ministrations, the griffin nudged the alchemist with its beak and let out an ear-splitting screech, a clear indication that it was hungry.

Both men covered their ears and burst into laughter, their joy becoming jubilation. Despite its accelerated gestation, the griffin looked healthy.

Farzan pointed to the plate of cookies on the table. "Well, go ahead, *Madar*. He's your baby."

And with those orders, Adarbad did his maternal duty, feeding his new 'baby' with the tenderness of a loving parent.

Meanwhile, Farzan carried the terracotta pot to the garden terrace wall and emptied the liquid waste into the alley. Even amid the griffin's sharp chirps and clucks, he could hear Adarbad reprimanding the creature for its gluttonous impatience. Chuckling to himself, he set the pot down and assured his prized falcon—screeching and perturbed by all the clamor—that he had nothing to fear from his much larger brethren.

Despite Minoo's raucous protests, Farzan caught the distant rumbling of hooves. He passed through a narrow gate and peered down his alley toward the citadel gatehouse. Though the city's buildings obscured much of the view, he caught fleeting glimpses of riders on horseback, their thunderous approach muffled by the surrounding edifices.

Farzan hurried to the laboratory and called out his friend. "The king has returned. Come."

After securing the griffin with a thread of frayed rope, the men exited the lab through the back door. So eager to share their good fortune, they walked and shuffled in turns until they rounded the corner to the gatehouse.

When they arrived at the council chamber, Delawar was seated on his throne while attendants offered him fruits and pastries. He was about to reach for an orange wedge but noticed the two alchemists rushing the dais.

"Can a king ever have a moment?"

"I'm sorry, my lord," Farzan said. "You must be exhausted."

"You have no idea."

"I'm afraid we do." Farzan shot Adarbad a side-eyed glance with a hint of a smile.

"What did you say? Speak up, for my ears are still ringing from the pounding of hooves."

Farzan cupped his hands at his chest, grinning in anticipation of delivering the good news. "We've done it, my lord. We've succeeded in making a griffin."

Delawar sat forward. "This is the best news I've heard in days."

"It's only one," Adarbad said, adding a cautionary note. "Whether we can replicate this success remains to be seen."

As Delawar rubbed his chin, his thoughts wandering, the pushtigban-salar entered the council chamber. "My lord, General Numdor of the kingdom of Jarak is here to see you. Shall I escort him in?"

The king resumed a more dignified posture in anticipation that the envoy from the southern kingdom had brought good news. "Yes, Vasna. By all means."

In walked a short and stout man carrying something in his hand. He walked oddly, taking strides longer than his legs seemed to permit. Other military personnel filed in behind him.

"Greetings, Delawar, King of Raydur. I've come at the behest of King Mazad in honor of your request for reinforcements, but an ill wind has hastened my arrival."

"What sort of ill wind?"

"In the valley of the Rud-e Hayat, we came across a gruesome scene. Horses and soldiers lay dead, including what appears to be a manticore. We fear there must have been an ambush. Amid the carnage was this scroll casing. It is my understanding that the message within was intended for you."

Numdor pulled a parchment from the casing and handed it to Delawar.

For such a short message, the king seemed to labor over the wording. When he finished reading, he addressed the Jaraki general. "Next to water, my daughter is the most sought-after commodity in the land. Do you even know the nature of your king's request?"

"I'm not privy to that information, Your Majesty."

"Well, allow me to fill you in. It appears your king is quite taken with my daughter, so much so that he's made his aid conditional on securing her hand in marriage." Delawar reached for a few dates and snickered. "Your young king has proven a quick study. I can admire that. Never offer anything without getting something in return. Your premature departure from Jarak suggests he was counting on an affirmative response."

"My troops are a day away from arriving. Shall I send word to King Mazad that you agree to the terms?"

Delawar crumpled the scroll and tossed it at Numdor's feet. "You can tell your king to go to hell. I've just returned from Zad, where, as we speak, my daughter is imprisoned, shackled, and half-starved. In two weeks, she's to wed King Kamran, the mere thought of which makes me wish for the specter of death."

Farzan and Adarbad exchanged looks of disbelief.

Numdor bowed politely and left the council chamber, followed by his retinue.

As if yielding under an enormous weight, Delawar slouched and drooped his head. His wrists hung over the armrests.

Farzan approached him. "My lord, how did this happen?"

"And what of the others?" Adarbad asked.

With his chin sunk into his chest, Delawar recounted the details of the abduction to the alchemists. "Anyone not killed immediately had to fend off approaching brigands."

"What are you saying?" Adarbad asked, alarm in his voice.

"What I'm saying is that nobody survived except my daughter. And as it stands, her survival isn't even guaranteed."

"But I thought you said she was to marry King Kamran?" Farzan asked.

"That's only half of it."

"With all due respect, my lord. I don't follow."

"Queen Lilya upped the ante. She demands we send two caravans of provisions—one of ours and one of theirs. The Zadian caravan will be backed by force. If I don't comply, Mahz will be executed."

King Delawar nodded toward Vasna, who had been observing the discussion. The commander of the pushtigban slipped quietly into the hall.

Adarbad began pacing the room, mulling over the few details he had to work with. He turned to the king. "Did anyone see General Jangi or Queen Shanaz get killed?"

"My understanding is that there was nowhere for them to flee. You can draw your own conclusions."

"What will you do about the princess?" Farzan asked. "Surely, you can't leave her in the hands of those monsters."

Before the king had a chance to reply, Adarbad interrupted. "I know what I'm going to do. After all, we did make a griffin. Until someone can say with certainty what happened to our brave emissaries, I intend to search for them."

Before he could leave, Delawar intervened. "Alchemist, you're not going anywhere."

Adarbad stopped, perplexed by the king's demand. "With all due respect, you don't understand. I was at death's door in the desert—naked, sunburnt, carrion for all creatures that crawl in the sand. And that woman, whom you presume dead, saved my life at great risk to her own. I intend to return the favor."

Led by Vasna, several of the royal guards entered the council chamber and flanked the alchemist.

"What's going on?" Adarbad asked.

"I'm sorry," Delawar said.

Adarbad tried to squeeze between the bodies blocking his way, but was roundly apprehended. "Take your hands off me! King Delawar, you can't treat me like a prisoner. I demand you release me."

"That will not be happening."

"But I'll return. That I promise. Just let me look for Queen Shanaz. Are you not the least bit interested in finding General Jangi?"

"Right now, my primary concern is my daughter, and you're going to help me bring her home."

"But how?"

"Queen Lilya agreed to release Mahzarin in exchange for you."

To alleviate his guilt, the king chose to rewrite the history of the conversation. Indeed, it was he, under considerable duress, who first proposed the swap.

Adarbad's woeful eyes sought out his friend for comfort. "Then I'm a dead man."

Farzan pleaded with his king. "My lord, there must be another way."

Delawar shook his head. "It was a decision I took no pleasure in making."

Adarbad stared at the floor, his eyes darting side to side as his mind searched for any way out of the web in which he was caught.

The king waved his hand. "Take him away. We leave in three days with the first caravan."

As Vasna and his royal guards pushed Adarbad toward the double doors of the hallway, the alchemist resisted. "Wait!"

"There is nothing further to discuss," Delawar said.

"Oh, yes there is. War is coming to Raydur whether you like it or not, and without the griffins or forces from Jarak, you will be decimated."

Delawar was hardly convinced. "Farzan can make the griffins."

"Have you confirmed that with him?"

Delawar raised a hand to stay his pushtigban-salar and turned his attention to his alchemist. "Farzan, speak to that insinuation?"

"He doesn't need to," Adarbad said. "Before making the griffin, Farzan briefly left the laboratory. While he was gone, I made some adjustments to certain applications to fix a problem. You arrived just as I was about to tell him what I had done."

Delawar looked at Farzan, who corroborated the facts with a nod.

"I guess we have three days to make you talk," the king said.

"I held my silence with Queen Lilya. I'll hold it with you, too."

"Either way, you're going home. I'll take my kingdom's chances against Zad."

After Vasna and his guards led Adarbad away, Farzan approached the king, who had sunk into his throne. "I know your heart is heavy, my lord, but what Ada says is true. We cannot survive an attack by Zad without a defense of the skies. It's been common knowledge since hybridization was first theorized that whoever ruled the sky would rule the lands. Our walls and ramparts will be breached, our arrows and spears out of range."

The king's thoughts were adrift, his eyes filled with sorrow. "I'm hurting, Farzan. My heart is torn asunder. The thought of my precious daughter with that monster makes me—" Delawar rubbed his forehead as his lip quivered. "She's still so innocent."

Farzan knelt beside his king and held his hand.

Through his tears, Delawar looked like a man bereft of hope. "Have I been a good king?"

"You've been a great king. The people have always trusted your judgment, and never have you failed them."

"Then why does my judgment betray me now? For the first time in my life, I don't know what to do. For the first time in my life, I'm frightened."

"May I offer a suggestion?"

The king nodded.

"We must create griffins if we're to have even a chance against a kingdom the size of Zad."

"Are you saying I should have Adarbad tortured for the information?"

"No," Farzan said. "There might be another way, though it's not without peril."

"By all means. I'm willing to consider anything at this point." Delawar leaned in to hear what his alchemist had to say.

WRESTLING, II

Since their fight against Lilya and her jackals, Yaya and Baba had pressed on with nary an encounter. They passed through the Rud-e Hayat valley and trekked up the adjoining mountain ridge until reaching the watershed. From their high vantage point on the divide, they observed dappled fields of wild sunflowers in the lower elevations. Beyond those was an arid savanna of tall grasses and clover stretched out like a soft tapestry.

Like a sentry on watch, a lone volcanic neck marked the southern edge of the Great Plains of Namak. Yaya knew the descent would bring much warmer temperatures, but he took comfort in the fact that he and Baba would at least be going downhill. After studying his map, he felt confident that the kingdom of Jarak—located south of the Green Mountains—was no more than a two-day journey away.

So down they went.

For much of the day, the companions traversed the foothills and skirted the periphery of the savanna. A change in foliage at the bottom of a long, gradual slope marked the end of the grassland. The ground became sandy and carried the scent of salt. Trees—uniform in their appearance and rising no more than twenty feet—peppered the landscape.

As they entered a sparse forest, it became clear to Yaya that there was more to the trees than met the eye.

"Pistachios!"

Though still early in the season, the excessive heat and lack of rainfall had ripened the nuts ahead of schedule. Many had already fallen.

Yaya scooped up a few and tossed one in his mouth. He managed to crack the shell but winced as a sharp pang shot through one of his teeth. It certainly wasn't worth the reward.

Meanwhile, Baba stood upright, his paws pressed against a tree. After a few nudges from his powerful arms, a bounty of nuts cascaded to the ground, many pelting him like tiny hailstones. Dropping to all fours, he began rooting amongst the bounty, searching for those with open shells.

Yaya joined him.

As the supply dwindled under one side of the tree, the competition for the remaining nuts intensified. Wherever Baba moved, Yaya shadowed him like a thief, often snatching up nuts before the bear could.

Bears were solitary by nature, and the idea of communal dining didn't sit well with Baba. "Hey, do you mind? I was here first."

"But you have a knack for this sort of thing. I'm trying to learn."

For Baba, nothing mattered more than his stomach, especially when he had to compete to fill it. He tried all manner of deception, sometimes leaning one way only to lunge the other to scarf up an open pistachio. Unfortunately for him, the prince caught on.

"That does it," Baba said, pushing Yaya aside. "I've about had it with you."

Yaya ignored the warning and took to plucking up pistachios, whether open or not. He became slap-happy, his limbs weak with giddiness.

Around the forest floor, they foraged shoulder to shoulder like conjoined twins. Baba's expression was so manic that Yaya half expected the bear's eyes to pop out of his skull. Funnier still was the extent to which Baba knocked him down to scrounge a few nuts. Yaya could barely contain his laughter.

Seeing another nut, Baba bowled Yaya over before he could reach it. "You seem to be forgetting—I'm much bigger than you."

Dazed and slightly disoriented, Yaya wasn't about to argue. One knows when he has been bested.

The prince took refuge under a tree, sitting against it with his legs splayed. As he inspected a bloody elbow, a sudden gust of wind swirled sand and shook loose pistachios from the branches. Yaya shielded his eyes with his haversack while Baba lowered his head until the blast of air passed.

In its wake came a beautiful sound—the rhythmic cooing of a bird, unlike anything the prince had ever heard.

Yaya followed Baba toward the sound, excited to see what creature made such the song. Little did he know, the bear had other concerns.

"That sound is a ringdove," Baba said. "Rarely do they sing in the company of other birds."

The hint of danger stopped Yaya in his tracks. "If not other birds, then what?"

As they wound around a knoll, the song grew louder, its melody even more enchanting.

Baba led the boy to a thicket of brush. Through the tall grasses, they spotted the ringdove, the desert crooner joyfully perched atop the horn of an enormous beast.

"Don't make a sound or sudden movement," the bear whispered. "One wrong move and we'll wind up either trampled under its hooves or skewered upon its horn."

The creature was not unfamiliar to the boy. "I know this animal, Baba. It's a karkadann. I've heard stories about them."

"What did you call it?"

"I thought they were a myth. I can't believe I'm looking at one."

The animal was as large as any that walked the earth. Its hide was black and scaly, with a pendulous flap of skin drooping from its upper lip. Thick legs supported its enormous bulk, each buttressed by yellow, three-toed hooves. The ringdove sang its sweet song perched on a horn as long as Yaya was tall. To the layperson, the animal looked like a cross between a wildebeest and a rhinoceros.

Yaya recounted to Baba what he had heard in his youth. "The story is that the karkadann will do anything to protect the ringdove. There's something about the bird's song that soothes the beast. If threatened, it will strike with enormous force. Some can even hoist elephants upon their horns."

"That last part is news to me. All I know is they're usually in pistachio forests like this one. To them, the nuts are a delicacy, shells and all."

Indeed, unlike its observers, the karkadann wasted no time distinguishing ripe pistachios from unripe—they gobbled them all the same. Once the beast's mouth was full, its mighty jaws set to work, grinding and churning like a grain mill.

The animal raised its head and relaxed, eyes half shut, and swayed ever so slightly to the cooing of the ringdove. Then the bird stopped singing. The karkadann's eyes snapped open.

Yaya gasped and turned away from the animal's gaze.

"Don't move," Baba said.

The karkadann sniffed the air before turning its attention to another pistachio tree. Unsatisfied by the sparse bounty, it trotted off, crashing through bushes and stomping on cacti.

For a brief moment, the ground shook beneath their feet until the ringdove, bouncing up and down above the treeline, disappeared from sight.

"I need my bag," Yaya said.

The prince led the way back and found his haversack where he had left it—next to the pistachio tree.

As he slung it over his shoulder, he noticed his amulet was missing. Suddenly panicked, he scoured the ground until, to his relief, he spotted it where Baba had barreled into him. He marched over and picked it up, letting his companion know with subtle head shakes and sighs that he was responsible for the near mishap.

"Don't blame me," Baba said. "You were the one messing around. I was just going about my business."

"Yeah, well, you didn't have to knock me over so hard, did you?"

Baba shrugged.

After donning his amulet, the prince skipped over a furrow and bounded up a slope, anxious to be on the move.

But with his belly still grumbling, Baba was thinking more about nuts than anything else—least of all another romp through the woods. Nevertheless, he made haste and caught up.

"You seem to be forgetting something, light-foot. I'm about seven of you big. Now, I've never been too good with numbers, but I think that means I need about seven times as much food as you. You had at least half as many pistachios as I did back there. So that makes me three and a half times as hungry as you."

"Enough with the math already. Good grief, you act as if you're starving."

"I *am* starving."

The prince turned around, only to burst out laughing at the bear's expression.

"What's so funny?" Baba asked.

"You are. You've got the most bad-tempered face I've ever seen."

Baba refused to make eye contact.

"Oh, so you're going to pout about it? Well, I've got news for you—you can keep on pouting. That act won't work on me."

The bear changed tactics, moving from grumpy to sad.

Yaya knew his stance was a losing proposition. "Ah, come on, Baba, don't do that to me. Are you going to cry?"

"Maybe," Baba said, looking away and sniffling for effect.

"If I'd known you would get this upset... listen, I'll make a deal with you. Next time we find food, you can eat until your heart's content. Just keep it together, all right?"

With those words of encouragement, Baba brushed past the prince and led the way. At the top of the slope, they turned around and scanned the vast pistachio forest below. They tried to find the karkadann among the many trees, but it seemed to have moved on to greener pastures.

For a time, they plodded along, each happy in his own thoughts and musings. Then Yaya began to hum a melody, which soon turned into a song:

> The queen is gone, she's woebegone,
> gone down the road on a karkadann.
> She sang of love near the little ringdove,
> "He's left my life for the world above."
> "Don't fret no more," said the bird. "We'll soar.
> To heaven, we'll ride on a manticore."
> But the queen did warn, her voice forlorn,
> "From life's short breath does love... get born."

The forest grew denser from the addition of soaring evergreens and poplars. In the understory were woody shrubs and an occasional briar patch.

Baba had his nose out for food, but the few patches of greenbrier they came across had been picked clean—no doubt the result of drought-induced scarcity. Already annoyed by Yaya's off-key crooning, the bear found an easy target for his frustration.

"Hey, Ringdove. Mind giving it a rest? I fear these songs are going to haunt me long after we part ways."

Yaya obliged, turning his attention instead to plucking leaves off bushes and tossing them at the bear.

Baba shook his head at Yaya's latest antic, more or less tolerating the boy's attempt to amuse himself. But he didn't have to for long.

"Akh!"

"What happened?" Baba asked.

Yaya held out his finger. A drop of blood pooled under the nail. "Another thorn got me. But, hey," he said, pointing to the bushes, "look at the bright side."

Baba's mouth fell open in sheer delight. Before him were clusters of ruby-red smilax berries. He closed his eyes and breathed in the aroma, savoring the scent as it tickled his nose.

Yaya wasted no time filling his mouth, juice dripping down his chin. "Are you going to eat them or sniff them?"

"You don't understand," Baba said. "These berries can no longer be found where I live. The mountains used to be full of them, but not anymore. Just look how far we've had to travel to come across these."

With unbridled bliss, Yaya and Baba picked through the bushes for the better part of an hour. This time, Yaya went to the far end of the patch to do his picking, unlike in the pistachio forest. Knowing Baba's passion for the berries, he figured it would be unwise to pester him. Besides, he remembered his promise to let the bear eat his fill.

At times, he waved to his companion, both of them enjoying their newfound bounty.

By his count, Baba was on his tenth bush when he saw a doe traipsing through the evergreens.

Trailing close behind her mother was a fawn, her ears twitching nervously. Having spotted a patch of grass, both deer paused to forage. Every so often, they lifted their heads to assess threats, but any sounds were drowned out by the rustling limbs and swaying treetops.

By this time, Yaya had noticed their presence and sublime beauty. It was nature unfettered, and he felt himself a spy. He wondered how something so gentle could survive nature's cruel indifference, especially the baby with her still fragile limbs.

He didn't wonder for long. Before he knew it, Baba charged toward the deer as if shot from a wound-up catapult.

Both deer made a mad dash. The mother bounded through the brush with relative ease.

Fortune, however, did not smile on the fawn. Given her slight frame, she became tangled in a knot of thin branches covering the forest floor. Like a spider's web, they trapped her. Only through a raft of desperate contortions did she manage to free herself.

But it was too late. The bear was upon his prey, delivering a crushing bite to her neck.

Baba carried the dead fawn in his mouth and dropped it at Yaya's feet. He gave it a good sniff and licked it a few times.

Yaya was repulsed. "The berries weren't enough for you?"

Baba pinned the the animal down with his claws and began tearing pieces of flesh with his powerful jaws.

Such gore was not intended for front-row viewing, so Yaya walked over to a storm-shorn trunk and sat down. He toyed with his amulet to pass the time.

Once Baba had finished eating, he sauntered over and joined the prince. His demeanor reflected satisfaction. A belly full of berries and blood will do that.

Ready for a good nap, he proceeded to groom himself. He wiped his mouth and cleaned his fur. He rubbed his paws and picked his teeth. To top it off, he wandered behind the trunk to urinate. When he returned, he nestled into the leaves and needles, belched, and rested his head on his paws.

Yaya lowered himself to the ground and covered his eyes with one arm. "You, my friend, are all bear."

Baba didn't hear him. He was already dozing.

------◄O►------

As it was wont to do, the sun gathered speed upon its descent as if an inordinate pull tugged at the edge of the horizon.

The forest grew dark, and shadows expanded. Sounds changed, too, as the nocturnal animals began their shift. Songbirds and deer settled down while rodents, the forest's floor managers, went to work rummaging for food. Not to be outdone, eagle owls scoured the ground for small mammals.

A loud shriek startled Baba. He rose from his oval-shaped depression and walked past Yaya, who was curled up asleep on his side, hands folded under his cheek.

The bear ambled on for some time. Now and then, he stopped and jutted his moist nose into the air. Sometimes, he altered his path to traverse the terrain. In one case, he skirted a ravine, then loped down a long slope of maple trees. Eventually, the ground leveled.

Baba pushed through cattails and tall rushes until emerging onto a dried-up lake bed.

On the other bank, faintly visible in the moonlight, stood another bear. It was a female—the sow smaller than Baba, but with a lighter coat.

They exchanged sniffs, though the female remained a little wary of the newcomer. Only after Baba lowered himself onto his forearms, a position of submission, did she feel comfortable enough to approach.

She padded across the lakebed and motioned with her paw in a cajoling manner, testing her suitor, who was all too eager to play along.

Baba walked toward the sow, sometimes tossing his head in a frolicking, non-threatening manner. He made sure not to slouch, recalling what his mother told him about the importance of good posture.

When the bears met, they came nose to nose, as animals often do. The female nuzzled Baba's snout, which happened to be his first kiss. Too excited to reply in kind, he plopped down in the dirt and rolled around.

The sow, unimpressed by the ostentatious display, wandered off.

Baba knew he had overdone it.

Hoping for a second chance, he brought himself to his feet and strutted the sow's way. But a different scent halted him in his tracks. He peered toward the other bank. A figure emerged from the grasses and onto the lakebed—another brown bear, who had also caught the sow's scent.

The boar was a bit smaller than Baba but no less formidable. What he lost in girth he made up for in being battle-tested, as evinced by a puncture wound on his snout and a missing tuft of fur on his silver-tipped shoulder hump.

After sizing up his opponent, the bear darted onto the flat and sauntered toward Baba. Face to face, they snarled. The boar even issued a threat, hoping Baba would back down and cede the prize.

Baba was clearly confused. He couldn't understand the reason for all the anger, so he turned away, hoping to lower the temperature.

But the moment he did, the other bear nearly coldcocked him with a blow to the head.

Baba's knees buckled. Shaking it off, he turned back to face his competitor, resolute in what he had to do.

In a blink, both animals came together—chest against chest, snapping at each other's necks.

The bears rose like two plates of Earth's crust colliding, two mountains grappling with mighty arms pushed by even mightier shoulders. A stalemate briefly ensued.

Then Baba scored the first takedown, pinning his adversary. But it came at a cost: the boar had hold of Baba's ear, the one the jackals had already injured. The pain was excruciating. Baba defecated from the shock, and the more he tried to pull away, the more it hurt.

Desperate, Baba unleashed a pulverizing rash of blows on the boar's body. The tip of his ear, still clenched in the other bear's jaws, finally gave way. Reeling, Baba backed off.

The respite allowed the boar to hurry to his feet and brace for another round. He advanced slow and methodically.

But Baba, worn out and frightened, had had enough. He turned tail and fled.

Baba's flight made the sow's decision for her. Yet before following the victor into the rushes, she hesitated, turning to regard Baba as he made his way up the opposite bank. Despite his slumped shoulders and long face, part of her wanted him to return and try again. But Baba failed to muster the necessary nerve. The female grew impatient and walked off to join the bear she had decided was the proper suitor.

Baba's return journey took longer than he expected. Losing a fight will do that.

As for Yaya, he was none the wiser as to what had happened. He lay curled up, sleeping just as Baba had left him.

Relieved to be in familiar company, Baba settled into his nest. Though bone tired, he didn't feel much like sleeping—nor could he, with his ear throbbing as it was. So the bear lay awake, thinking of home. He missed his woods and streams and pictured his favorite eating spots in his head. This longing led to thoughts of abandoning Yaya. After all, he had already accompanied the boy much farther than he had promised.

Feeling sad and lonely, but mostly humiliated, all Baba could do was close his eyes.

FLIGHT OF THE DAEVAS

The sun had yet to crack the horizon, but enough light spilled over to stir the forest's melody-makers. A pair of reed warblers, eager to start their day, called out to one another from separate perches. Not wanting to be outdone, a brown-speckled thrush on a pine top let it be known that his voice—if not the most varied and melodic—was certainly the strongest. The bird's fourth go-around awoke Yaya, whose tousled bangs lay draped over his eyes.

The prince hadn't had a haircut since his father's death, nor had he committed himself to the routine bathing and grooming expected of someone of his royal station. To say that his hygiene habits had fallen into neglect was an indisputable fact, even to the casual observer. As the boy scratched his armpits, he longed for a good soaking. Skin rashes, bug bites, and nights spent sleeping on the dirt can spur even the most dispirited teenager to want to feel clean.

Anxious to get the day's traveling underway, Yaya roused his furry companion. "Baba, wake up."

The bear rolled onto his side and licked the morning from his mouth. "Do I know you?"

"I should hope so." Yaya stood. "Come on—we have to get going."

"Do we?"

"That's the longest stretch of sleep we've had."

"Speaking of stretches..."

Yaya turned toward a shrub to relieve himself. "I bet we'll find some delicious berries along the way. Isn't that enough to get your wheels turning?"

Baba rolled onto his back and extended his limbs this way and that. He twisted his spine, turned his wrists, and curled his claws. If ever there was a full-body stretch, this was it.

To Yaya, the bear looked like he was dancing. As he watched him writhe in the dirt, he noticed that Baba's nipped ear looked worse for wear—prompting a closer examination.

The prince knelt and ran his fingers through Baba's coat. Parts of it were caked in blood, and a few tufts were missing.

"If I didn't know any better, Baba, I'd wager you were attacked by more jackals."

"I wish."

"What do you mean? How'd this happen? Your ear is in tatters."

Baba sat up. "Well, if you wanna know... after you fell asleep last night, I picked up the scent of another bear. I followed it until I spotted her on the banks of a dry lakebed. We played for a while, and then—let me just say, before I go on—girls are weird."

Yaya nodded in agreement. "And then what?"

"Another bear showed up, that's what. I wasn't sure what to expect, but then the jerk said some mean things and hit me. So we fought. That's when he bit my ear." Baba shook his head, still dismayed. "And to make matters worse, the girl left with the idiot. Can you believe that?"

Yaya thought of Gulzar and Afshad. "Yeah, I can believe it."

Baba stood on all fours and shook in the manner the prince had come to expect. It was the same every morning, starting with his head. Like the wave of a temblor, the motion rolled through his torso and ended at his rear, and always just as he started to walk.

Yaya thought it must be unique to four-legged animals. If humans shook while walking, they would either be dancing or crazy, and Baba was no dancer.

"Does it hurt?" Yaya asked.

"What do you think?"

"I know, dumb question."

"I've had better nights of sleep. But if I ever get a second crack at that bear, he's going to get a thrashing. Baba doesn't make the same mistake twice."

"From how you handled my grandmother's jackals, he must have been one tough animal."

"I don't know about that. But he was angry. And for what? A girl? I don't get it."

For a couple of miles, the two companions walked toward the rising sun. They didn't speak much. Baba was sullen, his mood soured by an empty stomach. Even when he did speak, he didn't abide by his habit of stopping to do so. At times, the aspen forest opened up to meadows of thick grasses, dappled with the yellow and purple flowers of yarrow and larkspur. Unfortunately, the aroma only made Baba hungrier.

Yaya knew his friend was hurting, his pride bruised by his fight with the older bear. To show he understood, he recounted how Afshad had given him a drubbing over Gulzar.

The bear stopped and sat down in the flowers. "Why didn't you fight your cousin after he let go of you?"

"I'm no match for him."

"Maybe not, but you can hurt him. You have fists, don't you?"

Yaya shook his head. "You should see this guy. He's built like a battering ram."

"A 'battering' what?"

"Put it this way: if I ever fought him, I'd get my face smashed in."

"If this Afshad is as handsome as you say, you know what you do next time? You hit him where it hurts—right in the nose. That'll teach him."

Yaya pictured himself on the chogan field in the scenario Baba had described. Even with his imaginative gifts, the ending only got worse.

At the bottom of a gentle slope, Yaya and Baba came upon a brook trickling down from the foothills of the Kuhha-ye Sabz. More hungry than thirsty, Yaya recalled what his bear friend had said about food along the banks. After some searching, they found a small patch of wild blueberry bushes. They were sparse but still ripe for the picking. Baba's mood brightened as his tussle with the boar was all but forgotten.

While the bear pruned the branches, Yaya pulled out the few remaining nuts he had collected in the pistachio forest. He counted what was in his palm, giving Baba twenty and keeping three for himself.

"That's all the food I have, big bear."

"I'll find food. I don't have this snout for nothing. I only wish it wouldn't smell so much sometimes."

Yaya switched to eating berries. "By the way, what did she look like? I'm curious what bears look for in girlfriends."

"Woah, she was beautiful. She had bronze fur and smelled amazing. I wanted to eat her up. But after she kissed me, she walked away and ignored me. I've been trying to figure out why, but for the life of me, I can't put my paw on it."

"And you probably never will."

The prince smiled. He was proud of what he considered a pointed observation.

After picking the bushes bare, the travelers saw a translucent wrap of silken fibers dangling from a branch under a shelter of leaves.

Yaya noticed it moving. "Look, there's a pupa inside. I think we've arrived in time for the show."

A small hatch at the base of the wrap vibrated open. What emerged from the chrysalis was an orange butterfly known as a Painted Lady. It unwound from its coiled sleep and began to flutter itself dry. And just like that, the butterfly was ready for flight.

"Happy birthday," Yaya said.

The prince patted Baba and wandered to a clearing alongside the brook. He dropped to his knees to rinse his hair and wash his face.

When he sat up, the bear chuckled.

"What's so funny?" Yaya asked.

"You look like a soggy lynx."

Baba's description was fitting. With his distinguished nose, wide-set eyes, and growing whiskers, the boy did resemble the animal.

"Well, I'll take 'soggy lynx' over 'shotor.'"

"Shotor?"

"It used to be my nickname. Shall we keep moving?"

"Sure thing... Shotor."

A few miles later, Yaya and Baba wandered into a forest of towering trees framed by sheer cliffs of white granite. They had to crane their necks to see the tops of the conifers. The smooth, branchless trunks stretched for half their length, reminding the prince of the torches that lit the corridors of Zad's citadel. The diminutive evergreens beside them appeared like children tugging at their parents' shirts.

The two companions walked among nature's monoliths in contemplative silence. Such was the power of these unusual trees. They were sublime and regal in their countenance. Yaya imagined the ages passing by while the giant conifers, rooted and still, watched them go. In the scope of time measured in stump rings, the notion of a boy and a bear wandering together was perhaps nothing they hadn't seen before, however absurd.

A drop in temperature from the shade gave way to a blast of much cooler air. It reminded Yaya of walking through the doors of a yakhchal. The boughs rustled, the limbs creaked, and the canopies closed in, shutting out most of the light. Like the moorings of a large vessel, thick vines wound their way high into the trees.

Yaya began to shiver, and it seemed their presence had not gone unnoticed. "I don't like these woods," he said, tying his bootlaces. "They remind me of where I met you."

Baba agreed. "Then let's get out of here. You lead the way."

Like a sprinter crouched before the race, Yaya took off. He ducked under limbs and hopped over vines. Besides the aberrant chill, the forest had become a labyrinthine mess of obstacles.

Baba did his best to follow, but his forearms and hind legs lacked the dexterous skill of his mammalian brethren to negotiate the vines and shrubs knotted across the forest floor. Forced onto a more linear path, he crashed through as many woody obstacles as he could.

The further they ran, the darker and denser the forest became. The vines reached ever higher into the trees, wrapping around limbs like fingers around an unsuspecting throat. Small evergreens struggled for light, while others lay on the ground, constricted and snuffed out.

Yaya stopped by a pine tree shorn of many limbs, its trunk in the grip of a thatch of tentacles winding all the way to the top. He scanned every direction for an end to the interminable darkness, but saw only shadow.

Baba sat down to rest. "Any idea which way to go?"

"None whatsoever. But if we keep on this course, we'll get out eventually. Don't you think?"

"That would be logical, but I don't think logic applies in this dreadful place. I thought my forest had grown strange. Heck, this one seems to be at war with itself."

Baba didn't mention the hint of sulfuric odor he had noticed.

As he thought of the demons they had battled in the temple ruins, a high-pitched squeal pierced the air overhead.

"Help! Help! Don't leave, please."

Yaya looked up and saw a stick cage suspended fifty feet off the ground, held by cables of ivy.

Peering through the gaps in the base was a spritely figure, her face wrought with tension. Her hair was long and lavender, with yellow-tinted tresses danging through the grate. Each time she flapped her wings, an aura of light pulsed, casting the colors of the rainbow.

The fairy pressed her face to the cage's makeshift bars. "Hurry, before they come back."

"Before *who* comes back?" Yaya shouted. "And what are you anyway?"

"I'm a *pari*. Can't you help me?"

Baba frowned. "The last time I chased a girl, I got my butt kicked."

The pari was unlike anything Yaya had ever seen. It seemed impossible that anything so radiant could have malicious intent. "We have to set her free, Baba."

"Oh, brother. I had a feeling you'd say that."

The pari bounced around the cage in a panic, occasionally gripping the bars and scanning the forest. "What are you waiting for? You must hurry."

Yaya decided the pine he and Baba stood under could get him close enough. "Wish me luck?"

Baba shook his head. "Don't expect me to catch you if you fall."

"I've come to depend on it, big bear." Yaya grabbed the lowest branch and hoisted himself up. "Well, here goes nothing."

With relative ease, the prince made his way up the tree. Where there were no branches to grab or step on, he used the vines in their place. Gaps were plentiful, as were strands of ivy, which he deftly utilized as handles. As he neared the top, his hands and hair sticky with sap, he glanced down through one of the few openings and saw Baba watching him, the bear upright and leaning against the trunk.

Yaya stepped onto a large vine that bridged two giant conifers. Thinner vines coursed alongside it, and he used them as guide rails, inching forward until he was a few feet from the bottom of the cage. Clothed in a silken blue dress and golden-laced slippers, the pari was mesmerizing. A scent he had never known before filled his lungs, leaving him feeling a little lightheaded.

The sprite pressed her face against the bars. "You have to open the latch on the door."

Yaya tried jumping, but he couldn't reach it.

The pari looked into the woods, her face tense. "Will you hurry? They're coming. Use a branch—anything."

"You keep saying, 'they're coming.' Who's coming?"

"Blood-sucking murderers."

Yaya didn't like the sound of that. He darted over the vine to the crown of the evergreen and returned with a thin branch. Though he could reach the latch, the twig's tip wasn't strong enough to lift it.

The pari stuck her hand between two bars in the base. "Give it to me."

Yaya readily obliged.

As she worked the latch, a sudden blast of wind swayed the trees. "They're here."

The sprite flung open the cage door, swooped down to Yaya, and handed him the branch. "Don't stand there. Run!"

With the pari pushing from behind, Yaya nearly fell off the vine. It didn't help that one of his hands was occupied with a weapon, however crude.

"You may not realize this," he said, glancing at the distant ground below, "but unlike you, I don't have wings."

When they reached the crown of the evergreen, a swarm of winged shadows, shrieking and hissing, descended upon them.

Yaya swatted at what he first took for giant bats. But that was only true of their wings. They were humanoid—about the size of toddlers, with emaciated torsos and limbs. At the tips of their knobby fingers were claws. Their skin had a gray, deathly pallor, and their beady eyes were as dull as slate. To Yaya, they fit the magi's description of underworld demons, or daevas, as they were commonly known.

From their snapping jaws, the daevas released a noxious odor.

The pari clung to Yaya and urged him on. "Swing! Hit them on the wings."

"What do you think I'm trying to do?"

No sooner had those words left Yaya's mouth than a daeva pulled his feet out from under him. Down he cascaded, into vines and through limbs, like a pinball bouncing bumper to bumper. Around and around, the forest swirled until a pillow of pine branches—the lowest on the tree—broke his fall. As they bent under his weight, he rolled off and landed on his back, settling on a bed of cones and needles.

Yaya gasped for air, stunned to still be alive. He barely had time to savor his luck before one of the daevas, fangs bared and mouth open, swooped down above him. All the prince could do to stave off the aerial attack was to extend his foot. Fortunately, his heel caught the beast's head. The daeva careened to the side and crashed into the earth. Yaya rolled away only to see Baba in a pitched battle with several of the creatures.

Like circling wolves sensing the more formidable foe, the daevas worked in unison to attack Baba's flanks.

But the bear retained valuable lessons from his skirmish with the canines. He had learned to feign and to be less predictable with his counterattacks. In doing so, he caught one of the daevas with his paw, the force hurtling it into another. Before it could recover, Baba pounced, pinning the creature by its wings. He bit down hard and tossed it aside, sending it skidding through the pine debris.

Meanwhile, a large daeva chased the pari from one trunk to another.

Yaya rushed to her defense but was knocked down from behind. Icy, cold hands gripped his ankles, and before he knew it, he was upside down and being carried aloft. He managed to catch his amulet, but he fumbled his haversack which fell to the ground. With no other options, the prince twisted the cap on the amulet until the symbol of air—a wavy inscription—was visible. He aligned the metal stopper with an opening and lifted the lid.

"*Havâ.*"

A whirlwind burst forth and engulfed his captors. Like the sand devils he used to see in the Dasht-e Marg, a howling twister took shape, sucking up dirt, cones, and pine needles.

The daevas could not hold on against such a force and were flung out of sight.

Yaya plummeted.

Before hitting the ground, a lateral gust flung him into Baba, who, along with the pari, clung to one of many thin vines. The bear shielded the prince, and had it not been for his hefty bulk, the winds would have blown the boy away.

The funnel cloud grew in strength and size, sucking in more needles and dirt. The sky darkened. The debris field widened, swallowing everything in its wake.

Then, as quickly as it started, the tempest vanished. Shafts of light pierced the canopies above, and silence returned.

Baba lifted himself off Yaya. "Are you all right?"

The boy sat up and leaned against the vines, one hand pressed against the side of his head. A low moan escaped his lips.

Despite his discomfort, the hovering pari was not keen on loitering. "We must flee. The fanged-wings won't be gone for long."

Baba was less amenable. "Hold on here, Twinkle Toes. Can't you see the boy is hurt?"

"But they'll return. Next time, we won't escape."

Baba relented. He lowered himself beside Yaya and prodded him to climb on.

The boy took hold of the bear's fur but couldn't summon the strength.

Baba glared at the sprite. "Can you lend a hand here?"

With extra flaps of her wings, the pari lifted Yaya by his tunic and helped him atop Baba.

The prince hesitated. "Wait. We can't leave. I lost my—"

"No time for talking, kid. Hang on." Baba popped up from the forest floor and bounded away. "Come on, Twinkle Toes."

With the pari keeping pace, the trio dove deeper into the woods.

The last image in Yaya's mind before he blacked out was the daevas twirling up high toward the treetops. He remembered seeing his haversack hovering in the air with them, and he remembered it falling toward his outstretched hand, ever so close, before the twister's updraft sucked it away. Lost with it was his bottle. The elements of the water cycle he had collected—the bits of haoma plants and blessed water—were gone.

FALLEN

Sitting at an inlaid table, Princess Mahzarin took her last bite of sweet bread. As common as the morning snack was throughout the lands, none she had ever tasted were as light and flaky as those from Zad. Except for her first day in captivity, when she had been denied food altogether, she had found herself looking forward to breakfast. But her feeling of disloyalty in desiring the food of the enemy was so dreadful that she rarely finished her allotted rations.

After wiping her mouth, the princess removed her necklace and rubbed its bronze pendant between her fingers. She remembered the day she received the heirloom, sitting on her bed in Raydur with her mother.

"The center circle, or sun, represents Ohrmazd," her mother had said. "The rays of light dividing the rest are his six divine sparks. This gift we pass to you, my dear. May you forever dwell in righteous mind."

With the ribbed edge of the pendant, the princess carved a seventh scratch on the wooden table—marking the seventh day of her imprisonment, and the number of days until her forced nuptials.

The mere thought of marrying Kamran made her bury her head in her arms. She looked at her chaffed toes. Never one for the *henna* and nail-painting rituals of her peers, she felt an unbidden desire to partake in the frivolity of a make-up party.

Mahz refastened the necklace and carried her tea onto the balcony. She wondered about Shanaz and Jangi. Sadness came over her, along with shame, as she recalled the queen's words about there being worse fates than exclusion from the heavy cavalry. Now that she had been kidnapped, imprisoned, and promised to a man she abhorred, the princess understood that Shanaz's warning had been right.

Lost in thought, Mahz was startled by the sound of someone clearing his throat.

Behind her, lounging against the doorway to the balcony, was King Kamran. He held a tunic, trousers, and a belt in his arms. "I happened to pass a servant bringing these for you. I'll leave them on the divan."

The princess followed him back into the chamber. "What's your real reason for coming here?"

"I think that's quite evident," Kamran said, adjusting his boot on the sofa. "You're going home."

Mahz was stunned into silence by the announcement.

Kamran walked over to her wearing a phony look of concern. "I know how you must feel. When I heard you were going home, my heart—like yours—was broken. But don't fret, my love. Consider this a mere delay of our nuptials."

Mahz refused to be baited and checked her impulse to respond with sarcasm. After all, she had hope that she might soon be free, and Kamran's words, more than ever, meant nothing.

But the king, disappointed by the princess's refusal to play his game, went for more vulgar provocations. "There's something I've been meaning to ask you, though I'm not sure how."

Like a shy teenager, Kamran folded his arms, stared at the floor, and slid the toe of his boot back and forth. His face was fraught with mock tension.

"What is it?"

"Well," Kamran said, "it's been a week since you arrived, and a day less that you've had the leisure to reflect on our wedding."

"Your point?"

"No point. Just a simple question—and I'd appreciate an honest answer." Kamran stepped closer. "With all that time on your hands, especially as you lay curled up in bed—scared and lonely—did you ever wonder... *really* wonder what it would be like, you know, our special night?" He looked her up and down. "Because I did."

The princess turned away in disgust.

Amused with himself, the king headed for the doorway. "Get dressed. The guards will return to escort you to the gates."

"First, I have a question."

Kamran paused, tapping his fingers on the door frame.

"How did my release come to pass?"

The king hesitated. "It hasn't yet. That all depends on your father." As he left the room, he added over his shoulder, "We shall know soon enough."

⚬

Mahz soon found herself standing behind the battlements of the southern gatehouse. From the west, the magenta and golden flags of Raydur, unfurled and secured to their wagon supports, fluttered in the breeze. The caravan was drawing near, and if the princess's freedom depended on her father, all the better. Mahz had no doubt he would save her, and she reflected on the words she had spoken to herself when first captured.

"I knew you would save me, Pedar," she muttered, scanning the lead wagon for King Delawar.

The driver, however, pausing to stretch, was a man of nondescript bearing.

As the caravan passed before the gatehouse, Mahz's eyes darted from one wagon to the next—a dozen in all. Dutifully, the pachyderms plodded on, with nary a soul seated in the elevated perches at the front of each flatbed or box wagon.

The princess's hopes faded until she saw two seated figures on the second-to-last wagon. One sat taller than the other. His slender frame and long raven hair left no doubt who it was—Hemog.

The other man was hunched over, head down, his hands behind his back.

Mahz moved along the rampart as the caravan passed, hoping to glimpse the mystery person from a different angle. But it was unnecessary—Hemog spoke a few words to his companion, who lifted his head to respond. The princess recognized him. It was Adarbad.

The sight of the alchemist made no sense. Mahz, aware of his contentious history with Lilya, knew that his very presence put his life at risk. Then she remembered Kamran's words: "That depends on your father." The pieces began to fall into place. She recalled the image of her father shaking hands with Lilya and Kamran and realized what they had agreed on. "He made a deal—me for Adarbad. He must have."

The notion of marrying Kamran made her stomach turn, but allowing the exchange to move forward would be like sealing the alchemist's fate herself. That, she would not accept. Her confusion morphed from anger to defiance.

"I can't believe you would do this, Pedar," she thought, as the guards—who had allowed her to watch the arrival from the gatehouse at Lilya's behest—escorted her down the rampart stairs.

Outside the city wall, Lilya and Sarvin observed the procession of wagons.

The queen noticed her alchemist fidgeting with his fingers. "A little nervous about seeing your old friend?"

Sarvin bristled. "Please, what reason could I possibly have to be nervous? *He*, on the other hand—well, I wouldn't want to be him for all the gold in the world. Can we skip the torture this time and do away with him?"

"There are some things I must know first."

"My lady, the last time you took that approach, he escaped. I beseech you—kill the treasonous lout. We have no use for him anymore."

Lilya found her alchemist's dour expression amusing. "This is making you uncomfortable, isn't it?"

The final few wagons approached as Kamran barked orders to several soldiers about transferring the water to the *ab-anbars*, or cisterns.

And for the first time since being left in the *boats* to be eaten alive by desert vermin, Adarbad locked eyes with Lilya, his would-be murderer. They stared at each another until the wagon rolled to a stop. His aspect was glum, his shoulders sunken.

"Welcome home, Adarbad," the queen said. "It appears trust is a commodity hard for you to come by."

"Indeed, it is," the alchemist said, his hands bound, "but then again, she who swims with snakes is bound to be bitten." Adarbad grinned at Sarvin. "Forgive me, my friend. I've taken to speaking in metaphors. By 'snake,' I meant you."

"Very clever," Sarvin said. "A little too jovial, aren't we, given what's in store for you? Or has your memory failed you—like your loins?"

"Your wit is as predictable as your alchemy. Isn't it time you graduate beyond the shallow jabs of the juvenile?"

Sarvin rolled his eyes at the rebuke, which only confirmed what Adarbad had implied.

While soldiers fanned along the caravan, opening cask spigots to verify the water supply, Lilya watched as a fretful Princess Mahzarin was escorted through the gates.

Kamran joined his mother's side. "It's a shame the old crank couldn't even show up to claim his daughter. He's less of a king than I imagined, and even less of a man."

"Don't forget, Afshad and our forces are at his doorstep. I'm sure King Delawar has more on his mind than a routine exchange."

Mahz halted, defying her escort. She fixed her eyes on Hemog, who had pulled himself onto the roof of the water cask and was working to loosen the bung. She studied his body language, searching for clues to what she had concluded was an unacceptable transaction. But Hemog offered nothing. Instead, he went about his task professionally, while the alchemist beside him remained hunched in apparent discomfort.

Unable to contain her growing impatience, Lilya motioned to the princess. "Enough dawdling. Surely you've figured out what's going on."

"If I'm to be exchanged for the alchemist, I won't do it."

Lilya marched over and squeezed Mahz by the arm. "You don't seem to understand. See that shriveled little wretch on the wagon perch? He escaped me once. He won't escape me again. And you, young lady, are the reason why, despite my son's physical yearnings."

Lilya turned to the Rayduri General. "Hemog, let's finish this. Release the prisoner."

Hemog climbed onto the seat and ordered Adarbad to lean forward so he could cut the leather straps that bound his wrists. When the alchemist refused to budge, the general smacked him on the back of his head.

Lilya delighted in the abuse. "More stubborn than a mule, isn't he?"

Less enamored with the transfer was Sarvin, who had been observing the soldiers checking the spigots. He shook his head, his eyes narrowing with suspicion. "My lady, I think it would be wise to check the water levels from the tops of the casks. For all we know, King Delawar filled them only as high as the outtake valves."

"And in doing so, forsake his daughter? I highly doubt it." When her logic failed to assuage Sarvin's concerns, Lilya ordered a soldier to climb atop the cask.

"It won't do any good," Hemog said. "I just tried to open the bung. They've been forced in too tightly."

"Then I'll do it," Kamran said.

The king bound up the spokes of the rear wheel and climbed up the slatted ladder nailed into the casks' staves. He strode over to the bung and wrenched it loose with his superhuman strength. Water shimmered at the brim. Satisfied, he shot Adarbad a look of contempt before making the fourteen-foot leap to the ground.

"It's full," he said.

Meanwhile, Hemog approached the leaders of Zad. "I've been reminded by King Delawar to use our siphons for the water transfer. They're inside the supply wagon with the clamps."

"That won't be necessary," Kamran said. "We have our own."

"But our spigots require special siphons."

Kamran folded his arms. "And what else is in that wagon? Seems a bit large for a few siphons."

"Not only siphons," Hemog replied. "There are spare iron hoops, rivets, staves, bungs, shovels—"

"Fine, Fine," Lilya said. "Get on with it."

Hemog gave a cursory bow and headed to the supply wagon, where the caravan driver was busy unlocking the double tailgate.

Lilya's eyes stayed fixed on Adarbad. "What are you waiting for? Step down from that wagon perch, or my men will drag you off."

"No need to get pushy."

Rather than obey, the alchemist climbed onto the roof of the cask and shuffled his way to the center. He squatted, settling himself on the bung.

Lilya shook her head in dismay. "Getting under my skin till the end. Seize him!"

As guards rushed the cask, the tailgates of the supply wagon swung open. From the shadows within came an ear-splitting screech. Soldiers recoiled as a griffin leapt out, bearing the King of Raydur in war costume dress. Two more griffins followed, one flown by Hemog with the caravan driver mounted behind him; the other by Farzan.

The alchemist led his beast toward the cask, swooping down on the guards climbing the slatted ladder to apprehend his friend.

Lilya looked on in horror as Delawar and his griffin made a beeline straight for her. Stunned by the sheer audacity of Raydur's surprise attack, she could only duck—too late. The griffin's talons raked her shoulder and scalp. She collapsed to the ground, blood dripping from her forehead as she crawled face down toward the cask. All around her lay her injured men, their cries of anguish filling the air.

Yet the queen's eyes remained fixed on the prize. As she sought cover under the flatbed, she commanded her guards forthwith. "Get the princess!"

But her order fell on deaf ears. Mahzarin stood all alone, her escort having scattered like rats fleeing a jackal.

Delawar pulled his daughter in front of him and onto the sturdy frame of his griffin. "Take hold of the reins," he said.

Like a coiled spring, the beast lowered itself, then sprang into the air.

Farzan and Hemog directed their griffins in a final assault to give King Delawar and his daughter time to move beyond any arrow's range. One stout-hearted soldier held his ground with a spear, but Hemog's griffin bypassed the tip and clutched the man's head between its talons. Up they rose, and as the beast made a sharp turn, the outward pull combined with the talons' razor-sharp points severed the soldier's head from his body.

Meanwhile, Kamran ran out from his hiding spot between elephants, his face wrought with fury, eyes filled with rage. He snatched a lone javelin from the sand and cocked it back.

"Damn you, Delawar."

Lilya crawled out from under the flatbed and watched the javelin rise into the bright blue sky. It homed in, as if gravity had yielded.

Amid the whirring wind, King Delawar leaned close, speaking into Mahz's ear, "You're coming home."

Just as he finished, his body lurched forward into his daughter's.

Mahz pushed herself off the griffin's neck and grasped the collar of her father's hauberk. Peering over his shoulder, she caught sight of the javelin impaled in his back. His arms fell to his sides, and his limp body started to slide from the saddle. Despite her desperate grip and pleas for divine intervention, the princess could not hold on. She screamed, watching in horror as her father's body tumbled through the air until his perforated corpse crashed to the earth.

A phalanx of Zad's savaran poured from the gates, followed by foot archers and a score of infantry.

Farzan and Hemog guided their griffins to Mahz's flanks. The general implored her to flee. "We must go, my lady."

"I can't leave my pedar."

"Then you will share his fate. He is dead. You are to be queen of Raydur. Now fly!"

Indecision gripped the young woman as arrows from composite bows began to find their range.

Amid the chaos below—the galloping horses, the running guards and soldiers—one figure moved with eerie calm. It was Lilya. Tall and sinewy, she walked in measured steps, a bronze-tipped spear in hand. Like a black shadow, ominous and foreboding, she drifted toward the fallen king.

When another javelin sailed past Adarbad's head, Mahz finally gave in. She ushered her griffin forward, leading her beleaguered retinue to the west.

As the griffins flew away, Farzan looked down and watched Lilya thrust her spear into King Delawar's corpse. He hoped the princess hadn't seen the pitiless display.

Fortunately, Mahz's eyes were focused on the horizon. Her wrists were wound in the griffin's reins as her plaited hair swirled in the wind. Her jaw was set. Her profile, stern.

The alchemist struggled to hold back tears for the young woman who would be queen. Like Prince Yaya, she was now an orphan—her charge determined, her course set, her fate as yet unknown.

BONE AND FLESH

Lilya retrieved the spear from King Delawar's bludgeoned corpse. Her shoulder, torn open by the griffin's talons, was soaked in blood. Part of her headscarf had been ripped away.

As she observed the three flying figures fade into the horizon, Kamran strode up beside her. When he saw that his mother was hurt, he turned to summon Sarvin, but the dutiful servant was already running toward them.

"My lady, are you alright?" The alchemist quickly examined the queen's wounds. "The cuts don't look too deep, but I should get you to the citadel for treatment."

"That can wait."

"But you're injured."

"Never mind. I want you to wrap and preserve Delawar's body. It wasn't the proper sendoff I had imagined for Princess Mahzarin. The *least* I can do is ensure she sees her father again." Lilya tossed the spear to the ground and started walking back to the caravan. "When you're finished, meet me in the stables."

"May I ask why?"

Kamran bristled. "Do as she says."

As several guards arrived, the king ordered them to help Sarvin with the body, though not before scolding them for their incompetence during Delawar's attack. By the time he caught up with Lilya, she was stepping out of the caravan's roof-covered supply wagon, the very one from which the griffins had emerged.

The king peered inside. There were no hoops, staves, or any of the other items Hemog had listed. Apart from animal droppings, it was empty.

"Fools," Kamran said. "We were damn fools."

Lilya wiped the sole of her shoe in the dirt. "We stepped in it, alright."

"Any word on the other casks?"

"They're being inspected as we speak."

"And the box wagons? They looked full of grain."

Lilya shook her head.

"What do you mean?"

"I've just been informed the first was packed with grasses and straw and covered with a bed of glossy-leafed ivy. On top of that was a thin layer of barley. I've no doubt the other two are the same."

A thorough inspection of the other casks and box wagons confirmed Lilya's hunch: Zad had been deceived.

Afterward, she and Kamran walked toward the gates.

Meanwhile, ordinary citizens had begun to emerge from the villages. The arrival of the caravan and subsequent battle had piqued their interest. Cautiously, and careful not to interfere with the soldiers, adults gathered in small groups, chatting idly, while children played tag among the wagons. Another gang of youths, predisposed to finding humor in all things crude, erupted in laughter, amused by the sight of a defecating pachyderm.

"I'll give orders to have the elephants slaughtered," Lilya said. "Our people can use the meat and whatever water we can siphon from the casks."

Kamran was less than satisfied. "I knew we should never have bargained with Delawar. The whole deal reeked from the beginning. I think you underestimated him."

Lilya stopped and looked her son in the eye. Her rusari no longer veiled her acid-burned face, which was made all the more gruesome by the dried blood that had stained her skin like pomegranate juice on leather.

"Allow me to enumerate," she said, her temper palpable. "First, we've come into possession of a caravan of wagons. Second, we have enough food to feed hundreds and water for half of that. And lastly, lest you forget, we have a dead king. The only loss was your new romance. So yes, it all smells good to me."

Chastened, Kamran tried to deflect. "Well, it was I who killed him. Don't I deserve some credit?"

The queen resumed walking, followed by royal guards. "If you want to impress me, have your horse readied for a four-day journey and meet me at Sarzamin-e Mordegan."

"What do you have planned?"

"I observed how my father used fear and intimidation as tools of coercion. I hoped I could do the same with Delawar and get from him what we wanted without sacrificing men and treasure. But his ruse terminated any such possibility. We must attack Raydur and take the city down while it reels from the loss."

They entered the stable grounds, where Sarvin was waiting.

The alchemist shuffled toward them. "I've arranged for Delawar's corpse to be chilled in a yakhchal, which should buy me time to prepare the embalming *mumiya*. But a word of caution—this isn't part of our tradition. I can't guarantee it'll work."

The queen took Sarvin by the sleeve and led him to the newly added manticore stall in the primary stable. A pride that had once numbered four had grown to a dozen.

"Where are we going, my lady? You need treatment."

Lilya flung open the gates and uttered a command. In response, the oldest of the brood trotted toward her from the feeding area. Another command prompted the beast to lie in a prone position. The queen took hold of its mane, climbed onto its back, and motioned with a tilt of her head for Sarvin to sit behind her.

"My lady, you know I have a deep-seated dread of heights."

"It's time you faced your fears, Sarvin."

"But there's no saddle, no bridle. And need I mention I've never even sat on a manticore."

"Were you this lily-livered with your other firsts?"

With his manliness questioned, the alchemist reluctantly mounted.

With a sharp kick to the haunches, Lilya ushered the manticore into flight. The beast ascended above the stable and high over the city wall.

Overwhelmed by his phobia and the uneven motion of winged flight, Sarvin began to feel dizzy and nauseous. "I think I'm going to get sick."

"Don't look down," Lilya said, her voice muffled by the wind. "You'll get used to it."

The alchemist went a step further, closing his eyes and trying to divert his mind from the soaring heights. Having been reacquainted with Adarbad, he imagined various scenarios in which his former colleague might be tortured. Some involved ancient techniques; others were more modern or altogether invented on the fly. While the methods varied, the one common thread was protracted torment.

While Sarvin was lost in sadistic reverie, the manticore landed on a worn outcropping near the ancient dakhmeh, jarring his eyes open. Outside the burial pit lay several rows of corpses, lives recently lost to starvation and cholera. Among them were scores of children and infants. Why they were not inside the dakhmeh was evident to the alchemist, who surveyed the area with distaste: the burial pit was already full.

Lilya dismounted and walked to the edge of the crag. Her presence startled a wake of buzzards picking at the bodies.

Sarvin, confused by the destination, followed. "In the name of Ohrmazd, what are we doing here?"

"This place was once a destination of heroes, a place of pride for feats of the fallen. It has since become a morgue for our starving children. I can no longer bear the cries of their mothers."

Lilya glanced southeast and saw a figure riding through the shallows of the Rud-e Barik. She knew Kamran was drawing near. "Give me some space," she said.

As Sarvin stepped back, Lilya closed her eyes and began to chant:

Ahriman, I summon thee.
Ahriman, come to me.
I give you air from my lungs
to see that my people breathe.
A dash of bone,
a pinch of flesh,
combine the two,

and let them mesh.

Lilya repeated the chant until, at last, her feet lifted from the ground. In the air, she hovered, arms stretched upward and back arched. Her mouth was open and drawn taut as if Ahriman himself was prying open her jaws with spectral fingers. She shook and bellowed a series of discordant wails until a belch of rust-colored mist escaped her lungs.

A tempest formed, widening so fast it engulfed the landscape in a swirl of dust and debris, including pieces of the deceased.

Kamran made his way up the hill until the stinging grains of the tumult became too much to bear. He sought refuge on the ground and crawled toward Sarvin, who was huddled against the low-lying manticore, its head covered by its wings.

From their vantage point, they watched Lilya collapse and slide several feet down the escarpment. When she came to a stop, she let out a woeful cry. The dirty air dissipated and grew still, letting the sunlight return.

Kamran hurried to Lilya and helped her to her feet. "What in the name of Ohrmazd just happened?" The king's inquiry was met with silence. He studied his mother's face for clues but gathered nothing from her stoic expression.

Finally, Lilya stirred, releasing a foul stench from her mouth. "I'll see that Afshad and General Baraz wage war on Raydur. You'll see to the destruction of Jarak."

"But that's impossible. I have no army."

Lilya took her son by the wrist and led him to the top of the outcropping. "Behold," she said, extending her arms. "This is your army."

Kamran gazed upon the burial pit and the broader cemetery in both repulsion and awe. Sarzamin-e Mordegan had been reanimated, brought to life by a goulash of ghouls. Semi-fleshed, their entrails partially exposed, the undead clawed, bit, and crawled over one another in their desperation to reach the king, their newly imbued leader.

"I have summoned them to be at your command," Lilya said. "Take the *Rah-e Faraz* through the mountains and destroy Jarak's eastern garrison. King Mazad will come to Raydur's aid, which will leave his city defenseless." The queen embraced her son. "Show me why you were meant to be king."

Kamran descended the rocky slope. Waiting below were the groveling throngs of undead who funneled around the outcropping like water around a stone.

The king walked unimpeded toward his horse as the ghouls yielded before him like supplicants. Once mounted, he steadied his anxious steed and drew the gleaming sword handcrafted by Bezan the metallurgist.

"One king has fallen by my spear," he said, looking up at his mother. "Another shall fall by my blade."

Lilya watched as her son led his army of disfigured cohorts onto the semi-arid plain and toward the Rud-e Barik. They numbered in the hundreds, each driven by a uniform hunger for flesh and bone. Rising from their ranks was a cacophony of growls and hisses that, to their summoner, sounded like the sweetest of melodies.

Beaming with pride, the queen turned her thoughts to the young King Mazad. "May the waters of the Rud-e Hayat swell with the blood of your children."

GLOSSARY

Ab: water

Ab-anbar: underground cistern used for storing water

Ab-Zohr: ritual offering made to the waters during the Yasna ceremony

Agha: sir; a respectful form of address

Ahriman: the Destructive Spirit; eternal adversary of Ohrmazd

Akh: an exclamation expressing pain or frustration

Al: a female demon said to prey upon mothers and newborn children

Amoo: paternal uncle

Apaosha: demon of drought and enemy of rainfall

Argbed (Argbedan): commander of a fortress or garrison

Ash-e anar: pomegranate soup

Avesta: the sacred scriptures of Zoroastrianism

Baad-bezan: hand-held fan

Bacheh: child

Bagh-e Shahryar: "The Sovereign's Garden," a traditional court song

Bagh-e Shirin: "Shirin's Garden," a traditional folk song

Booz-Rooz: an ancient communal rite of bonding and shared feasting

Chogan: polo; an ancient Persian sport

Daeva (Daevas): malevolent spirits or demons

Dakhmeh: Zoroastrian funerary structure used for exposure of the dead

Damad: son-in-law

Dasht-e Marg: the Desert of Death

Div: demon

Dram (Drahm): silver coin

Drakht-i Asurig: "The Babylonian Tree," a Middle Persian poetic dialogue

Faravahar: Zoroastrian spiritual symbol representing divine guidance and the human soul

Faloodeh: frozen dessert made with starch noodles, syrup, and rose water

Gheli-Khast: fortified garrison and trading post of Danzardani origin

Grand Magus: supreme religious authority of the Magi

Haboob: violent dust storm

Halva: sweet confection made from sesame, sugar, and spices

Haoma: sacred plant used in ritual; associated with healing and divine inspiration

Hava: air

Henna: plant-based dye used for body adornment

Jan-e del: "soul of my heart"; a term of deep affection

Jashn-e Tirgan: midsummer water festival honoring rainfall and renewal

Karkadann: legendary horned beast resembling a rhinoceros

Khaleh: maternal aunt; also a respectful term for an elder woman

Khormalu: date plum or persimmon

Khoshgeleh: affectionate term meaning "my beautiful one"

Koloocheh: traditional sugar cookie

Kuh-e Ab: Water Mountain

Kuh-e Sang: Stone Mountain

Kuh-e Sholeh: Flame Mountain

Kuh-e Zuzeh: Howl Mountain

Kuhha-ye Sabz: the Green Mountains

Kuhha-ye Siyah: the Black Mountains

Kulah: ceremonial crown or ornamental headdress

Madar: mother

Madar be khata: a severe insult invoking one's mother

Madar-bozorg: grandmother

Madar-shohar: mother-in-law (husband's side)

Magi: Zoroastrian priesthood

Mina: ancient unit of weight

Mithra: god of covenants, truth, and fellowship

Moosh: "mouse"; affectionate nickname

Mumiya: bituminous substance used for embalming and medicine

Naan: leavened flatbread

Nakas: contemptible or dishonorable person

Namak: salt

Ohrmazd: the Wise Lord; creator of all that is good

Pari: fairy or benevolent spirit

Pedar: father

Pedar-bozorg: grandfather

Pushtigban: royal guard

Pushtigban-salar: commander of the royal guard

Qanat: underground channel system used to transport water

Rah-e Faraz: mountain pass named after Faraz, second king of Zad

Rud-e Barik: Narrow River

Rud-e Hayat: River of Life

Rud-e Mah: Moon River

Rusari: headscarf

Samjari: northern brigands and raiders

Sang-e Pir: pilgrimage site at Stone Mountain

Sarooj: waterproof mortar made of lime, ash, and clay

Sarzamin-e Mordegan: Land of the Dead

Savaran: elite cavalry

Scaphism (the boats): a form of execution described in classical sources, involving confinement between two vessels

Sekanjabin: sweet-and-sour drink made from vinegar, honey, and mint

Shahpur: prince; literally "son of the king"

Shamshir: curved sword

Sharbat: chilled sweet drink made from fruits or flower extracts

Shotor: camel

Tishtrya: divine spirit of rainfall and fertility

Vastryoshan: common folk, especially farmers and herders

Visgari: southern brigands

Warahram: god of victory and righteous battle

Wind Catcher: architectural tower used to cool interior spaces

Yakhchal: domed icehouse for storing ice and food

Yasht: sacred hymn

Yasna: central liturgical texts of the Avesta

Yazdan: divine beings and forces of nature worshiped before the rise of strict monotheism

Zartosht: prophet who founded the faith of Ahura Mazda

Songs

Alloy

(Em) Copper and (G) Tin,

(D) how've you (A) been?

(Em) Get together and (G) have some (Em) kin.

(Em) Al-loy, loy, (G) loy, (D) Al-loy, loy, (A) loy,

(Em) You can't break the bonds of (G) my son, (Em) Bronze.

(Repeat)

Copper and Zinc,

what do you think?

That's too much haoma for you to drink.

Alloy, loy, loy, Alloy, loy, loy,

You're such a pretty lass. We'll call you, Brass.

Carbon and Iron,

it's your turn.

Fire the smelter; watch it burn.

Alloy, loy, loy, Alloy, loy, loy…

Let's seal the deal with another son, Steel.

Seal the deal with another son, Steel.

Seal the deal with another son, (A) Steel.

The Queen Has Gone
The (A) queen is gone, she's (F#m) woebegone,
(D) gone down the road on a (E) karkadann.
She sang of love near the little ringdove,
"He's left my life for the world above."
"Don't fret no more," said the bird. "We'll soar.
To heaven, we'll ride on a manticore."
But the queen did warn, her voice forlorn,
"From life's short breath does love... get (A) born." **[Capo 5th
fret]**

Acknowledgments

I wish to thank my two sons, Kaz and Rhun, for their unwavering patience and critical insights. To my wife, Ambar—without your endless support, *The Springs of Anahita* would not have come to pass.

Lastly, I must express my deep appreciation to Hamzeh for proofreading my glossary, Karina for bringing my map to life, and Jesh for designing my book cover.

ABOUT THE AUTHOR

Mark Howard Henderson is the author of *The Springs of Anahita*, the first book in the *The Yazdan Trilogy*. He and his wife live outside Washington, DC.

facebook.com/YayaAndTheWaterWars/

instagram.com/mark_howard_henderson/

linkedin.com/in/mark-howard-henderson-03553b101/

pinterest.com/mark11690025/

amazon.com/author/mark_howard_henderson

https://x.com/MarkHHenderson1